CANARY

RACHELE ALPINE

MEDALLION
P R E S S

Medallion Press, Inc.

Printed in USA

For my mom, who has always kept me supplied with a steady stream of love, support, and books.

Published 2013 by Medallion Press, Inc.

The MEDALLION PRESS LOGO
is a registered trademark of Medallion Press, Inc.

Typeset in Georgia
Printed in the United States of America
ISBN 9781605425870
10 9 8 7 6 5 4 3 2 1
First Edition

CANARY

RACHELE ALPINE

"A searing and tender portrait of the complexities of high school friendships, dating, and privilege. *Canary* is a testament to the power of the hard-won truths."

—Daisy Whitney, author of **The Mockingbirds**
and **When You Were Here**

"Rachele Alpine's *Canary* sings the truth about what happens when we put our high school heroes on a pedestal and give them the power to act like villains."

—Erin Jade Lange, author of **Butter**

"The subtle way Rachele Alpine addresses love, loss, popularity, and friendship makes this book a realistic and arresting read. For anyone who ever struggled with frenemies and fitting in, *Canary* is an important addition to contemporary YA discussions."

—Jennifer Brown, author of **Hate List**

"Alpine's *Canary* is a deeply felt, poignant account of someone trying to find strength in a world that has hurled its worst at her. Alpine has created a compelling narrator in Kate, and the challenges she must face are both realistic and heartbreaking."

—Colleen Clayton, author of **What Happens Next**

"This is a captivating tale that addresses a lot of contemporary issues in a sensitive and thought-provoking way."

—Nicki J Markus, author of **Time Keepers**

www.allmytruths.com

Today's Truth:

You can't count on anyone but yourself.

Your dad will leave you when you are twelve.

He won't empty his closet or pack up his car like you see dads do in old after-school specials.

He won't move in with a lover closer to your age than his, an exercise buff who wakes him at the crack of dawn for morning runs and wears short skirts and drinks martinis in bars while texting her girlfriends on her cell phone.

He won't spend his life alone and rent a room in a seedy motel.

He won't invite you and your brother to spend Christmas with him in the tiny, dingy space with a sad-looking, tinsel-covered tree in the corner on a rickety table over a stained carpet.

In fact, he won't leave the house.

He will stay right inside with you and your brother. You will eat dinners together, sit in the same room watching TV, have conversations about everyday matters like the weather and the dwindling supply of food in the fridge. You will do mundane things, such as passing each other in the hall as you head to and from the bathroom and riding in the car together when he takes you to school. Each day will blend into the next.

But from your life, he will be gone.

Posted By: Your Present Self
[Sunday, August 11, 12:36 PM]

My brother, Dad, and I do the majority of our communicating using Post-its. Whoever invented them must make a fortune from the three of us alone.

I'll find them stuck to the bathroom mirror reminding me that Dad *"Won't be home until late"* or on the kitchen counter with *"Money for groceries."*

If Brett and I need something signed or want permission to go somewhere, we'll leave notes in places we know our dad will see: the door to the garage, his coffee pot, the bathroom mirror, or his computer screen.

It's worked for us since Mom died. There have been only a few mix-ups when Post-its have fallen off and blown under tables or when one of us broke the regular routine and didn't walk past the spot where the note waited to be read.

But for the most part, we're able to communicate without really communicating. And in my household, nothing says family love more than a day without having to talk to each other. Dad thinks it's brilliant. I think it sucks.

The last Monday of the summer, I woke surprised to find a note stuck to my bathing suit asking, *"Meet for dinner at 6 at Garland's Pizza?"* When Brett finally dragged himself out of bed two hours later, he confirmed that he'd received the same message stuck to the bathroom mirror.

Garland's Pizza was a little ten-table place the three of us loved. It was only two blocks from our house, a quick solution when there wasn't anything else to eat. These days we ordered from there a lot, but it was always takeout. I couldn't remember the last time we ate in the restaurant together. Dinner at home didn't usually involve conversation. Dad would read the paper while my brother and I fought over the television remote.

I was surprised Dad wanted to meet us there, but I wasn't going to question it. Dad hardly ever spent time with Brett and me anymore. I practically had to tackle him to stay in a room with me for more than five minutes. He always claimed to have important things to do for work—stuff that involved hiding in his office all night, every night.

I spotted Dad as soon as I walked into the place. Even though I'd sat around and done nothing the whole day, I was the last to arrive. He was in the crowded restaurant at a small table. My brother slouched next to him, no doubt angry at having one of the last days of vacation interrupted. He wore his fatigue pants even though it was boiling outside. Brett practically lived in those lame pants.

People were everywhere. Families eating at tables covered in cheesy pizzas. Kids running around with their greasy fingers. Older siblings playing video games against the back wall. Babies wailing along with the music blasting from a jukebox that seemed to play only old Billy Joel songs. The place was such a dive, but that's why people loved it.

I pushed through the crowd and bumped into chairs shoved around tables. It was a major fire hazard, but everyone seemed willing to take the risk for the pizza here. Nabbing a place to sit at Garland's Pizza was a talent, and I was impressed Dad was able to do it.

I slid into an empty seat. "Hey." I picked up a menu and fanned myself. "I'm not late, am I?"

"You're fine. We haven't been here long. Brett already ordered a few pizzas: a cheese, a veggie, and a pepperoni. I figured you'd find something you like between the three of them."

I shrugged. "Sounds good." I pulled my brown hair into a ponytail. It was hot in the restaurant, and my hair was heavy on my neck.

The air conditioner chugged along, apparently wiped out from a full summer of work. Drops of sweat gathered in my bra, and I prayed I wouldn't sweat through my shirt and get nasty pit stains.

"How was your day?" Dad asked.

"Boring." I kept it short; he'd space out if I said much more. "What about yours?"

"Not bad. A lot of the team came to the gym today for a pickup game, and I got to see them shoot around a bit."

"Did any of them seem good? Or more importantly"—I leaned in—"were any of them hot?"

Before Dad could answer, Brett snorted. "I'm sure they loved having you there. Gives them a chance to kiss the new coach's ass."

Dad set down his drink and faced Brett, taking on that lecture look.

A waitress interrupted by setting down a pitcher of

Coke and piling napkins and silverware on the table.

I filled my glass and watched the sides sweat. I put my wrists against the moisture, trying to cool down.

"Listen," Dad said, "I've got some important news for both of you."

Brett crossed his arms and focused on the ceiling.

"I've been talking with the principal, Mr. Drew, for a few days now. About not only basketball stuff but other things too. He and the rest of the administration think it would be a good idea for the two of you to become Beacon students."

"You want us to go to Beacon?" I asked. I didn't think enrolling was a possibility. The school was superexpensive. Tuition was probably more than Dad's salary. But maybe I was wrong, and after everything that happened the past year, I liked the idea of leaving behind the memories lingering at my high school.

Brett opened his mouth, but before he could speak, Dad started again.

"You'll be able to start the new school year there. It should be an easy transition."

I nodded, willing him to go on, but he paused.

Brett seized the opportunity. "You promised we didn't have to leave Olmstead High."

Dad sighed. "Brett, wouldn't you rather go to Beacon?"

"No, I wouldn't," he spat back.

A group at a nearby table turned to stare.

I focused on my menu and wished that for once in our lives we could have more than two minutes of peace before Brett and Dad were at each other's throats.

"Calm down," Dad said. "Think about what I'm saying."

"There's nothing to think about. You said I didn't have to go there."

I kicked Brett under the table, but he kicked me right back. I knew he wasn't about to give up. Brett had been picking fights with Dad since Mom died, and it seemed as if they all revolved around basketball. Or, more specifically, the time Dad spent with basketball instead of with us. Brett would never admit it, but I knew he felt as hurt as I did when Dad grabbed a late dinner with some of the coaches or spent the weekend taking one of his star players to a college offering an athletic scholarship. Now that he'd landed his new position, it was even worse. We hardly saw him all summer.

"You promised," Brett hissed.

More and more people turned to look at my family's show.

I slumped in my seat.

Dad probably figured dropping the news in a public place would lessen the chance of a full-blown confrontation. Buzz, wrong answer.

Brett pushed back his chair and nearly knocked down the waitress passing behind him while balancing a pizza.

"Brett, sit down. I need you to listen to me," Dad whispered.

Despite the scene, my stomach fluttered with nervous excitement. Beacon was amazing. I couldn't even begin to imagine what it would be like to go there.

"How can I calm down when you tell me a week before school starts that I won't be starting my senior year at Olmstead High? Instead, I have to go to school with a bunch of rich kids who look down on people like us because we don't go sailing on our daddies' boats or attend parties at country clubs guarded by iron gates. That's not who I am, so why the hell are you doing this?"

"Why? I'll tell you why," Dad shot back. "Because people are talking. They're wondering what the new coach finds so wrong with the school that he can't send his own kids to it."

I tried to catch Brett's eye and said, "Why do you have to be difficult? If you gave Beacon half a chance, you might find out it's not so bad."

Dad looked relieved.

Brett gave me a dirty look.

"Kate's right. I'm sure you'll like it there if you give it a shot."

I felt good, as if I'd done something right and Dad was proud of me.

"How about I tell them exactly what's wrong with the school and why your kids don't want to go there?" Brett said.

Dad wiped his forehead, shiny now with sweat, and tried to discreetly glance around the restaurant.

"Don't worry." Brett threw the sharp-edged words at him. "I don't think your face has been in enough papers yet for everyone here to recognize the new Beacon coach."

He spoke loud enough that anyone who didn't

know probably knew now.

"Enough." Dad slammed a fist on the table.

I grabbed my glass as some pop splashed out.

"I get it," Brett continued. "This is about you. You and your position at your great big important private school. I may not be smart enough to score as high as the other kids on those fancy exams you have to take to get into Beacon, but I get it. I get it completely."

"Brett," Dad said, demanding a respect he had lost from Brett a long time before.

"You know," Brett said, "if Mom were still alive, she'd never expect me to do something like this." Brett marched away, winding through the obstacle course of happy families, and shoved open the door so hard it banged against the side of the building.

I turned to Dad to tell him how I felt about leaving Olmstead High to go to Beacon. "I know Brett's being his usual pain in the ass, but I really—"

"Not right now. The two of you really need to stop for a minute and think about what a great opportunity this is for you." Dad dug into a pocket, then pulled money out of his wallet and threw it on the table. "Can you take care of the bill? We'll talk about this later."

"Sure, whatever." I watched him leave through the same door Brett had stormed out of seconds before. This was so typical of Dad. He really hadn't listened to me, and I felt stupid for thinking maybe he would.

Transferring schools made sense, though. My old school was where Mom got sick and I sat worrying about her test results instead of my own tests and homework. The halls of Olmstead High held friends who stopped acting normal around me, as if I were the sick one; classmates who stared at me, as if I were a freak for losing my mom; and teachers who would put a hand on my shoulder and tell me I could talk to them anytime about anything.

Brett might have been fighting to stay at Olmstead High, but I was ready to run from it. Dad didn't need to convince me. Starting my sophomore year at Beacon was one of the first things in a long time that actually felt right.

www.allmytruths.com

Today's Truth:

Your life is about to change forever.

Michigan Central News   Sports Page 1

Beacon Preparatory School Names New Basketball Coach

by Robyn Moffat

Last year, Beacon basketball had a momentous season. The team brought the school its seventh state title and had five graduating seniors accepted to NCAA top-ranked schools, and legendary Coach Bud Simeon retired. While the school celebrated the first two events, the retirement of Bud Simeon was an upset to all in the Beacon family and raised the question of who would fill Simeon's shoes.

In a press conference last night, Beacon stopped the endless discussions of possible replacements by announcing Robert Franklin as the new head coach for Beacon. Even though Beacon held a nationwide search, they did not have to look far to hire Franklin. Franklin, the now former coach of Olmstead High, a Division 2 school, is rumored to have first been considered when his team beat Beacon in a pregame scrimmage last year. "We knew Franklin was the ideal candidate after witnessing the upset of Beacon by his team. We have been following his coaching for years, and we are confident he will continue to lead Beacon to more state victories," Beacon Athletic Director William Bennett commented when asked about what led to their decision to hire Franklin.

Franklin has an impressive record as a high school basketball coach at Olmstead High. The team made it to the state championship five out of the seven years he was coach and finished last year's regular season undefeated. His players have won scholarships and gained acceptance to numerous colleges to play basketball, and he works with Middleburg College's basketball team in their summer conditioning pro-gram. He has been coaching for sixteen years and when questioned about his thoughts on coaching a team that has won the state title seven years in a row, he stated, "I can't wait to make it number eight."

All we can say is, "Go, Beacon!"

Posted By: Your Present Self

[Monday, August 12, 9:14 PM]

Dad's car was gone when I got home from Garland's pizza, and a Post-it sat on the counter with a simple message: *"You both start at Beacon next Monday. I ordered uniforms from the school bookstore. I'll pick them up later this week."*

I changed into my bathing suit and dived into our pool. I couldn't stop thinking about Beacon and what it might mean to go there. I'd be able to leave behind everything that happened at Olmstead High and start fresh. I could be a different person. I moved through the water and imagined my new life.

I'd swum twenty-three laps when the lights lining the pool wall flashed, illuminated like round moons. They lit up four times, my brother's signal.

Dad was used to me swimming late at night before I went to bed. It was my version of a bubble bath or mug of warm milk. It calmed me. Brett, on the other hand, thought I was crazy to swim in the dark, and he always made me promise to knock on his door when I got out so he knew I hadn't drowned. I made fun of him for being so sensitive, but I always checked in with him after my swims.

When I surfaced, Brett sat at the side of the pool, untying his shoes and socks. "You could take a night off, you know."

"I do. October through May." I held onto the side of the pool, keeping my body under the water so I wouldn't get cold from the night air. "What are you doing out here?"

"Checking up on you." Brett put his bare feet into the pool and pulled them out immediately. "Damn it, that's freezing. How do you stand swimming in here when it's all cold and dark?"

"I can think of worse things than a cold pool at nighttime." I knew he understood what I was talking about. Mom had died more than a year before, but the pain was still strong. We had become good at moving through life avoiding conversations about her.

He turned away, not meeting my stare. "Me too, like the time you practiced cooking the breakfast casserole for class and Dad and I had to try it."

"My casserole was delicious."

"Sure, if you like runny, undercooked eggs."

I splashed him. "If you want scary, let me remind you of the time Mrs. Reynolds babysat us and asked me for a back rub. Now that's scary."

"Oh, shit, that would suck. She was gross with all the cat fur stuck to her and white spit hanging out the corners of her mouth."

"Exactly. My eggs were nothing compared to Mrs. Reynolds."

We laughed softly, the sound fading until all you could hear was crickets and the water lapping against the pool walls.

"But now," I said slowly, "those things don't seem scary at all."

"I know."

"Why are you making things harder than they already are, Brett? Fighting with Dad only makes it worse."

He sighed and stared into the trees bordering our yard. "How can you believe what Dad is doing is right? He's using us to make himself look good."

"Come on. He's not like that," I said, but we both knew I was lying.

"He's changed."

I wanted to tell him I agreed, that Dad had changed and nothing in our house seemed right now that Mom was gone. But I couldn't because a bigger part of me wanted to go to Beacon. If I said something, it might ruin it.

I pushed off the wall and swam to the deep end and back, holding my breath to see how far I could go without air.

"He won't even listen to us," Brett said when I surfaced.

I grabbed the wall near him. "I know."

"Each day goes by, and it's as if he forgets about us more and more. We're not his family. His team is. He cares more about those guys than he does about us."

"That's not true." But lately it did seem possible.

"It is, and he's screwing us over in the process."

I ducked under the water so I didn't have to decide if Brett was right.

www.allmytruths.com

Today's Truth:

If you're not in, you're out.

Beacon Is Excellence

This declaration written in gold letters on a large maroon board greets you from the bottom of the winding drive into Beacon's campus. It's there before you head up the hill lined with large black lights, before you make it to the ancient iron fence arching high over the entrance of the school, and long before you enter the manicured lawn covered in trees and brick buildings.

Beacon wants everyone to know they are entering excellence.

The sign doesn't state that Beacon is a school, the year it was founded, or show a picture of the mascot. Instead, it issues a simple yet firm declarative: *Beacon Is Excellence*. The statement seems to leave no room for anything else.

Beacon produces excellent athletes. The basketball team wins championships year after year, girls in field hockey go on to win college scholarships, and swimmers compete and break records in nationals.

Beacon produces excellent students. Dozens go to Ivy League schools and become doctors, lawyers, and stuffy managers. They continue their presence on campus by donating large sums of money as alumni.

Beacon also produces excellent musicians: students who join city youth symphonies, singers who open baseball games with the national anthem, and jazz bands who perform for senators.

Beacon announces its excellence to all who enter the school and continues to remind its students every day.

The sign stares you down as you arrive.

Beacon is excellence, and if you aren't, then why are you at Beacon?

Posted By: Your Present Self

[Monday, August 19, 6:08 AM]

Slipping into Beacon was easy for me.

The kids at my old school guarded the entrance to their groups, never letting in anyone new. I thought it would be just as hard to break in to Beacon's world, but I found friendships were flimsy and easily stretched to fit in a new person if her dad was the school's basketball coach.

Brett may have hated the team, but there was no way I shared those feelings. They were hot, and I would've been lying if I didn't say I was hoping to see some of the boys as soon as I walked through the main doors. I kept my eyes open but didn't spot them until PE when I arrived at the competition gym, their primal watering hole.

Construction paper stars covered in glitter lined the walls outside, each a message of encouragement to an individual player. A banner filled with signatures wished the team good luck in the upcoming season. Framed pictures of past teams holding trophies lined the walls. It was impossible to forget that Beacon was where champions played.

I pushed open one of the double doors and was welcomed with the smell of sweat, the screeching of shoes against the slick floor of the court, and the unintelligible yells from a group of boys playing basketball. I recognized the players from Dad's team. I'd met most of them briefly two days before at the faculty and alumni welcome-back picnic. Dad, as the new coach, had been one of the guests of honor, and I learned it was tradition for the basketball team to serve the staff and alumni. However, it seemed as if most of the men on the faculty had taken over the barbequing and the boys hung out in big clumps joking loudly and looking hot, hot, hot.

Brett refused to go, claiming he'd already made plans to go hiking. When Dad tried to argue, Brett stressed how important it was to see the friends he wouldn't be spending time with anymore because he was being forced to go to Beacon. Brett disappeared an hour before we were supposed to leave, so Dad, not wanting to be late, settled for just me. Together we'd create the image of at least half a happy family.

I stood next to Dad for most of the night, and he kept his arm around me, something he hadn't done in years. I was introduced to the team players: tall, lanky boys who grunted hellos and then turned their attention toward Dad, more interested in impressing him than me. I met their families, the other coaches, and the faculty. Names were thrown at me all night so that by the time people started coming over to say good-bye, it was all a blur.

Well, most of it was a blur. There was one face and name I kept thinking about.

Jack Blane.

I'd met him in the parking lot. I'd run to Dad's car for a sweatshirt, and his mom was dropping him off.

"Now remember. Coach Franklin doesn't know a lot about you."

I paused when I heard her mention Dad's name.

"You're a guest at this picnic. That means you take one serving. You may eat me out of house and home, but you don't do that here."

He threw his hands up. "Give me a break. I know how to act. Besides, I ate two peanut butter sandwiches at home."

"I'm sure you did. Just make sure Coach doesn't think you've been raised by a pack of wolves."

"I promise to be on my best behavior. Cross my heart." He made the gesture over his chest with his fingers. He headed toward the crowd and then turned back to her.

"Well, that is if they don't serve chocolate cake for dessert," the guy said. "If they do, I can't make any promises."

"Get out of here," his mom said.

I laughed out loud. I covered my mouth, but he heard me.

"Oh, man, I didn't think anyone was around."

"I was grabbing a sweatshirt, but I had to stop when I realized how dangerous you were."

"Dangerous?" He ran his fingers through his blond hair, making it all messy and sexy.

"Your killer appetite."

"Oh yeah, you're right. That has been known to get me in trouble before."

A couple of guys slammed car doors nearby.

He waved at them.

"I'm Kate," I said, seizing my chance before it was too late.

"Jack." He scuffed the dirt, a cloud of dust floating

around his old-school green and gray Nikes.

"Well, I guess I'll see you there." I pointed toward the cookout. "I'm heading over to make sure that if there's any chocolate cake, it's good and protected in case you get near it."

"Good idea," he said with a smile that made me hope I'd run into him again.

Now, two days later, I searched for Jack in the gym and found him under the basketball hoop. He was crouched in defensive position watching another guy to see if he would shoot. I stared at him and willed him to look back at me. No such luck.

A ball bounced near my feet, and I forced myself to look away from Jack as one of the other guys on the team ran past me. These boys were the only people I knew at Beacon, and technically I didn't even know them.

I snuck another look at Jack. He was deeply tanned, no doubt from a summer spent vacationing at some beach only a Beacon family could afford. A white line on the back of his neck divided his hairline from his tan.

I looked around the gym. All the boys shared the same new haircuts. Keeping up appearances was Dad's specialty. He wouldn't stand for scruffy, greasy, or sloppy appearances. Basketball was a three-hundred-sixty-five-day-a-year commitment, and his team needed to look serious.

I touched my own hair, already tangled from the humidity outside. I wished some of Beacon's magic would've rubbed off on me this morning and my hair would behave, but no such luck.

Brett was no different, but he opted to keep his blond hair shaggy, no doubt an act of defiance.

Dad's demands on his team didn't rub off on the two of us, but he didn't seem to notice anyway.

I took my gaze off Jack when a small, pretty blonde girl walked into the room. Her uniform skirt was rolled up to a level I knew wouldn't pass the fingertip rule stated in the student handbook, and she wore heels instead of the ballet flats most girls were wearing. Luckily she caught me looking at the team and not her outfit.

I gestured toward the boys. "Not a bad way to start the day, huh?"

"I could stare at them for hours," she said.

I pretended to look at my watch. "I think I already have."

"Hey, I won't judge," she said.

She was exactly the type of person I wanted to be friends with. "Really, I was trying to find the gym. I have class there now."

"*Our* gym is this way. This is the competition gym where the team practices. You'd think we'd all use the same gym, but they keep us regular students segregated from the greatness of the basketball team. Well, unless we're cheering them on and checking them out." She grinned.

I couldn't help but smile back. "Thanks." I slung my bag over my shoulder and followed her out.

Her long, blonde hair was caught behind her book bag, and she pulled it out and let it fan across her back, the light above making it shine.

I sped up to walk alongside her. For someone in heels, she sure moved fast. "I've been to this gym before for a game. I assumed it was for regular class too."

"Prepare to be shocked." She led me out of the gym, leaving behind the pack of boys who continued to dribble and make shots from all over the court. Their shouts and cheers echoed after us as we walked out the doors. I thought back to the days when Mom, Brett, and I were surrounded by the sounds of Dad's basketball games, but I quickly pushed the images out of my mind. Now wasn't the time to get upset.

We went down a hallway that curved away from the competition gym. I tried to take it all in. "How the heck does anyone find this place? It would be nice if they put up arrows or a sign."

"That would take away from the beauty of the shrine we've built to our gods of the basketball court. Beacon doesn't want to remind the world that there is life beyond basketball here." She rolled her eyes. "That there are regular students who walk amongst the champions."

We arrived at a door labeled *Girls,* and she pushed it open. "Here's the locker room, and beyond those doors is the gym. It was built over a hundred years ago when Beacon didn't allow girls. Now? Voila." She paused for effect and then flung the door open. "Lucky us, they've let us in. We're privileged enough to get the old gym floors."

I did a double take. The gym was old. Wait, not just old. It was ancient, as in Abraham Lincoln could have taken classes here. Wooden planks with small cracks between lined the floor. Some areas were repaired, and in those spots, the wood was different colors. I thought of the glossy, slick floor in the competition gym with Beacon's logo in the middle. I walked farther in. "This is awful."

"Isn't it? You just have to be careful not to sit on it with bare skin or you might get a splinter."

I laughed. "I'm Kate, by the way."

"Oh, geez, I never told you who I was. I'm Ali."

Groups of noisy girls walked into the gym. We followed them to the bleachers. A few girls waved to Ali as we took our seats.

"Remember," Ali whispered. "No bare skin on the bleachers, or you'll find splinters in places you don't even want to think about."

"Got it." I made a point of smoothing down my blue plaid skirt to cover as much of my skin as possible.

Ali did the same.

A redheaded girl in front of us turned toward me. "Are you Kate Franklin?"

"Yeah," I said quickly, knowing where this was heading.

People turned to stare.

"Is Coach Franklin your dad?"

I nodded.

"I thought so." She leaned in close. "I'm Michelle. I'd kill to be in your position right now. Do you get to see the team a lot? What do you think of them? Who do you think is the hottest? Does your dad invite them over to your house?" Her inquisition was cut short when a muscular woman walked in and blew a whistle to silence us. She introduced herself as our gym teacher, Miss Gallagher.

I turned away from Michelle as Miss Gallagher started to discuss the beginning of the school year and the class.

Clearly upset she'd been interrupted, Michelle tried to catch my attention again with heavy whispers.

I acted interested in Miss Gallagher's stimulating discussion of gym shorts versus sweatpants.

"You didn't tell me your dad was the coach," Ali said.

"It's not a big deal," I said, but I knew it was.

Michelle was going to strain her neck if she kept trying to get me to talk to her, and the other girls started looking at me too.

Ali whispered, "But the stuff I said about basketball before—"

"Don't worry about it. I'm kind of sick of

basketball."

"What? You don't like it?"

"It's not that I don't like it," I said cautiously. "I'm surrounded by it. It gets old sometimes."

"I'm not sure you can go to Beacon and not be a basketball fan." Ali shook her head.

For a minute, I thought I'd blown it. Beacon was basketball, and here I was putting it down.

But then her expression shifted into a smile.

"I know," I said. "I'll have to work on my school spirit. But from the looks of the team, I don't think that'll be hard."

"I have a feeling you'll soon enjoy basketball again."

"I think you're right. It does seem important here."

"Yeah, just a little bit."

I laughed with her.

Miss Gallagher paused from her oh-so-important speech and shot us a warning glare.

Ali leaned into me. "Beacon basketball is a whole new world, its own society. You'll soon learn the team has their own rules and way of living."

"Which is why they have swelled heads," I said. "I think I saw a few when I was in *their* gym."

Ali winked. "Their egos aren't the only things big about them, if you know what I mean."

I covered my mouth to keep my laughter in and tried to listen to Miss Gallagher. It felt good to laugh, as if I hadn't done that in a long, long time.

I left the gym and headed to lunch with Ali.

"You don't mind if I eat with you, do you?" I said as we started through the lunch line. I'd imagined Beacon having fancy food to match their fancy everything else, but it was the same old junk. One cafeteria worker slopped mashed potatoes onto a plate, and another handed out burgers apparently flattened by a steamroller. I reached for a peanut butter and jelly, thinking they couldn't mess that up, and continued, "I don't know anyone and—"

"Of course you can eat with me, but only if you promise to ignore what I said before about the basketball team."

"Forgotten," I said and vowed to make sure it was. I couldn't believe I'd told her I didn't like basketball. It was the type of thing people would flip out about, me being the coach's daughter and all.

What I didn't tell Ali was the real reason basketball wasn't my favorite—why I'd stopped watching it, playing it, loving it. She may have accepted that I was sick of it, but I had no idea how she'd react to the truth. What would she say if I told her about the night I fell out of love of with the sport?

Everything was going great that night as Betsy's parents drove us home from our basketball game. I was pumped. We'd won by over twenty points. The eighth grade team was on fire, and a win this big had put us all in good spirits. Betsy and I were singing along with the radio, making up our own lyrics, as we arrived at my house.

Both of our cars were in the driveway. Dad was never home so early during basketball season. Something wasn't right.

I walked in and saw Dad, Mom, and Brett at the table. I sat with them and waited for Mom to tell me I stunk and order me to take a shower before dinner.

Instead, she offered me a weak smile. "Did you win?"

"We did. I scored twelve points, Betsy scored eight, and the other team kept trying to foul us."

Mom leaned in.

Dad went to the oven to pull out whatever was cooking.

Brett slowly shredded a napkin.

Dad placed the serving pan on the blue and purple potholder I'd clumsily weaved in first grade as a Mother's Day gift.

"Lasagna?" I said and tried to figure out if I'd forgotten something important. Lasagna wasn't a meal Mom whipped up casually. She made the noodles and sauce from scratch, the process taking hours. Lasagna was reserved for birthdays, holidays, and when my grandma came to visit. "Why are we having lasagna? Did I miss something?"

No one answered, so I helped myself to a huge plateful.

Everyone else sat at the table not eating.

Mom cleared her throat a few times, Dad rearranged his silverware on the sides of his plate, and my brother built his mountain of napkin scraps.

I shoveled a forkful into my mouth. "I didn't mean that as a bad thing," I said, still chewing, wondering if I'd done something wrong by touching the food on my plate. After a day of school and basketball, though, I was starving. "I'm glad we're having this fancy dinner. Real glad."

Dad dropped his spoon on his plate with a loud clatter. "Your mother and I need to talk to you."

I paused between bites. "Bring it on. What do you have to say?"

"Kate, be quiet," Brett snapped. "You need to listen to them."

"Shut up. You're not the boss."

"We've talked to Brett," Mom told me quietly. "He was here when your dad and I got home. I didn't want him to sit and worry."

"What's going on?" I said, scared now because I was the one who was sitting and worrying. Something was clearly wrong. "What happened when I was at the game?"

"Your mother is sick, Kate."

"Sick? Sick from what? Will she have to go to the hospital?"

Mom let out a little noise, a cross between a cry and a wail, a sound like our old dog Rascal used to make when he heard something outside but couldn't see it. She put her hand over her mouth as if to keep the noise inside.

"Not sick like that. She's really sick."

My brother pushed back his chair, and it smacked the wall behind him. "I can't listen to this again. I need to leave."

"You need to sit down," Dad demanded.

Mom interrupted. "Let him go. It isn't right to make him stay here."

Brett left the room quickly.

I wanted to follow. I looked at my parents, a million questions on my lips, a trillion fears racing in my head, and zero answers I wanted to hear. The lasagna wasn't to celebrate my team's win or a birthday I'd forgotten. It was to help my parents tell me something too hard to say, something so important we couldn't wait for Dad to come home from practice or for me to shower.

"Your mother is sick," Dad repeated. "Very sick."

"How sick?" I whispered, not sure if my voice was loud enough to be heard. I wanted Mom to explain, but Dad continued to do all the talking.

"She has cancer. It's moving fast. The doctors are going to try to treat it, but they aren't hopeful." His words jumbled, gushed from his mouth like water from the faucet in the bath. "The doctors might not be hopeful, but we are."

Mom touched my hand. "We're going to try to act as we always have. I want us to be a family. I want us to be normal."

I wanted to ask what she thought normal was now that she was sick. This kind of normal couldn't be anything like what we all used to know. "How long have you known about this?" I demanded instead.

The heat from her hand burned into mine, yet I shivered. It didn't seem possible, but Mom now looked frail, as if right before my eyes, her sickness started to show. Or maybe she had looked like that all along, and I hadn't noticed.

"About a month," Mom answered, her confidence building a bit, as if saying the word *cancer* out loud was the worst of it. "We didn't want to worry the two of you before we talked to all the doctors, specialists, and people we needed to."

"So it's a big deal now?" I pulled my hand away from Mom's.

No one responded.

I thought about myself at the basketball game today and all the games I'd played this month. Running up and down the court, I'd cared only about winning these stupid games while Mom was sick and I hadn't known.

"It's a big deal now," Dad answered.

In that instant, when nothing more was said, when eyes remained clouded, when my entire life switched to slow motion and it was hard to move forward, it truly hit me just how big a deal it was.

"It's natural to want to talk about things," Mom told me gently after she and Dad finished explaining what they knew about the cancer. She tilted her head, waiting for my questions.

What the heck was I supposed to ask? Cancer was a word I'd heard before, but I'd never paid attention to it. Why would I? No one thinks they'll have to deal with it. But now, here was Mom telling me she had it and I was supposed to act as if I was *learning* something. I couldn't speak. What sort of questions do you ask when you find out your mom is dying?

"We want to continue to live as we always have. We don't want your life or Brett's to stop," Dad insisted, like that could happen, like we could continue as if Mom would live, when we knew she wouldn't.

I excused myself and went outside to do the only thing I could do well. I picked up the basketball that rested in the bushes next to the garage. I dribbled, the ball slapping against the concrete, echoing all around me. Really, it was too late to play outside. This was usually the time Mom would come out and tell Dad and me to stop and come inside. She'd say the neighbors didn't need our racket while they were having dinner, getting homework done, or watching the evening news.

But everything was different tonight. No one came out to tell me anything.

It was impossible to focus on what lay ahead. Instead, I continued to bounce the ball and wonder what I had been doing when my parents found out it was cancer. Where I'd been when they were getting tests done, seeing doctors, and worrying about what would happen.

I took a shot, pushing the anger out of me, smacking the ball against the garage just above the hoop. I thought about myself at the game that day. I shot again, missed again, the ball rattling off the rim. I remembered practices where I had joked with my friends. I shot basket after basket, trying not to think about all the times I'd had fun, all the times when I'd cared about nothing but the fight to win, while my parents were fighting to save Mom's life.

I slammed my basketball against the side of the garage.

I hated it. I hated basketball.

I hated it because I'd loved it. And by loving it, I hadn't noticed anything else happening around me. Basketball had made me selfish and blind.

The ball felt solid in my hands. The little bumps in the texture sunk into my palms as I squeezed it.

"I'm done with basketball," I yelled to the sky, a purple night where wisps of clouds brushed against the moon before moving on to taunt the stars. A night too nice for anyone to hear news like this. It should be raining and storming and awful out when you learn your mom is dying.

"I'm quitting basketball," I yelled to the windows in the neighborhood, some dark, some full of light, as people went on with their normal routines as if the world hadn't changed.

I waited for Dad to join me, to explain what was going on, to promise we weren't going to lose Mom. Dad always stood up for me. He was the one who sweet-talked Mom into letting me stay up past my bedtime to watch the end of a basketball game or skip a day of school to take a trip with him to scout a rival school's team. Dad was the one who explained the world when I was confused. Dad was always there when I needed him. So I waited for him to come out and be there for me on the night I needed him the most.

I threw the ball at the garage over and over, waiting for him, the bouncing of the ball his cue to join me.

Sweat dripped into my eyes and my arms ached, but I kept shooting at the hoop.

I waited for him until I finally collapsed in a heap of exhaustion, not sure if it was from the news about my mother or from Dad, who for the first time in my life had left me standing in the driveway alone.

5

Ali's friend Jenna joined us at lunch on the first day. I'd noticed her in my second-period class because she rushed in when the bell rang and took a seat in the back, leaving behind a scent of vanilla and cigarettes. She was tiny with long, thick hair so black the lights reflected in its shine. Her eyes were green like my neighbor's cat and her face was covered with freckles. I half expected her to say hello to me with an Irish accent.

"Jenna and I have been friends since seventh grade, when our parents forced us to take a junior lifesaving course at the pool," Ali said.

"But you were more interested in laying out in the sun than learning how to save lives," Jenna shot back. She sat with her legs tucked under her and a sketchbook on her lap. She doodled flowers all over a blank page.

"A lot of good that did," Ali muttered. "We had to wear one pieces, and I got awful tan lines."

I liked the two of them, and on the second day at lunch I headed to the same table. I didn't ask if I could sit but dropped my tray on the table as if I belonged there.

A few other girls joined the three of us. They gossiped about classmates, pointing out some of them, and tried to fill me in on the important stuff, such as who had a nose job, who cheated on who, who snorted drugs in the bathroom but denied it to everyone, and who might or might not be carrying a knife in his boot. I made a mental note to avoid the potential weapon carrier.

The third day at lunch more girls joined us, and the entire table was full, all eight seats. They talked a bit about their classmates, but it was now old news. Everyone seemed to be more interested in something else: the new girl.

It was uncomfortable to have all the attention on me, but a part of me kind of liked it. People were here for me. They wanted to get to know me.

The fourth day at lunch, another table was pulled up and some boys joined us. The conversation revolved around three things: basketball; the boys' hopes of making the varsity team; and, by association, me.

People kept joining our table the fifth, sixth, and seventh days of school, until we were our own section in the cafeteria.

I didn't have time to be lonely at Beacon. My life filled up before I'd noticed the holes.

It was weird to be surrounded by basketball again. I wasn't sure how I felt about it. I'd spent the last two years avoiding the sport and the loss it reminded me of. But if basketball was the reason Beacon was so welcoming, maybe I could give it a second chance.

Brett's first day of school was different from mine. He sat alone at a table by the frozen dessert cart. His table also had eight seats, but only one was filled. I'm sure he could've found people who'd let him sit with them, but he acted as if he didn't give a crap. He sat there with his head down, a scowl on his face, and posture that would scare even the bravest person from approaching him.

The second day of school Brett sat alone at that table, and the other seven seats remained empty. He did the same the third, fourth, and fifth days. I watched him sitting there by himself, looking angry as he paged through some recruiting catalogs from the two Marines seated at a table near the entrance of the cafeteria, the ones who tried to hand them to all of us when we walked in. Most of us shoved the papers into the garbage, but Brett studied them as if he were reading the secrets of the world or, more re-alistically, a porn magazine.

I kept telling myself someone would sit next to him, but every day he was alone.

The afternoon we started our second week at Beacon, I knocked on his bedroom door. Dad had left a Post-it on the microwave telling us, *"Don't wait for me to eat. I may be home late."* I figured I could get Brett to come out of his room if Dad wasn't around.

"Hey." I barged in without waiting for an invite.

I leaned against the doorframe, not wanting to venture in and navigate the mess of clothes and magazines scattered all over the place.

Brett sat on an old armchair he'd found in our basement. He didn't look up, just flipped through the television stations.

I cleared my throat. "I wanted to tell you that you can sit at my table during lunch if you want."

Brett didn't answer.

"Everyone is really nice. You'd have fun sitting with—"

"Oh, wow. How sweet of you letting me sit with *your* friends." He ripped out a page in his magazine, crumpled it in his hand, and tossed it against the wall.

"Sorry. I thought since you sit alone every day . . ."

Brett stood and headed toward me. "I don't need your help. I'd rather eat by myself than with your new friends." He pushed me back and slammed the door in my face. The lock clicked into place.

Brett's disinterest stung. I understood why he was mad at Dad for making him transfer to Beacon, but he could at least try to fit in. He acted as if he didn't care, but I knew how important it was to find a place where you mattered. And now that I'd found my place, I wouldn't do anything to mess it up.

www.allmytruths.com

Today's Truth:

**If you step too close to the fire,
you may get burned.**

September starts, and Dad breaks the vow of silence
he instituted when Mom died.

Brett is a hot topic on Dad's lips, and their arguments
rage through the house like a fire.

The flames climb the walls, the curtains, and wood-
en ceiling beams until they push into my room,
making it too hot to come out.

Their words burn.

I crouch in my room above, my ear to the floor, listening.

Dad's voice sparks, questions sounding like accusations, insults, threats burning my brother.

"Is there a reason why you don't complete your Spanish homework and won't speak Spanish in class?"

"Do you really think refusing to change into your gym uniform is going to get you a passing grade in the class?"

"You're failing math. If you don't get your act together, you're going to fail the grading period."

"Are you even trying to make friends at Beacon, or are you sitting around with the same pissed-off look on your face that you have at home?"

"Your English teacher called and said you didn't turn in your paper. Do you plan to stop sitting on your ass and complete it?"

"Do you care about your work? Yourself? Your future?"

"You've been caught four times in the parking lot during lunch. What are you doing out there? Do you want me to take the car from you? Search your room? Are you doing drugs?"

"You need to do something with your hair. Cut it. I didn't raise my son to look like a slob."

The words break through the calm of the evenings.

Fault after fault is flung at Brett, who says nothing back.

I think Brett's silence is his way of fighting fire with fire, using Dad's best tricks to give him a taste of his own medicine.

So while Dad breaks the long stretches of silence we're used to in our house, Brett manufactures his own.

Night after night, Dad comes at Brett asking him for explanations. He wants to know what changed. What made Brett's grades drop? Why he is behaving so unlike himself?

Brett never answers, but Dad keeps pushing.

And I sit helpless. I want to run down and extinguish the fire by sticking up for Brett, but I'll only cause smoke so thick no one would be able to see. You need to smother a fire to put it out; my fanning will only encourage the flames.

They scare me, these fires. Sometimes the night burns so hot I worry once the fire is out, all that will remain are the skeletons of the house frame, the rest stripped bare.

Posted By: Your Present Self

[Monday, September 2, 11:07 PM]

I learned about the winter equinox in Mrs. Dreiling's fourth grade science class. She'd explained it was the start of winter, the one day a year when the night is longer than the day.

September 7 was my winter equinox. It was the second anniversary of my mom's death. I didn't need winter with its freezing earth and everything icing over to believe this date was the darkest of the year. All day long I tried not to think about how much had changed, but it was hard to get my mind onto anything else.

Last year Brett and I went to the cemetery. He drove us there after school instead of heading home. He didn't say where we were going, but I knew. Dad was waiting at the entrance, and the three of us spent the afternoon at her grave, not talking, but for once we didn't need to.

Now, with Brett still angry at having to go to Beacon and Dad immersed in basketball, I was left alone to remember Mom. I heard an announcement earlier in the day reminding students of the basketball clinic after school. I wasn't surprised Dad agreed to a practice on the anniversary of Mom's death. It was so easy for him to lose himself in basketball that he forgot there were others around him who also needed help.

Brett drove me to school without speaking, and I told him not to wait for me when the day ended. Ali and Jenna didn't know what day it was, and I didn't feel like telling them. It wasn't something I wanted to talk about.

I took the bus home and walked around my empty house, not quite sure what to do. Finally I put on my swimsuit and dove into the pool.

I swam laps and thought about Mom and my family two years before. After people found out about Mom's sickness, they said we were lucky to have the time with her, time to prepare. But to me, it was a constant reminder of what was being taken away from me. Instead of being granted time to spend with her, we were granted time to watch her fade away from us. Summer vacation was spent in a haze of hushed voices, funny smells that made my nose twitch, the sound of pills falling out of bottles and water filling glasses.

She died right before ten that September night. I'd been sleeping in the common room of the hospice on a couch more often than in my bed at home. The TV was turned on quietly in the background to some news show. We'd spent the last few days there, trying to hold off time. Brett was still up, staring ahead but not really watching the images on the screen. Then Dad walked out of Mom's room. He didn't need to say anything. His face was empty. I could hear my aunt crying.

Brett shook his head, saying no over and over.

I didn't know what to do, how to act, what to say.

So I ran away from it all.

I ran out of the hospice into the open fields behind and turned my face to the sky, unable to catch my breath. I was choking in an open space. I tried to take in gulp after gulp of muggy, Indian summer air. I kicked off my shoes and ran. I reached the end of the field and kept going into the woods as the fire filled my lungs and objects pinched at my feet. I couldn't stop. I needed to feel something in a body that was numb.

Behind the hospice were trails that patients could walk. I followed one into the woods and broke out of the trees to the lake Mom used to love when she was strong enough to go outside. The moon was a sliver, making the world in front of me a dark hole. I waded into the water with my clothes on, the thick mud squishing between my toes. When I was younger, Mom would put socks on me when I went swimming in our pool. I was scared to lift my feet off the bottom, to suspend myself in the water, so instead I would walk, scraping my toes as I pulled myself across the concrete bottom. The socks protected me from those injuries, while still letting me keep my feet on the bottom of the pool. Now I welcomed the soft earth below that I sank into, not caring what I was stepping on. I swam to the middle of the lake with strong strokes, feeling the burn in muscles I'd forgotten since I stopped playing sports and stayed home with my mom. I swam as Mom had, cutting through the water and pushing forward, blocking out my thoughts, and only focusing on the physical pain in my body.

I reached the middle and floated on my back, trying to slow my breath, lost in the middle of a lake with a whole new world hidden under its waters. I stared at the sky, wanting to yell, but my voice was trapped in a tight fist of choking sobs. I lay there, the waters pushing me around, until I saw thin beams of flashlights coming through the woods. I slowly swam back to shore.

When I waded out, my brother wrapped a blanket around me and Dad picked me up, carrying me to the car where my aunt was waiting to drive us all back to a house that would never feel like our home again. I curled up in the backseat, my chest bursting and body shaking.

We entered a dark house, and Dad turned on every light. When all the rooms were ablaze, he came back down. I hadn't moved from the couch. He pulled me close to his heart and let me cry. I fell asleep with him there, waking the next morning to find him gone.

If you asked me to pinpoint the moment it happened, I'd say that was it.

That was when I lost Dad.

When I walked into the kitchen the next day, he was on the phone and glanced at me briefly with sad eyes.

The days passed, and the silence grew.

We took each day as it came, but that was all. We lived, but it was as if we were sleepwalking. We moved ahead, but we didn't look back. We didn't talk about my mom; we didn't talk about the loss; we didn't talk at all.

Olmstead High told him he could take the season off, but he insisted he wanted to work. He threw himself into the games, starting a streak of wins that would eventually attract Beacon's attention.

He became basketball.

To me, to Brett, he became lost. He was gone.

Those days still pulled me down now, even when I tried to fight the reminders creeping into my mind. I pushed my head up into the crisp air, gasping for breath. I couldn't hide from the memories even underwater. It all kept crashing against me. I clutched the side of the pool, goose bumps popping up on my arms, and waited for my heart to slow down.

A voice came from across the pool. "You were swimming like something was chasing you." It was Brett, standing there in jeans and a hooded sweatshirt.

I wiped my eyes. "What are you doing out here?"

He walked toward me with a towel in his hand. "From the looks of things, I think I made it right before the hypothermia set in."

I climbed from the pool, shivering. "It's not so cold."

"Take this and go change into something warm. We need to get going." He threw the towel at me.

"What are you talking about? Where are we going?"

"Do you really need to ask?" He stared past the treetops. "The cemetery."

My voice caught in my throat. I'd told myself I didn't need to go to the cemetery or think about Mom. "You want to go with me?"

"Of course I do. We shouldn't be alone today."

I pulled the towel tight around me. "Let me go change."

He nodded.

I started toward the sliding doors but then stopped.

"Is everything okay?"

"Yeah," I said. "I'm just really glad you're here."

"We need to look out for each other. Mom always told me that." Brett's lips curled up into a half smile. I could see his pain, but I could also see the brother he used to be. I thought about all the times he had come to my rescue. He hadn't forgotten how important family was to me.

www.allmytruths.com

Today's Truth:

People are often glad they are not you.

Words Overheard at Mom's Wake . . .

I am sorry for your

loss is hard for

anyone can see how much you loved

her body is at peace

now you hurt, but the pain will get

easier since you could prepare, say good-bye, rather

than have her

taken from this world so

young, you are too young to lose your

mother was an amazing

woman like her leave their imprint on you and it's a

shame they're taken too

soon this loss will get easier for

you two are holding up so

good that she is done

suffering is not the way to live your

life with her heavenly

father has been so strong throughout her

illness took us all by surprise and

shock it is to everyone to have to say

good-bye is not forever; you will see her again one

day by day the pain will start to go

away from the suffering and hurt she was

feeling as if you can't go on, but you can, and you

will keep in touch and let me know how you, Brett,
and your father are

going to figure out how to handle all her items, the
beautiful pieces of knitting she

created a world where you knew she cared about you
with her whole

heart breaking to see everyone full of

grief will turn to memories of the good times you
had with your

mom will be proud of the young woman you grow
up to

be strong for your father and your

brother told me you want to try to go back to school quickly, instead of sitting around the

house is full of food so when you go home today you won't have to worry about having things to

eat something; you look so skinny and need to keep up your

strength, and faith will get you through these next few

weeks ago I talked to her and told her how special she was to

me and your mom grew up together; we were best friends in high

school will help you catch up; don't worry right now about those

things get better, life goes on, and you'll be able to handle your mother's

death is inevitable; your mom's just came way too

early on it will seem impossible to go on, but you will move

on the last day of her life, she still continued to fight for another day with her

family will be here for you.

Words blended oneintoanother;

words of sympathycondolencecareandlove,

as people morphed into more and more and more
people,

the hours dripped by at Mom's wake.

Brett and I hugged everyone as they shuffled past,

awkward embraces with people we didn't know.

What we didn't hear were the words of relief, held
tightly inside.

Secret words not meant for my family.

Words revealing that they were glad they were only
here for a short while,

glad they could still go home to their loved ones who
were still living,

to their families who were still safe

and

whole.

Posted By: Your Present Self

[Friday, September 6, 9:36 PM]

The second time I talked to Jack, I spent the night with him.

Beacon was having a basketball scrimmage, and I wanted to go. Brett was bugging Dad about transferring back to Olmstead High, but I loved my new school. The excitement of basketball was starting to rub off on me. I felt the familiar thrill of the sport, which had been absent for so long, and I liked the comfort of emotions I once knew so well.

The scrimmage was going to be at Saint Edward's, the all-boys boarding school three hours south of us. It was one of Beacon's biggest rivals. Although recruiting was restricted, everyone knew that rule was a joke. The school got some of the best players in the country. They enticed student athletes with hefty academic scholarships that continued to be awarded all four years even though the recruits spent more time in the gym than in any classroom.

Dad's bedroom door was open and the room was

empty late one night when I got up to go to the bathroom. I found him in his office. He turned toward me and yawned, his glasses resting on the top of his head. He was doing the same thing he had been when I went to bed two hours earlier: feverishly studying tapes of Saint Edward games, memorizing plays.

"You need to get some sleep. It won't do you any good if you're too tired to coach."

"I will, I will."

"Dad, you can't stay up all night."

It was a useless battle and he'd spend at least another hour in his office, but to walk by without saying anything didn't seem right. This was the first time his team would play another school this season, and I knew Dad felt he had something to prove. I could've told him he'd already proved it, beating out of hundreds of other coaches for the job, but I doubted he'd listen. It was obvious he saw this scrimmage as his first test. Everyone at Beacon did.

Caravans of people would trek to the scrimmage, eager to see the new players and coach, but Brett refused to go. He was adamant about staying home. Jenna didn't want to go either and miss the Saturday art class she took at the local college, but Ali acted as if her life would end if she wasn't at the game.

Ali convinced me to try to get Dad to let us ride with the team.

"Think about watching all those hot sweaty boys running around on the court trying to show off the first time they play for a crowd this year."

I wrinkled my nose. "Sweaty boys?"

"Believe me, you'll agree there is nothing better after the game."

Ali and I went to Dad's office when the day ended. We planned to beg him into submission, but we didn't have to.

He put his papers down, his attention completely on me. "You want to go to the game?"

I shifted my weight, suddenly shy. I glanced at Ali before I answered. "Yeah, if it's okay. We promise we'll be good." I was about to go into the speech the two of us had prepared about how great it would look to have his daughter cheering for him right from the bleachers, but he cut me off.

"Yes, yes, of course you can come."

"Really? You don't mind?"

"I'd love to have you there."

I looked at Dad, and instead of the sadness I usually saw in his face, for a minute it was as it used to be. He was excited for me to be a part of the sport that just two years ago had been so special to both of us.

Ali and I promised to keep out of his way, to stay out of trouble, and to be full of Beacon spirit. After Ali's parents agreed to let her go, he booked us a hotel room to share.

We rode on one of the school buses decorated with signs the cheerleaders made. Dad and the other coaches were seated behind us, and the team was behind them. Ali and I spent the whole ride peeking at the players and discussing who was the hottest. I watched Jack when he wasn't looking and wondered how Ali wasn't blown away by his crazy sexiness.

We arrived late Friday night. The players were told to go to their rooms; wake-up was at seven so they'd have time for breakfast and warm-ups before the noon scrimmage.

Shortly after I'd fallen asleep, I woke to a muffled blaring sound. I wrestled out of the tangle of sheets, trying to figure out what was going on. The shapes around me seemed hazy. Ali was buried under the covers in the twin bed next to mine, oblivious to the noise.

The shrilling of the phone next to my bed added to the noise. I fumbled for the receiver.

"Hello?"

"Kate, it's Dad. The fire alarm is going off. We don't think there's a fire, but you and Ali need to come outside. Find me when you do."

"Where will you be?"

He hung up, saying something about calling the team members.

I woke Ali as I slipped on my flip-flops, and we followed a stream of people toward the stairwell.

"Thank goodness we're only on the fourth floor," I said to a half-asleep Ali as we hurried down.

She grunted. She was a self-proclaimed marathon sleeper, waking for nothing.

Outside, people stood away from the building alone or in small groups. I didn't see any smoke or sign of a fire, but the employees worked hard to keep us out there, just in case there was one. Most people wore jackets or wrapped the scratchy hotel blankets around their shoulders. I wished I'd thought to grab something. The night was cold, and all I had on was a pair of sweatpants and a T-shirt that I'd worn so often it really was decent only for bed, where people wouldn't see me.

I crossed my arms over my chest and looked around for Dad. There were moms and dads holding sleeping kids and frazzled businessmen using the time to e-mail even though it was after three in the morning. A few basketball players I vaguely recognized huddled together, bumping shoulders.

"Kate," Dad yelled across the grass.

I weaved through the crowd, leaving Ali curled up on an empty bench near the front of the hotel as if she were a piece of luggage someone had dropped off. She'd thought to bring a comforter out with her, and I was willing to bet she'd be asleep in less than five minutes.

Dad placed a hand on my shoulder for a quick moment. "I'm glad you're here. We're missing four people, but I sent two of the boys to search for them on the other side of the hotel. I think we'll be fine. No one sees any smoke, but we have to stay out here until they let us go back in."

"Okay," I said, trying to keep my teeth from chattering. "I'll go wait over there." I pointed to the parking lot where people sat on a rock wall that stretched along the hotel's edge.

Dad tapped his pen against his clipboard.

"Sounds good. Just make sure to stay out here." He walked toward a group of his players.

I balanced myself on the narrow wall. The cold seeped through my sweatpants. I wrapped my arms around myself and considered talking Ali into sharing her blanket with me.

"You look like you're freezing."

I jumped, startled by the boy's voice, and lost my balance.

A pair of hands wrapped around me. "Whoa, I got you." He let go.

I hoisted my knees up and turned around on the wall. There was Jack, right there in front of me, pulling off his Beacon sweatshirt. His T-shirt stuck to his sweatshirt and came up a little. I caught a glimpse of his muscular stomach, and my heart raced. I could look at his abs forever. I considered grabbing his sleeves and tying them together so he could never find his way out.

"Hey," I said and knew I sounded lame.

He tossed his sweatshirt at me. "You need to warm up. Put it on."

"Thanks," I said, obviously wowing him with my witty conversational skills.

"Kate, right?"

I nodded and thought I might start hyperventilating. He remembered my name. I ran my fingers along the inside of his sweatshirt sleeves. They were still warm from his body heat.

I tried talking again. "Yeah, my dad is your coach." I winced. I sounded like a loser. Had I really mentioned my dad as a way to look cool? "I mean, I know you from the team. My dad's talked about you."

"Oh, he has, has he? I hope it was good stuff."

"I didn't mean just you," I said quickly. "He talks about the whole team a lot."

Jack grinned, and I relaxed a little.

"Actually," I said. "He mentions you guys more than a lot. The team is almost all he talks about."

"Well, I hope he mentions my name once in a while."

"He does. Not as much now, because I think he realized I was sick of hearing about you. I told him you're not the only person on the team."

Jack laughed, catching my joke, and we fell into a conversation about basketball, specifically Beacon basketball. I was afraid he'd leave to join his teammates, but it didn't happen. In the distance, sirens blared. We watched as the red trucks showed up and a bunch of firefighters went into the hotel.

They came out about fifteen minutes later, and we were all waved into the building. I waited for Jack to stand and head in, but he didn't. Instead, he moved closer to me. I casually bumped a shoulder into his. I could feel the heat through his sweatshirt. I tried not to freak out that his leg was touching mine. He wore plaid flannel pants; pajamas never looked so sexy.

"So how come I don't see you at any of the practices?" he asked.

"I'm not sure. Maybe I'll start going."

"I think you should." He grabbed my hand, and my stomach dropped. "Come on. We better head inside." He pulled me up from the rock wall and then let go.

I sighed, mad at myself for thinking he'd wanted to hold my hand.

We walked toward the hotel, but then he stopped. "Damn, this is going to be a killer for my game today." He pointed in the distance. "The sun is coming up."

I smiled at the light creeping upward in the sky. "Good morning, Jack."

He grinned, and I thought, *It is a good morning.*

I thought about my night with Jack the rest of the weekend. I held it with me deep inside, my own little treasure. Even when Ali asked why it had taken me so long to come back to the room, I never told.

Jack Blane.

I rolled his name around on my tongue like candy, tucking it in the corner of my mouth to preserve its sticky sweetness. His name left a taste in my cheek, a whisper on my lips, a thin thread floating around my head and then evaporating into the air.

Jack Blane.

The mere thought of what his name could do unnerved me.

The name of a boy I would've never had the guts to talk to at my old school. A boy other girls laid claim to, his name on their strawberry-glossed lips as they flirted with him. A boy a town cheered for and hung their hopes for victory upon. A boy who might never know anything more about me than my name and status: Kate Franklin, the coach's daughter.

But I would change that. I would find a way to make sure Jack Blane never forgot my name.

When Dad and I got home from the scrimmage, I waited until he was lost in work in his office before I pulled open the sliding door. It was cool out— too cool, some might argue, to be swimming—but this was the one place I could go and forget about everything. The place where I could let the inky water cover my head, surrounding me so I couldn't see or hear the outside world.

I kept the lights off and dove in, feeling the water rush past me as I pushed deeper. The pool was heated, but the air whispered cold across my face when I surfaced. I was the only one who used the pool anymore, and I liked to swim at night, as Mom had.

Back when she was alive, Dad had teased her: "You won't get any use out of a pool in the Midwest. Most of the year it's winter. You'll be lucky to get three months straight of warm weather. The other nine months, it'll be a big eyesore reminding us how cold it is."

He and Mom loved retelling the story of her in-sistence on finding a house with a pool. They joked about it with us when we'd sit outside during the lazy days of September as the heat lingered and it seemed too hot to do normal things like homework, house-cleaning, and cooking. Mom always said, "I guess you were wrong, Bob. It looks like you can use this thing well over three months."

"True, true. That's why it was my idea to get a pool. Can you imagine how miserable these days would be without one? We'd all be running through the sprinklers or walking around naked."

"Disgusting," Brett would yell.

I'd plug my ears and make a show of singing loud enough to block out all noise and images created by Dad's comment.

Mom would splash water at Dad. "Yeah, yeah, it was your idea. It's always your idea until the cold sets in and you can tease me again."

On days like that I'd lie next to them, one hand dipped in the water, listening with my eyes closed, the bulb of the orange sun impressed on my eyelids. We wouldn't head inside until it had sunk low and pulled down some of the heat with it.

Mom was officially diagnosed in early March when the days were warm in the teasing way that encouraged you to wear short sleeves or flip-flops. A day when you opened all the windows in your house and wanted to submerge your feet in the pool but the bare branches and muddy brown earth made you think otherwise. The water would be cold and biting when you peeled back the cover, not yet warmed by a summer sun. It was the time of year when you were taunted by hot days that could easily roll into freezing ones.

Life around us continued the year Mom was diagnosed: the seasons progressed, the weather warmed, but that year the pool remained hidden under its thick plastic shell, a reminder.

Mom retreated into a shell of her own.

Outside, she seemed to be trying to stay the same. She joked and laughed.

There were days she didn't have to try hard.

Days she had to try really hard.

And days she didn't seem to want to try at all.

We all continued to do normal things, even though they seemed anything but normal because Mom was dying. Stuff like shopping at the mall, game nights, and trips to restaurants where we didn't have to order because the staff knew our usual dishes.

There were things we did that we hadn't done before: firsts Mom wanted to experience, such as visits to museums, nights watching classic movies, and family photos in funny poses with Dad and Brett as James Bond and Mom and me as Bond girls. Firsts we knew would also be lasts for Mom, lasts for us as a family.

We tried to make memories and cram it all in. We tried to pretend time wasn't running out. We tried to be a family, but there were some family traditions that stopped.

Like the swimming pool.

For months, late into the summer, the cover stayed on, the water still. Until one night when, in the late hours, something woke me. It was that time between the night and the morning. The time when light inched up in the sky and you could almost call it dawn. The air was calm, the house quiet, the world still.

I moved my curtains to the side, turned the metal knob along my window, and cranked the screen open to watch the neighborhood, lights off, houses slumbering.

Then I heard a noise. It was slight. If I had been sleeping, talking, or even moving, I wouldn't have noticed it. If I hadn't stopped to catch it again, I might have dismissed it as the creaking of the house, someone rustling in bed—the usual sounds.

I looked outside at the pool where the noise had come from.

The lights outside were off, but the cover was folded to one side.

I saw the water moving before I saw Mom. There were dark ripples, disappearing in the areas the moon's light didn't touch.

Mom swam laps soundlessly, back and forth, turning her head slightly to draw in breaths, making small gasping noises.

She swam from end to end, in what seemed a continuous line of movement to nowhere.

I watched, far away, until she climbed out and wrapped her frail, thin body with a towel.

I looked the next night, and she was there.

Each night I watched her as she navigated the same path, and each night the tears fell, leaving their own slippery tracks down my face.

She was always there when I woke and went to the curtains. It was an automatic response, and after the first few nights, my body didn't need an alarm clock.

She swam constantly, urgently. She swam on rainy nights when lightning crackled through the sky and lit her up for brief intervals. She swam on nights when the air was thick with heat and you could hardly breathe. She swam on nights when the wind shrieked so loud you didn't know if it really was the wind or yourself, calling out for someone to hear you.

She swam all through the summer, her path shorter and shorter.

She swam until she had to stop sometimes, clinging to the side of the pool in a short respite.

She swam until, instead of the length of the pool, she swam the width.

She swam until she could only sit on the edge of the steps and stare into the water.

She swam until she was too weak to make it outside and only saw the pool through the large guest room windows that faced it.

She swam until she could no longer stay in her own house and we had to move her to a hospice and it was not her body swimming but her mind, her body slowly pulling her down into the choking waters of her illness.

Now that she was gone, I swam to find her. It was my way of coping. I moved through the water, remembering moments I spent with my mom: the ice cream sundaes she bought for Brett and me when it rained because we needed something happy on a gloomy day, the nights we pitched a tent in the living room and curled up in sleeping bags, the movie marathons with popcorn and root beer floats. I remembered it all as I swam and vowed I wouldn't forget any of it.

But as I slid through the water that night, after we got home from the scrimmage, I didn't think of my mom. Instead, I thought of Jack.

I replayed our conversation outside the hotel over and over again. I held on to the words he had said, the feel of his hands on my back, and the warmth of the sweatshirt he offered. I held tight to all of this and let myself believe Jack could be something.

www.allmytruths.com

Today's Truth:

If you don't learn to survive, you will drown.

The day after Mom died

.survive to laps swimming started I

I swim toward the deep end, dropping the days that follow into a dark abyss.

.was once Mom what feel to, past the touch to end shallow the toward swim I

I swim through the water

.strokes strong, strong strokes

I swim back and forth,

.forth and back

I swim until I am exhausted

.more some swim to myself push and

I swim to feel the pain in my arms, my legs, my thighs.

.being my, heart my, head my in pain the numb to swim I

I swim toward the shallow end to reach for images of Mom and me.

.death of, loss of feeling the away kicking, end deep the toward swim I

I swim back and forth,

.forth and back

The day after Mom died

.survive to laps swimming started I

Posted By: Your Present Self

[Saturday, September 14, 10:13 PM]

The Monday morning after the scrimmage began two hours before my alarm usually went off. I had set my cell phone on vibrate to wake me, afraid Brett would hear my regular alarm and wonder why I was up so early. I'd never live it down if he knew I was trying to impress a guy.

My sleep had been fitful. I woke off and on to make sure my phone hadn't fallen out of my hand, slipping into my covers so I'd miss the alarm and wake at the regular time or, worse, late and I'd have to rush to school, bypassing a shower and the hair dryer. I sweated under my sheets, tossing with strange dreams that evaporated as soon as I woke and tried to remember them.

It turned out the alarm wasn't necessary. I got up before it went off. I was anxious to see Jack at school. I had watched him play Saturday in the scrimmage, but he was with the team and I never had the chance, or the nerve, to say anything more to him. Today I would see him at school, and I planned to talk to him.

I needed to prepare. Usually, sleep overruled my morning beauty routine, but today, and maybe for the rest of the days this year, it was more important to look good. No matter how long that took.

I grabbed a towel and my shower caddy and crept past Dad's room and then Brett's to get to the stairs. Dad had installed an extra shower in the basement shortly after my parents had bought the house, and while I usually didn't shower there, it was perfect for me today. I took my time shaving my legs, covering myself with fruit-smelling lotions and leaving the deep conditioning mask in my hair long enough to hopefully make it smooth and shiny. The extra two hours gave me enough time to blow-dry and straighten my hair and try to make my makeup look good. I couldn't do much with my school uniform, but there were enough other parts of me that could use a little work, and I wanted to make sure they were perfect or at least decent before I saw Jack.

Once I was convinced my hair was as straight as it would get, I headed into the kitchen.

Brett waved a hand around his nose. "Whoa. If you think I'm letting you in my car smelling like you bathed in a gallon of perfume, you're delusional."

"Shut up." I grabbed one of the bagels from the bag he'd left open.

"Seriously, we're driving with the windows open." Brett tossed his plate in the sink, even though the dishwasher was right next to him.

I finished my bagel, brushed my teeth again, and headed to the garage, where Brett sat honking the horn.

Thankfully, he didn't make me ride with the windows open.

The morning sped by. I weaved through the halls on adrenaline, half-excited and half-terrified of running into Jack until it was time for lunch, when running into him wasn't a fear but a certainty. He had the same lunch block, and I knew exactly where he and a bunch of basketball players sat.

I pretended to listen to everyone at my table, nodding once in a while to look interested, but I was really watching Jack. I planned to follow him out of the cafeteria, and I hoped he wouldn't leave in a group.

Luck must have been on my side because he got up when there were about five minutes left.

I jumped out of my seat and grabbed my stuff. "I gotta go," I told everyone.

"What? We still have a bunch of time," Ali said.

"You haven't even finished your lunch."

"I forgot I had to print a paper for English."

I rushed out before Jenna, who had English with me, could question the paper we didn't have due. I threw my food in the trash and followed Jack. I must have looked like a crazy woman dodging tables and students. I probably took out two or three freshmen.

"Jack, wait," I yelled when I'd nearly caught up to him.

He turned and stared at me blankly.

My stomach dropped. This was a mistake. He didn't even remember me.

And then he did. "Kate, what's up?" And everything was perfect in the world.

I grabbed his sweatshirt out of my bag. It killed me to give it back, but I needed a reason to talk to him. "Your sweatshirt. I thought you'd want it back."

He took it and shrugged. "Thanks. I'd forgotten about it."

"I wanted to give it to you . . ." Now that I'd used my excuse to talk to him, I couldn't think of anything more to say. "Well, okay. I gotta go to class."

He nodded and turned to walk away.

I closed my eyes and let out a slow breath. I'd blown my chance.

But I was wrong. When I opened my eyes again, Jack was facing me. "Are you going to Joe's on Friday?"

I shrugged and pretended to act casual, as if I obviously knew who Joe was and had been planning for weeks to go to his party. The bell rang, and students spilled into the hallway.

"Maybe I'll see you there," he said before he turned to catch up with another sophomore I recognized because he always walked around with a basketball in his hand.

"If you're lucky." The words slipped out, and I was surprised at how natural it felt to flirt with Jack.

"I hope I am," he said over his shoulder.

Somehow, by some divine miracle, I did come to know about Joe's party.

I finally told Ali and Jenna about my conversation with Jack outside the hotel, and they didn't protest when I told them I wanted to start watching practices.

"You should totally hook up with him. He has a legit sensitive side. I remember when we were in third grade, he smuggled his new puppy into school. He hid the dog in his book bag. Who can resist that?"

I laughed and agreed.

The three of us started attending practices after school each day, sitting in the bleachers, joining parents and girls who were dating team members. One of the girls was with the now infamous Joe Radcowski and started to talk about the party he was throwing while his parents visited his brother in college.

"It's going to be crazy," she gushed. "Have you

been to a Beacon party yet?"

I shook my head. There was no way for me to lie. It had only been a few weeks. I didn't know which past parties to even pretend to have attended.

She didn't seem to mind. "You have to come to this one. What's your number? I'll text you the address. You'll love it. Joe's parties are always a good time."

I gave her my number and wondered what I'd gotten myself into. I'd never been to a high school party. After Mom died, high school things didn't seem important, especially parties full of people I didn't talk to anymore. My version of what went on at these parties came from the images I'd seen on TV or in movies. The ones where everyone dances like a maniac, the alcohol flows, and you either throw up, pass out, have sex, or get arrested. None of these options appealed to me, but I agreed out of curiosity.

There was also the little fact that Jack would be there.

Who was I kidding? Jack being at the party was the reason I agreed.

The next day, when Ali and I were sitting in my kitchen making plans, Brett walked in and stood with the refrigerator door wide open. He pretended to search for something, but I wasn't stupid. He was listening to the two of us. After Ali left, he tried to get me to change my mind.

"Why would you want to go to a party with people like that? Why don't you hang out with your old friends anymore?"

I shrugged. I tried not to think about my old friends, about how easy it was to forget people I'd gone to school with for nine years. Friends I had declared besties forever. The people who ditched me when Mom got sick.

"These are my friends now."

Brett frowned. "I'd be careful calling some of those people friends."

"You'd find out they're not so bad if you gave them a chance."

"Just make sure you keep things in control when you're at the party. Don't assume they're watching out for you."

"Geez, you act like something horrible is going to happen."

"I know what can happen, and I don't want it to happen to you."

I kicked at the floor tiles and told myself to drop it. Brett was acting like this because he cared about me. Without Mom, he was the one who watched over me and worried. Dad was so busy with his basketball that I could probably hitchhike across the country before he realized I was gone. I wouldn't admit it to Brett, but I didn't mind him playing the big brother routine.

"Promise me you'll watch out for yourself until you know you can trust these people."

"I *can* trust them," I said, but I wondered why I felt so sure. I really hadn't known Ali or Jenna long.

"If you're going to drink—"

"Really, Brett? A lecture about drinking."

He raised a hand. "Hear me out. I'm not going to tell you not to drink. I'm not stupid. Just make sure you keep an eye on your drink and eat something before you go to the party. You won't know what hit you if you start to drink without anything in your stomach."

I gave him a thumbs-up. "Food and guarding my drink. Got it. Anything else, or are you satisfied with my safety?"

"Yeah, the most important thing—"

"Of course there's one more thing."

"Call me if you need anything."

"Okay, Dad."

"Seriously, Kate. Call or send me a text if you don't feel comfortable. I'll come get you."

I gave him a half smile. This was the type of conversation you were supposed to have with your parents. "Thanks, but I'll be fine."

"Just in case," Brett said and grabbed his car keys off the kitchen table.

"Okay, just in case," I promised but knew I could take care of myself.

Despite Brett's warnings and my nerves, there was no way I'd miss Joe's party. If Jack was going to be there, I'd make sure he found me. I was excited about what might happen. Especially if that something involved running my hands through Jack's hair.

I was also scared out of my mind.

The plan was to meet up with Jenna there. She'd been complaining for days that her grandma's birthday party was seriously cramping her style, forcing her to arrive at Joe's late. She claimed we'd all be guzzling beers and having the time of our lives while she had to wait for her grandma to find enough air in her lungs to blow out all her candles.

"Tonight is going to be amazing," Ali said from the front passenger seat.

Her brother, Jeff, drove like a maniac and kept yelling at us to stop giggling. Ali had blackmailed him into giving us a ride, threatening to tell her parents about the party if he didn't. He made us promise we wouldn't drink. Ali winked at me as she promised.

There was no way I'd admit it to Ali, but I'd never gotten drunk before. The taste wasn't completely foreign to me; I'd had sips from glasses during the holidays, and once I found Brett with a beer out by the pool and talked him into letting me try some. But the idea of going to a big party—one where people probably drank until they puked and then wiped their mouths with their sleeves before slamming another beer—scared me.

But ready or not, Jeff swung the car into an open spot on the street and turned off the engine. The party was packed. You could hear everyone from two blocks away, which was where we had to park because of all the cars.

"The police are going to be here soon," Jeff warned, a weak attempt to scare us away.

Ali pumped her arms as if running. "Then we need to walk fast."

"Be careful." He sighed. "Don't do anything that's going to get you in trouble."

"Yeah, yeah, yeah." Ali slowed to walk beside me and let her brother move ahead of us.

She and I were dressed identically in jeans and

long-sleeved T-shirts with tank tops underneath. Ali, however, wore a pair of shiny red heels while I wore flats like the rest of the girls we passed.

"Do you ever not wear heels?"

Ali slowly made her way up the front walk, trying to avoid the cracks in the concrete. "Nope. When you're as short as me, you gotta make sure you work it some way."

A boy from Dad's team greeted us when we walked inside. I couldn't remember his name, but it probably wouldn't have made a difference. The music was so loud, we wouldn't have been able to hear each other talk. He put an arm around my shoulders and directed us to the beer before he disappeared through a mass of people. The house wasn't as crowded as the cars outside led me to believe, and Ali and I found our way to the kitchen without having to elbow past everyone. Getting to the keg was a different story. The space around it was crammed with people putting their cups under the nozzle and pumping vigorously, as if that would make the beer come out faster.

"We're not getting a drink from here anytime soon," Ali said, opening the refrigerator door. "Here, take one of these." She handed me a can and took one for herself. "Let's go outside."

The cold drink cooled my sweaty palms. "Do you think it's okay to drink these?" I didn't want to seem like a loser, but I also didn't want someone to bash my face in because I took their beer.

"Relax. It's fine. When my brother has people over, I take their beer all the time. It tastes a million times better than the stuff in the keg, and usually whoever brought it is too drunk to notice." She popped the tab and gestured for me to do the same. "Enjoy yourself. Tonight is going to be a good, good night."

I opened my can and held it up.

"Cheers." Ali clinked her beer against mine.

I took a tentative sip, wrinkling my nose. When I saw that Ali was watching, I took a bigger one. "Cheers," I responded, feeling the sour liquid bubble down my throat.

We made our way to the backyard, which was packed with bodies. I looked around for Jack, but there was no sign of him.

The night was windy, but with so many people bumping shoulders, it felt warm. Perfume, sweat, beer, and cigarettes mixed in the air, creating a unique scent that wasn't good but wasn't all that bad either. Ali spotted Jenna, who must have escaped from her grandma's party early, and we fought our way over to her, trying to move fast so they wouldn't disappear into the sea of people. Plastic cups cracked under my feet, and the cuffs of my jeans were quickly soaked from the wet grass blades, the cold ends like slippery fingers grazing my feet. Music pulsed out of a second-floor window, so loud the song was distorted and hard to decipher. Cigarette butts sparked in the backyard like fireflies, flashes of light, glowing for a second with each intake of breath and then disappearing in a haze.

Jenna stood with a group, flinging her arms wildly as she talked. She introduced me to some kids I'd seen around school, an unusually tall boy and two girls who spoke alike, their sentences coming out rushed and ending with giggles.

Ali fell into conversation with them about someone who would be showing up at the party later. I tried to follow, but it was hard to pay attention when the music was so loud and people pushed past me. I sipped the beer, trying to act busy, bringing the can up and down so I wasn't just standing there silent.

My cell phone vibrated in my purse, and I dug it out. There was a message from Brett: U R NOT DANCING ON TABLES OR SMOKING OUT OF STRANGE-SHAPED TUBES, R U?

I laughed softly and texted him back: THIS PARTY IS CRAZY! IM ABOUT TO BONG BEER NUMBER 10!

The phone vibrated again. NOT FUNNY.

IM FINE. FIND SOMETHING 2 DO BESIDES STALKING UR LIL SIS.

I thought I'd be annoyed at Brett for checking up on me, but it was kind of nice to know someone had my back.

I put my phone in my purse and focused on the group. More people had joined, and someone handed me another beer. I drank it slowly, feeling a bit light-headed. I tried to get Ali's attention to let her know I was going to find the bathroom, but she was in the middle of telling a story about her brother and some family vacation they'd taken a few years ago. I slipped away, hoping she'd be in the same spot when I returned.

The path to the house was almost impossible to walk through. Two or three people stood on each stair leading to the deck, and with my unsteady feet, I didn't think it was a good idea to try to climb up them. Instead, I elbowed my way to the side of the house, where concrete blocks formed a walk-way. I pushed through the bushes and low-hanging branches, following a sort of tunnel, feeling the branches grab the sides of my shirt. I broke free and stumbled onto the driveway, where I ran into the back of a guy leaning against the garage.

"Whoa, sorry." I nearly tripped over my own feet. "You have to fight to get anywhere at this party. There sure are a lot of people here," I said more to myself than to him.

The guy faced me, and his gaze fixed on mine. "Where else would we be tonight?"

My face heated up when I realized who it was.

Jack Blane.

"So we meet again," he said, drawing the words out.

My stomach flipped. The one person I'd wished to see had seemingly appeared out of thin air.

Why was he on the driveway? He didn't seem like the type to hang out alone at a party. He should be surrounded by girls. Pretty girls who wore tiny swishy skirts and tight tops. Girls who painted their toenails bubble gum pink and had long glossy hair. Girls who screeched as boys chased them through the hallways trying to tickle them.

Girls who weren't like me.

Girls I had no idea how to be like.

I tried to figure out what to say. "I meant there are a lot of cars here, parked all over. The neighbors must notice what's going on."

He laughed and touched my arm.

"I don't think most of the people here will care if the neighbors notice. Joe might, when his parents come home, but as for us"—he grinned—"we'll be long gone. You don't have to worry."

I must have looked as if I didn't believe him because he stood right in front of me, so close I could see the small freckles across the top of his nose.

"Don't worry," he said. "I was joking. You don't have to be so serious. I wondered when you'd show up."

"You were looking for me?" The words came out before I could stop them. *Way to go, Kate. Nothing like sounding calm, cool, and collected.*

"Of course I was. Why do you think I mentioned the party? After all, we have some history. We spent the night together." He raised his gaze and ran a hand through his hair.

"We did, didn't we? I wanted to see you here too," I said quietly, unexpected courage surging in me.

"Good." His hand found mine, and then the two of us were moving toward each other. Suddenly talking to Jack became nothing.

The memory of the first time we talked—the cold bench, his warm sweatshirt, the early morning—was erased.

The conversation we had outside the hotel wasn't important.

The feel of his arms when he had caught me from falling off the wall was brushed away from memory.

The solidness of his hand when he helped me up from the wall was forgotten.

Because nothing came close, not an inch or an ounce, to what it felt like when Jack kissed me.

We broke apart. We stood still. It didn't matter that we were separated, because it felt as if we were together. A truck screeched up next to us. Before we could say or do anything, someone laid on the horn.

"Where the hell have you been, Jack? Get inside," a passenger yelled out the window.

Jack started to say something, but the driver honked the horn again. Jack turned and climbed into the truck, which peeled out of the driveway, kicking dust in my face.

14

I went back to the party, even though all I wanted to do was sit still and think about the kiss. I found Ali in the living room hanging off of Luke, a stocky, dark-haired basketball player I'd seen Jack with the other day. She was pressed up against him, and his muscular arms were wrapped tightly around her.

I wished Jack's friends hadn't shown up and stolen him away. I felt a pang of regret for a moment, but as Ali broke away and tottered toward me, I pushed the feeling aside.

"Kate, there you are," she slurred. She stood unsteadily and wrapped her arms around me in the same way she'd been doing to Luke. "I've been trying to find you."

"Here I am. Safe and sound."

"Yes, yes, you're here, and my brother is over there." She swept an arm around, and I had no idea where she meant her brother was. "It's time to go, my brother demands." She broke away to give Luke a wobbly kiss, and the two of them started making out.

Jenna came alongside me. "What have you been up to while Ali's been sucking face with Luke over there?"

"Just hanging out," I said, not wanting to share with anyone what happened. "Talking with people."

"Sure you were. You have that look on your face like you've been up to something bad." She smirked.

My stomach dropped. She knew. I imagined her lurking behind the bushes watching us, and I wondered who else might have seen us. Did Jack and I have a whole audience?

Jenna tilted her head. "Are you okay? I'm just kidding."

"Yeah, of course." I exhaled slowly.

"We need to go rescue Ali. Luke is a walking STD, and what's going on over there is not good. If there's anyone to avoid at Beacon, it's Luke. I don't even want to think about how dirty and nasty he is from all the girls he's slept with." She grabbed my arm and pulled me toward the two of them.

She tapped Ali's shoulder. "It's time to say good-bye."

Ali waved us away, not even bothering to detach from Luke.

"Your brother is going to ditch us if we don't get outside." Jenna grabbed Ali's wrist and pulled her away. I was impressed someone as small as Jenna had enough strength to pry Ali's death grip off of Luke. "Sorry to break up the party."

Ali allowed us to take her away, but she reached toward Luke as if begging him to grab on and keep her with him.

"I give him five minutes until he's shoving his tongue down someone else's throat," Jenna whispered to me. "That guy is repulsive."

The three of us made our way out the door, and a car was in fact sitting by the curb with its lights on and horn blasting. We opened the door and pushed Ali inside.

"Mom is going to shit when she sees you," Jeff said.

Ali fell into the passenger seat, oblivious to Jeff's grumbles. She rested her chin on her chest, and by the time we turned out of the development, she was snoring softly.

I leaned against the window and pressed my

head to the cool glass, watching house after house, most tucked into the dark, everyone asleep. We drove farther and farther away from the party, and I ran a finger over my lips, remembering.

www.allmytruths.com

Today's Truth:

A moment can change everything.

Smoky breath, meet sour beer.

Chapped lips, meet glossy moistness.

Exploring tongue, meet smooth teeth.

Firm hands, meet sweaty palms.

Bristly cheek, meet red-flamed blush.

Jack, meet Kate.

Kate, meet Jack.

Posted By: Your Present Self

[Saturday, September 21, 1:13 AM]

Monday morning I was in the kitchen eating breakfast when a car pulled in to the driveway. Giant arcs from the headlights cast shadows on the living room walls. I could see them from the kitchen, where I stirred soggy cereal in the bowl. Dad had left twenty minutes before, and Brett was banging around upstairs doing who knew what.

Outside, two short beeps startled me and sent a neighbor's dog into a barking fit.

I crept to the door, pulling the ratty, faded blue robe I'd had since I was eleven around me. Peeking out of the corner of our curtain, I saw a large truck in the driveway, its motor sending up steam as it struggled with the crisp October morning. The headlights made it impossible to see who sat in the driver's seat, but the truck was unmistakable.

I closed my eyes. This couldn't be happening. But there was no denying who was here; the red truck in my driveway was the very same one that had picked up Jack from the party.

"Kate," a voice outside the door yelled.

I dropped the curtain and slid to the ground, trying to hide.

Jack was on my front porch.

I stared down in horror at the robe I always wore in the morning. The one I wore only in front of family. The one Brett made fun of. The one stained with nail polish and an unidentified breakfast item that had hardened and refused to be scratched off. It had a giant hole in the back I'd jokingly patched with a scrap of Disney princess sheet I'd outgrown. A robe I'd never let anyone else see me in.

Especially Jack.

But I didn't have time to run upstairs and grab something else. Jack was still knocking on my door and clearly wasn't leaving anytime soon.

I took a breath and turned the knob. "Hey," I said, unable to hide my surprise. "What are you doing here?" The question sounded more accusatory than I meant it to.

Jack seemed unfazed. He smiled slowly, as if he knew I'd been hiding behind the door, as if he'd caught me doing something secret. "I thought I'd give you a ride to school."

Like an idiot, I stared at him.

"Since we go to the same place and all." He smiled again, as if it was that easy, as if of course he would show up and take me to school.

My heart pounded, and I thought about what it meant to have him here. I knew what was going on. This was a big deal. It was freaking amazing. Jack wasn't here because he thought I needed a ride to school. Jack was standing at my door because he liked me. I felt light-headed.

"Usually I go with Brett," I said, stalling but not knowing why. Realizing he might not know who Brett was, I added, "Brett's my brother."

"Let's give Brett a break. Come with me today."

I couldn't hide a smile anymore. I wanted to jump and celebrate, but instead I said, "Sure, that would be great. Let me tell him and change. I'll be ready in five minutes." I pushed the door all the way open, allowing him in, and turned to run upstairs, giving him a full view of my Disney-princess-clad ass.

But I didn't care.

Jack had come to pick me up. He'd kissed me the other night, and now he was waiting for me to get in the truck with him. I danced into my room, shaking my butt in the mirror to imaginary music, and threw my hands in the air.

Jack Blane liked me. It was as simple as that.

Suddenly, almost as if had you had blinked you might have missed it, I became JackandKate, a name merged like movie star couples'.

I wasn't plain Kate, new girl Kate, or Coach Franklin's daughter Kate. I was something more, something powerful and brilliant. I was Jack's Kate.

I was ecstatic. The two of us together as a couple was a monumental event to me, giant as the erupting of a volcano dormant for decades or the burning of a piece of toast and finding Jesus's image in the charred remains.

But to everyone else, our new relationship seemed simple. Ali even commented, "It was as if one day you were together—poof. You were never anything but together."

It was simple, that coming together. Jack picked me up each morning for school, waited outside my classroom, and came over to our table with some other guys on the team and ate lunch with me. By the end of the week, we were a couple. When he asked me Friday after school in front of my house, it was easy to say yes to being his girlfriend.

I'd never really wanted to be a part of a couple before. The idea of having a boyfriend didn't cross my mind much except for a few short-lived crushes on boys in my class who quickly proved to be either gross or uninteresting. Mom used to ask which boys I thought were cute, but I always ignored her, embarrassed to be talking about stuff like that with her and more interested in sports than boys.

But with Jack, it was different. I wanted to be with him. I wanted to be one of those girls who had a boyfriend, who was attached to him, who talked about nothing but him.

My life with Jack clicked. Our lives merged, one day blending into the next, all with such an easy movement that I didn't even notice the transition. It seemed there wasn't a time before there was a time with Jack.

www.allmytruths.com

Today's Truth:

**Don't expect anything. It's never
what you think it's going to be.**

Being with Jack isn't just

his hard urgent kisses that leave me

starving for more.

Or

his blue-green eyes,

as if viewing earth from space.

Or

his smile,

which grows across his face when I walk over.

Or

his smell,

a mix of

deodorant,

fruit bubble gum

and laundry detergent.

Or

the way he always asks to kiss me,

pausing as if worried I might say no,

even though there is nothing I could ever say

except yes.

Or

his laugh,

loud and stretching across a room,

causing people to turn to see what they're missing
out on.

Or

his jersey,

the practice warm-up I wear over jeans,

his name on the back so everyone can read

who belongs to him.

Or

the way he says my name

when I pick up the phone,

as if hearing my voice is what he waits for all day.

Or

the late-night phone calls,

the early-morning drives to school,

all my time spent with Jack so I'm never thinking
about who I miss.

Or

the way his hand hangs around me,

when we're at a party, after a game, or with friends,

as if he's letting everyone know I'm with him,

and I eagerly claim the position.

Or

the pride I feel

when people learn I'm dating Jack,

that I'm with Jack,

that Jack is my boyfriend.

Being with Jack isn't all of these things;

it's more.

And more and more and more.

It's opening door after door after door into another world,

the world of Beacon, the world of privilege.

Posted By: Your Present Self

[Monday, October 7, 7:18 PM]

In mid-October, a few weeks after we started dating, Jack grabbed my hand as I walked out of English class.

"Let's go get something to eat," he said and pulled me in the opposite direction of my next class.

"Now? I have precalc."

"You told me the other day how easy the class was. You'll be able to catch up."

"Jack, I can't cut," I told him, but really, who was going to stop me? Besides, it would be a lot more fun to spend the day with Jack than to sit in a boring old math class.

"It's not a big deal. I cut every once in a while, and it's fine. If anyone says something, I'll sign a pass for you. I have a whole pack of them. Come on. It'll be fun."

I didn't bother to ask Jack where he got the passes. I didn't want to know. What mattered was that Jack was here waiting for me to make up my mind. I glanced down the hall toward my class and back at Jack. He stood there with a half grin almost as if he were laughing at me.

That sealed my decision. "What the heck," I said, pulling my bag higher on my shoulder and turning away from my next class. "Let's get out of here."

I followed him out the doors of the school. I expected someone to stop us, ask us where we were going, and demand an explanation. No one did. We walked right out and got into his car.

Jack leaned over and gave me a kiss.

I almost pushed him away but thought better of it. I was living dangerously today. I pulled him all the way to me and gave anyone who might be watching a show.

He finally broke away and put the key into the ignition. "I may have to cut class with you more often."

We drove out of the gates and wound down the hill. I pushed the button to open my window and held my hand out, the cool wind rushing past.

"Where should we go, rebel?"

I swatted at him. "Stop it. If I'm the rebel, you're the one who corrupted me."

"I can handle that. I wouldn't mind corrupting you some more."

I rolled my eyes and sat back. "Let's get some ice cream."

"Ice cream?" Jack laughed. "It's nine forty-five in the morning and October."

"The perfect time for a hot fudge sundae."

"Okay, then, ice cream it is."

We stopped at a little café still serving breakfast and talked them into putting the ice cream into Styrofoam coffee cups so we could take them to the park. It was one of those perfect autumn days when school, work, and doing anything inside—especially eating ice cream—seemed wrong.

Apparently everyone else had the same idea. Moms chased toddlers around, kids shrieked with delight as they ran on the playground, and dogs followed balls across the field. Jack pulled an old green blanket out of his truck and spread it on the ground. We ate back to back, giving each other a place to lean.

"Okay, you were right about this ice cream. It hit the spot," Jack said, his hand reaching around and finding mine.

"Yeah, it was good." I turned around to face him and pointed to a big blob of hot fudge on his sleeve. "It looks like it was so good you're saving some for later."

"Hey, you never know when you'll get hungry. Thanks for running away with me today."

"Of course. This sure beats sitting through one of Ms. Carmody's boring old lessons."

"So it was worth it? Breaking out of class and being on the run?"

"Totally." I took a deep breath and found the courage to keep talking. "You make me happy. And that's not always easy . . ."

Jack knew about my mom. I'd only mentioned her briefly one afternoon when he'd dropped me off at my empty house. I hadn't been ready to open up, and he hadn't pushed any further. Instead, he'd grabbed my hand and squeezed it, which was enough for the moment.

"Why, Kate, I do believe you're getting all mushy on me."

I bit my bottom lip and closed my eyes, embarrassed. I willed myself to look at him. He leaned toward me, and then we were kissing.

I let Jack pull me onto the blanket, and I thought about how much better this was than precalc.

I was happy about opening up to him. It wasn't hard at all. Maybe I still tripped over my words when I had to look at his face, and maybe I had a difficult time staring into his eyes without breaking the gaze first, but I grew more confident. I was able to talk about the type of things I usually kept inside since Mom died. Slowly, I was able to let him know how much he meant to me without being scared he'd leave.

The next day, Brett and I got a ride to school with Dad. Brett's car was in the shop getting new brakes. We settled into our seats in silence, the smell of Dad's coffee and aftershave attacking the small space. Brett cracked his window open, and Dad cranked up the heat in response.

"Listen," Dad started. "I have to go out with some alumni tonight, so I thought you'd like these." He tossed an envelope to me.

I pulled out two tickets to the Pistons' preseason game.

"This is amazing. How did you score these?"

"The athletic director passed them on to me. He couldn't use them and thought I knew someone who would want them."

"Who are they playing?" I held the tickets close to my face to check. "You're kidding me. These are courtside seats."

Brett grabbed the tickets. "You got courtside seats, and you're giving them up?"

Dad winked at me via the rearview mirror. "I figured Kate and Jack would enjoy the game."

"You're kidding," Brett said. "The tickets are for Kate and *Jack*?"

Dad seemed confused. "I didn't think you'd use them, Brett. After all, you're not into basketball like Kate is."

Brett threw the tickets back at me as if they were hot. "You're right," he muttered. "I don't give a shit about basketball."

"Good," I told him. "Because I do." I clutched the tickets and thought about what Dad had just said. Basketball was a part of my life again. It made me feel guilty to think how easy it was to love the game again, but it felt right. What mattered was that Dad was excited about it, and I remembered how basketball once connected us instead of separating us.

Quitting basketball hadn't been as simple as giving it up that lonely night in the driveway when I learned Mom was sick. It was a lot bigger than that and something everyone was able to witness.

When Mom and Dad said they wanted life to go on as normal, I didn't believe it. I mean, come on. How many people can really go on with their lives as if it's no big deal that someone they love is dying?

But that's the way it was for them. Dad wasn't having anything to do with my decision to quit basketball. There were only a few games left in the season, and we'd made it to the play-offs. Before I found out about Mom, I thought winning was a huge deal. But after, I realized how stupid it really was. We were only a middle school team. No one cared if you were the eighth grade champions. No one except Dad, that is.

"I'm not playing in the game," I told him when he knocked on my door with my uniform in his hand.

"Of course you're playing. Your teammates are counting on you."

I snorted. My teammates didn't give a crap about me. I'd stayed home from school for three days after I found out about Mom and had missed a week of practice. Not one of my so-called teammates called. I made excuses that they were focused on the big game, but it still hurt. These girls were supposed to be my friends. Didn't they wonder where I was?

"I'm not letting you abandon your team." He stood in my doorway, all strong and imposing as if he could bully me into playing basketball.

"I don't care," I said, and I didn't. There wasn't a lot I cared about after Mom's news.

"Well, I do, and I'm sure Mom does too. She's not a quitter, and I think you owe it to her to show you aren't either."

I froze and clenched my teeth so I wouldn't scream. That was a low blow. I grabbed my uniform from his hand. "Whatever."

"We need to leave in about twenty minutes. Don't take too long."

"We?"

"Your mom and I will be ready."

"Mom's coming?"

"This isn't something either of us would miss. It's your first play-off game."

"Whoop-de-doo," I said and walked out to get ready in the bathroom.

The gym was packed when we arrived, and Mom and Dad separated from me with hurried good lucks so they could find some seats.

I headed over to the team, who paused one by one when each noticed me. They gave me mixed looks full of nervous sympathy, and I knew someone had told them about Mom.

"I'm here. Now we can get the winning started," I said, trying to break the ice.

No one said anything.

I wanted to scream at them all for acting as if I was something broken. These girls were my friends, but not one of them seemed to know what to do. "Cheer up. I'm not the one who's dying."

"Kate, how horrible," Tina said. She was one of my best friends, or at least I thought she was, but I hadn't heard from her at all.

I ignored her and shot layups. I tried not to look

at them, and I knew they were relieved. I concentrated on the sound of the ball bouncing against the floor until the buzzer sounded.

"Kate," Coach Drew said, "are you okay to start?"

I shrugged and looked out at all the people in the crowd instead of at him. "Yeah, sure."

I walked onto the floor and searched the crowd for my parents as I waited for tip-off. I spotted them in the middle, almost at the top. Dad saw me looking and held up crossed fingers. Mom rested her head on his shoulder and waved.

I turned back to the game. The ref tossed the ball, the other team got possession, and we were running across the court.

I was lost in the game for the first quarter and a half. We were ahead, and the high of the crowd, mixed with the excitement that we might win the first play-off game, allowed me to forget everything else.

That is, until I looked back up at my parents. Or at least where they *should* have been. I paused and scanned the bleachers. The scuff of shoes on the court brought my attention to the game. Amy, our center, threw the ball at me, and I twisted right, then left, looking for someone to pass to. I didn't focus on a teammate, though. Instead I saw Mom and Dad walking out.

Mom was leaning against Dad. She wasn't doing well. They moved slowly.

"Kate," Amy shouted, "pass the ball."

"Shoot, shoot, shoot," the crowd chanted, but it didn't mean anything to me.

The shot clock was running down—00:08, 00:07, 00:06—but all I could think about was Mom. She and Dad were out of the gym now, and I had no idea what was wrong. What if she needed an ambulance? What if something really bad was happening? What if we were going to lose her even sooner?

I couldn't stay there on the floor. I needed to make sure she was okay. Time ran out with a loud buzz. The crowd booed. I felt a hand on my shoulder. It was Tina, and I knew she'd understand.

"What the hell? You just screwed up the game."

I took a step back. I was unsteady. "My mom," I started and gestured toward the door. "I need to see if she's okay."

"Wah, wah, wah, poor Kate." Tina stuck out her bottom lip. "We all had to hear about your mom when Coach talked to the team. It sucks, but it sucks more that you can skip practices when we're busting our asses every day. Then you just walk back onto the court, and Coach makes you a starter. That's bullshit."

"I never asked for any of this." I dug my nails into the ball. Sweat dripped into my eyes, but I didn't wipe it away. It was better to see the world all blurred.

A whistle blew, and I was aware again of where we were.

"Miss? Are you okay?" the ref asked.

I looked at him and then all around.

The gym was silent. Everyone was watching. Everyone except my family.

I took the ball and heaved it as hard as I could into the middle of the bleachers. Someone gasped, but I didn't care. I didn't care about any of this.

"Forget you," I said to the team. "I'm done with this."

And I was.

I ran outside the gym and spotted Mom on a bench. She was drinking a bottled water.

Dad was standing beside her, talking on the phone. He said a few more words and hung up.

"What are you doing out here?"

I knew he was confused, but I didn't have the energy to say anything. He'd find out soon enough when everyone started talking about it.

I turned to Mom. "Are you okay? I saw you walking out, and you didn't look good."

"I'm fine. I got a little hot and dizzy."

I started to cry. I couldn't help it. I was scared.

"What happened to the game?" Dad asked.

I just shook my head. "There won't be any more games, and don't bother trying to change my mind." I clutched Mom's hand. "Can we go home? I don't want to be here anymore."

We stood and walked to the car.

Basketball was never mentioned again. Not by me. Not by Dad. Not by the teammates who walked past me every day for the next year and a half as if I didn't exist.

Jack and I were sitting outside the school a few days later, waiting for Luke to finish a history test so we could give him a ride home. The leaves were changing, and we watched as red, orange, and yellow ones twisted to the ground.

I pulled my hoodie's zipper up to block the cold air, and my necklace caught in it. I worked to pull it out but couldn't seem to get it loose.

"Here, let me help," Jack said and stood in front of me, gently tugging on the necklace. He got it out and let the chain drop outside my top. "Is this new? I've never seen it before."

I shrugged. "It's not new. I just don't put it on often."

The truth was I didn't wear it a lot because I was afraid something would happen to it. It was my baby locket. Mom bought it for me when she was expecting me, and there were pictures of me wearing it the day I was born. I'd gotten a longer chain for it, and I wore it on days when I was missing Mom really bad.

"So why are you wearing it now?" He tugged at it again.

I gently pulled it out of his hand and made a fist over it. I moved the locket side to side against the chain, listening to the faint zipping sound it made. "My mom gave it to me," I whispered.

"What was she like?"

The perfect response. Usually when I mentioned Mom, people acted all sad or asked me how I was doing.

"Well, she was nothing like Dad. I mean, she watched his teams' games to be supportive, but she liked doing crafty stuff more. She was always sewing quilts or knitting us scarves and hats. I swear, I have enough winter items to keep the whole city warm during a blizzard."

"Great. It's good to know I'll stay warm during any massive snow storms."

"She was crazy about us. She loved to do things with Brett and me. Cooking, trips to the zoo, movies and popcorn in our basement. We were always doing something with her. I'd come home from school, and she'd be waiting there, so excited to have us back."

"She sounds like my mom. She used to have a snack ready for me in the afternoons."

"Mine too." I felt good sharing stories about Mom and was surprised how easy it was to talk about her without getting upset. "You'll think I'm crazy, but when I saw you that afternoon in the parking lot before the cookout, your mom reminded me of her."

"When did you see my mom?"

I bumped his shoulder with mine. "Remember? She warned you not to eat all the food."

"Oh, geez, that's totally my mom."

"And totally you. I had to guard my dinner the other night so you didn't devour it."

Jack pulled me against him. "I bet I would've liked your mom."

"You would have." I didn't feel sad but happy Jack was willing to talk to me about her. It made me feel a little bit guilty that I hadn't brought her up before.

We both turned when someone yelled our names.

Luke headed toward us. I thought about what Jenna said about him and wrinkled my nose. Ali talked about him nonstop, and they'd hooked up a few more times when we'd gone out with Jack and some of the guys on the team.

"Thank you," I said before Luke reached us.

"For what?"

"For letting me talk about my mom. Most people either don't listen or get all weirded out when I bring her up." *Like my Dad,* I thought but didn't say it.

"She's your mom. It would be strange if you didn't talk about her."

Jack stood and offered a hand to me. I took it and stood, and we walked to meet Luke.

Brett came down the steps Saturday afternoon wearing khaki pants and a dress shirt with a sweater a bit too small for him. He also had a new slicked-back haircut and a piece of Kleenex stuck to a section of his chin he'd cut shaving.

I spurted milk from my mouth, surprised at his appearance. "Whoa, sexy," I said. "Don't tell me your jeans and T-shirt are in the laundry. Better yet, where's the wedding?"

"Shut up." He stopped in front of the mirror, trying to straighten his collar.

"Really, why are you dressed like that?" I asked a little nicer, hoping this strategy would get me an answer.

"Don't worry about it."

Brett walked out of the kitchen and stood in front of the closed door of Dad's office. "I'm going out. I'll be home later tonight."

"Dad, get out here. You need to see this," I yelled, unable to resist.

"I gotta go, Dad. I'll see you tonight," Brett said louder.

Dad's door opened, and he walked into the hallway. "What's so important that you had to interrupt me?"

"Listen, I have to go," Brett said, shaking his keys and backing out of the hall.

It was then, apparently, that Dad noticed him. "And where is it you're going? A wedding?"

"Good one," I said, reaching to pull the tissue off Brett's face. "I asked him that too."

Brett swatted my hand away. "Leave me alone. I'm going out with someone. I'll be back by eleven."

"No way. Are you going to homecoming?" Believe it or not, Beacon did have a football team, but they didn't get much support. The school celebrated homecoming, but my friends said it was lame and not worth their time. Brett must not have gotten that memo.

I shook my head at him. This was my brother. Brett hiked in the woods and played warcraft games. Brett didn't date. "How much did you have to pay her to go out with you?"

"I'm leaving. I'll be home by curfew." Brett made his exit quickly, before we could say or do anything else.

Dad and I were left standing in the hallway.

My nose twitched at the lingering cologne.

"Well," Dad said, smiling slightly, "I guess if he forgot to put on deodorant, that'll cover the smell."

"True," I said, happy to be joking. I wanted to stretch the moment out. "And if he's not back by curfew, we can just follow our noses."

"I didn't know Brett was dating anyone."

"I didn't know he was aware girls even existed," I added.

Dad frowned. "I better get back to my work. I have some plays to go over."

"Right, plays. Very important plays," I said, knowing he would miss my sarcasm.

"Yep," he said and dissolved into his office as quickly as he had appeared.

22

"Your brother is a flick," Luke said at lunch. He was all over Ali. His hand rested in her lap, and she kept giggling and slapping his hand away when he tugged on her uniform skirt. He used his other hand to toss carrot sticks at a bunch of freshmen boys sitting near us.

The five of us crowded around the table. Lunch trays, drinks, cell phones, homework papers, and other odds and ends covered the surface. Our legs tangled in the mess of book bags and purses beneath it. Jenna was writing on the bottom of my shoe, drawing stars across the sole. Other people watched us, and I liked it. It felt good to be part of a group, especially the group other people would die to belong to.

"A flick?" I watched my brother move through the lunch line. The same line I just cut with Jack. He'd pushed past about twenty other students and joked that the basketball team didn't need to wait to eat. It was kind of badass to be able to do stuff like that. I felt a twinge of guilt, but Jack and the rest of the guys did it with such ease that it seemed the natural thing to do.

Brett's book bag bulged on his back, and he walked slightly hunched as if the weight pushed him down. His shirt was untucked, and I wondered how long he'd go until a teacher would give him a discipline slip for breaking dress code. White cords snaked out of his collar and up to his ears, his iPod no doubt hidden in his shirt.

"Yeah, a flick." Luke flicked at Ali's ear. "Get it. You could flick him out of your face. He's such a loser. I can't believe you're related to him."

"That's harsh," Jenna said, pausing in the middle of filling in a shooting star.

"Are you sure he's your brother? He can't even make a basket in gym. Everyone tries to pass him the ball to see how bad he'll mess up. He never disappoints."

"Seriously?" I asked. "Are you for real?"

"Come on, Kate," Luke continued. "You can't tell me you haven't noticed."

"Why do you even care about my brother?"

Luke scowled, and I was glad I'd put him on the spot. No one was laughing with him. He just looked like a jerk.

Jack put an arm around me. "Forget Brett. What matters is that we have the best Franklin at the table with us." He kissed me in front of everyone.

Jenna whistled while the rest of the group groaned.

Brett walked toward our table on the way to Julia, a girl in my choir class he'd started to sit with. The same girl I assumed he'd gone to the dance with the other night. I willed him to go a different route, but he was walking straight to us.

I gave him a brief smile as he neared, and he nodded slightly, refusing to show any emotion toward the people he disapproved of the most. He headed past us to Julia.

"What's up, Flick?" Luke said. "Too good to say hi?"

Brett paused, probably confused by Luke's lame nickname. I kicked Luke under the table, hoping he would get the hint. Instead, he stood and grinned at all of us, as if to say, *And for my next trick, I'll screw with Kate's brother.* He stuck a hand out, apparently planning to flick Brett's neck, but caught his headphone cord. The buds were jammed deep in Brett's ears. Luke tugged harder, causing them to fly out and smack Brett's face.

Brett's hand went to the spot they'd struck. "Asshole," he hissed.

Luke wasn't listening. He was too busy laughing with Ali.

"Do you really think that's funny?" I looked straight at Ali. Luke was a lost cause, but I couldn't believe Ali thought it was okay to join in. I wanted to say something in my brother's defense. I remembered all the times he'd stood up for me: when I was six and the boys next door made fun of my height, when his friends wouldn't let me play soccer with them, when I hit a home run on the playground and one of the boys tripped me as I rounded third base. I wanted to repay Brett for all the times he'd fought for me.

Ali stopped laughing. She wrapped a piece of her hair around a finger and shrugged.

"If you don't know why you're laughing, then why would you?"

Jack placed a hand on my shoulder. "How about we go grab some fresh baked cookies?"

"Yeah, sounds good." I knew what he was trying to do. I pushed back my chair and grabbed my stuff, but before following Jack, I turned to Luke. "Brett's my brother. You're an asshole."

"Why do you hang out with those freaks?" Brett asked me as we headed toward the parking lot after school. Jack was staying late to work out in the weight room, and Ali had to babysit, so I followed Brett to catch a ride. He walked quickly, head down, straight toward the car. If I stopped to wave at people or make a comment about weekend plans, Brett muttered for me to hurry up.

To spite him, I walked slower and talked to more people.

He leaned against the trunk of his car, waiting for me.

"Beacon is changing you, Kate," he said when I caught up. "And it's not in a good way."

I knew Brett was talking about what had happened at lunch, and I didn't blame him for being mad. He had every right to hate Luke. I would've felt the same way, but I wasn't about to be the one who brought it up.

Instead, I questioned Brett's new view of me. "What's wrong with wanting to have a life at Beacon? I like being at a school where I fit in. You know how awful everyone treated me at Olmstead High when I quit the basketball team."

"Couldn't you have picked a better group? Maybe people who don't treat me like a big joke."

I closed my eyes. His words stung, even though I'd known they were coming. "Luke's a jerk, but not everyone is like him."

"Really? Because I don't buy that." Brett threw his book bag into the trunk. He closed it but kept talking to me instead of unlocking the door. "It looked to me like the entire table thought Luke was a goddamn comedian."

"Maybe *they* did, but *I* didn't think he was funny, and I let him know that."

"Yeah, a lot of good that will do."

"Do you really think I'd stoop to Luke's level? That hurts. You know me better than that."

"I thought I knew you, but now I'm not so sure. Did you ever consider they might be hanging out with you because Dad's the coach?"

"You mean they might be using me?" I'd be lying if I told him the idea hadn't occurred to me. Sure, some of my friends might not have been sincere, but Ali and Jenna were and Jack liked me for who I was. There was no denying how great it felt when he kissed me or when Ali and I laughed forever over the phone. They were my friends. Even when they pissed me off, as they had today at lunch, it was because I knew they liked me for who I was, not who Dad was.

"Exactly," Brett said. "These people wouldn't hesitate to pretend to be your friend if they could get something out of it."

"Well, what's so bad about that? My real friends aren't like that, and maybe I'm getting something out of the other relationships too."

I knew Brett didn't like to hear that, but it was true. I wanted to be a part of Beacon just as bad as some of them wanted to hang out with the new coach's daughter.

Brett shoved his key into the car door. Unlike the rest of Beacon students, we didn't have a new car. In fact, we didn't even have power locks or windows.

I waited for him to pop my lock. I climbed in and

fastened my seat belt. "I get that you don't like some of the people I'm hanging out with."

Brett stared straight ahead.

"Ali and Jenna can be a bit much sometimes," I said, "but I trust them."

Brett started the engine and drove down the hill. The leaves had fallen from the trees. It would soon be November. We'd been at Beacon for over two months.

Keeping his eyes on the road, Brett said, "You need to be careful. Make sure you don't become Dad, kissing up to people who don't care an ounce about you and only want to benefit themselves."

"I won't. Just because I'm hanging out with a new group of friends doesn't mean I have to be like them. I'm not going to make stupid choices. I'm the same old Kate."

"Just make sure you don't lose yourself."

"I won't," I said firmly.

"It's just that you're not so bad for a sister, and I'd hate to see that change."

"Not bad for a sister, huh? I think my brother likes me."

"Yeah, yeah, yeah. You know what I mean."

I put my head against the seat and grinned. I did know what he meant, and it felt good to be reminded he was the same old Brett.

www.allmytruths.com

Today's Truth:

To ensure success, please follow instruction manual exactly.

PROPER CARE AND HANDLING
OF A BEACON BASKETBALL
PLAYER BOYFRIEND

Congratulations! You are now the proud owner of a Beacon boyfriend. We want to thank you for choosing Beacon as the place to select your boyfriend and for upgrading to the Beacon basketball player boyfriend. Well done. Your superb selection will benefit you in many ways. Make sure you read all the instructions to ensure the proper care and handling of your Beacon basketball player boyfriend. Enjoy!

CONTENTS

Your Beacon basketball player boyfriend comes with the following items:

- Weekends that are never empty. You will have parties, games, dances, and double dates to fill your nights.

- Compliments. You will have girls telling you every day that they like your hair, jewelry, makeup, and anything else different from the same plaid skirt and white blouse every girl in your school wears.

- Access to tables far away from the lunch tray return and garbage cans in the cafeteria, next to the large picture windows overlooking the campus. Seats in the back of the classroom, in a spot where you can hide your phone when you're texting and you don't have to sit next to boys who don't seem to know what deodorant is and girls who raise their hands every ten seconds.

- Friends who vacation on islands in houses their families own and drive cars that cost more than the total of the three cars your dad has ever owned.

- Teachers who know your name and who you are dating and will comment on the points your Beacon basketball boyfriend made during a recent game when they should be teaching.

- A secret excitement that people envy you, people want to be you because of who you are with, because you are the one your Beacon basketball player boyfriend picked.

- A power that will put you at the top of the ladder at school, allowing you to tower over your classmates as you begin to rule aside a Beacon basketball player and the rest of the basketball team and their girlfriends.

INSTRUCTIONS

The proper care and maintenance of your Beacon basketball player is of the utmost importance if you want to continue to own him. Please follow the instructions below carefully:

- Keep him supplied with kisses, hugs, caresses.

- Be ready for sex. It's expected when you are with a Beacon basketball player.

- Eat lunch with him.

- Attend all his practices and games.

- Do not talk to other boys at the school if he is not around.

- Maintain a perfect appearance. You should

stay fit, make sure your hair and makeup are always fresh, and keep up on the current clothing styles.

- Maintain a happy attitude, even if you feel sad. Smile and laugh often. Let him know life is perfect for you when he is around.

- Agree to what he wants to do, be where he wants to be, watch what he wants to watch, and become interested in things that interest him.

- Remember constantly how lucky you are to have acquired a Beacon basketball player boyfriend.

WARNINGS

The following negative side effects may result from dating a Beacon basketball player. Please contact your best friend if any of the following occurs often in your relationship:

- Others may try to steal your Beacon basketball player boyfriend.

- Others may be jealous of your new Beacon basketball player girlfriend status.

- People may try to use you for purposes of personal gain.

- Your Beacon basketball player boyfriend may demand a large amount of your time.

- Your Beacon basketball player boyfriend may start to lose interest in you if you do not treat him properly.

BEACON BASKETBALL PLAYER BOYFRIEND INTERACTIONS

Having a Beacon basketball player boyfriend might interact with the following character traits:

- Morals

- Common sense

- Good judgment

- Ethics

- Principles

- Values

You may start to lose the person you once were as you date your Beacon basketball player boyfriend, but if you follow the directions above carefully, you will transform yourself as a Beacon basketball player girlfriend.

PLEASE SEEK EMERGENCY HELP IF your Beacon basketball payer boyfriend decides to no longer be with you.

EXPIRATION DATE

As long as you can properly care for your Beacon basketball player boyfriend, there is no reason this relationship should expire.

Posted By: Your Present Self

[Thursday, October 17, 4:03 PM]

After Brett challenged my friendships at Beacon, I made sure I didn't have to depend on him to get home anymore.

I started to hang at Ali's house while she babysat, and it was a lot better than my place, where Brett would sulk around, giving me dirty looks whenever I came into the room.

Ali's home was the complete opposite of my empty and quiet house. The moment you entered her place, your ears rang with shouts, jokes, and name-calling coming from every room. Ali along with her mom, dad, older brother, and sister made five. If you wanted to get specific, you could also add the two labs and the goldfish to make seven. I loved hanging out at Ali's.

The day after I got into it with Brett, I headed to Ali's after school to study with her.

Ali's five-year-old sister, Heather, cracked the door open and belted out an enthusiastic, "Hi."

The two dogs stuck their panting faces out the door. I helped Heather hold onto them while I walked into the house.

Heather grabbed my hand. "We have a hamster at school, and Mom said if I keep my room clean I can bring it home for a weekend. We're allowed to do that, you know."

"Wow, sounds fun." The dogs ran circles around me and didn't calm down until I gave them a proper hello. I bent to pet them, and they covered my face in drooling kisses.

"I'm not sure Jack would like you kissing someone else," Ali joked, walking into the room. She'd changed out of her uniform into white yoga pants and a Beacon hoodie. Her hair was pushed back in a headband.

"Yeah, well, he's going to have to fight these two off if he wants to get to me."

Ali grabbed my bag and steered me through the chaos of her house: blocks all over, a jump rope hanging from the banister, water guns and a headless doll on the floor. We walked into the kitchen.

"Let's sit in here. My mom said she'd order pizza for dinner."

The kitchen was my favorite room in Ali's house. Her mom loved to cook, and the kitchen was the center of everything. It was one of the biggest rooms, with an open cooking area on one side, a huge old wood table with benches and chairs, and my favorite part: a fireplace. I'd never met anyone with a fireplace in their kitchen. It was between the kitchen and the living room, open to both sides. The kitchen was so big that two comfy chairs fit next to the fireplace. Everyone hung out in there while Ali's mom cooked. They'd do their homework at the table, read in the chairs, or lounge around the island and talk.

We worked on our homework for an hour when my phone vibrated. I checked the screen. "Jack."

"Answer it. I don't mind."

"I'll call him back later. It's no big deal." I went back to reading a passage of my book and writing notes on what I thought it meant, notes that were most likely the opposite of what it really did mean.

"Pick it up. You know he can't live without you."

I grabbed the phone and walked into the hallway. "Jack?"

"Where have you been?"

"I'm at Ali's, finishing my English assignment. I told you I'd be here tonight."

"Can you get away?"

"Not really. I have to get this done."

"I need your help. My essay questions for history are a lot harder than I thought."

"We can go over them at lunch." I rolled my eyes at Ali, who was watching me now.

"It's due *tomorrow*," he said.

"Tomorrow?" I tried not to sound angry. "Why do you leave this stuff until the last minute?" I closed my eyes and rubbed my temples with my free hand.

"I thought I could do them, but I can't. I need your help. Please? I'll come to your house. Just for a little bit."

"Okay. I'll leave in twenty minutes. Give me some time to get home."

"Thanks, Kate—"

"I'm the best."

"You are."

"I'll see you in a little bit."

I hung up and turned to Ali. "Jack needs help

with his history assignment that's due tomorrow. He thought it would be okay to put it off until tonight."

"So what else is new? That boy can't live without you," she joked, but I caught a bit of an edge in her voice. This wasn't the first time Jack had called, and I'd left Ali because of something he needed.

"Yeah, yeah, I'm sorry. He says he doesn't understand it, but how much do you want to bet all he's done is put his name on the paper?"

"Yeah, first name only. If it asked for the last, he'd need your help too."

I closed my book and collected my stuff. "You're right. Where would he be without me?"

"Without you and everyone else who helps him?" Ali smirked.

"What's that supposed to mean?"

"My guess is Jack and the rest of the team would be warming the bench quite nicely if their playing time depended on their own work. Now he's got you doing his dirty work too."

"I'm not doing it for him." For a second, Brett's comment in the car flashed in my mind. I pushed it aside. My friends weren't using me.

"He just called, and now you're running right over there."

"To help him. Like I was helping you." My tone was hard. It was obvious what Ali was getting at, and I wasn't letting her get away with it.

"Okay, okay, call me later if you want."

"If I have time. I may be too busy *working* with Jack." I didn't wait to see if she took it as a joke or a dig.

Jack and I never got to his homework that night. Dad stayed late at Beacon with the other coaches, and since Brett was somewhere with Julia, we had the house to ourselves.

We made out for over an hour. Neither of us wanted to separate. We were wrapped up in each other, all hands and feet and lips. I told myself this was the way it should be. This was Beacon. This was happy. This was my life.

It was getting late, and Dad would be home soon. I knew Jack should go. We'd pushed the time limit, but I didn't want him to leave. Not yet.

"You don't have to worry," I said, rolling over and trying to wrap my arms around him, although he was already pulling his shirt on.

"Your dad would kill me. It's almost the start of basketball season. I'm supposed to be focusing on the game, not the coach's daughter."

"It's okay. Seriously, he wouldn't know you're here even if he comes home. He'll lock himself in his office."

"Right. I'm upstairs in his daughter's bedroom while he's not here, and he wouldn't think it was a big deal?"

"Really, he doesn't care."

Jack fished around for his cell phone, which neither of us could find. "Damn it, where the hell did it go? I need to get out of here."

"It's okay. We'll find it. It's gotta be somewhere in here."

We pulled pillows off the bed, shook out the comforter, and made a bigger wreck than we'd started with. I purposely tried to bump against Jack, giggling each time we touched.

A door slammed downstairs, and Jack froze.

"Shit," he whispered. "That's why I didn't want to stay." He grabbed the rest of his stuff, pushing my arm away when I tried to help. "Let me figure this out."

Jack raked his hands through his hair, messing it up in the sexy way that drove me crazy.

"Relax. It's okay." I put my hand against his chest to stop him. "Wait. You'll see. Trust me."

We both looked at the door when we heard someone coming up the steps.

"Didn't you say he wouldn't come up here?"

Someone reached the bedroom door and knocked.

"Kate? Are you in there?"

I let myself relax. "Hey, Brett. I'm here."

The door opened, and he walked in. "Is the rest of the pizza for me?"

"Sure. I had a few pieces . . ."

Brett looked at Jack. "What is *he* doing here?" He said it as if Jack had crawled out of the deepest, darkest hole and trailed slime everywhere he moved.

Jack took a few steps toward the door. "That's the same thing I said when you walked into my school, asshole."

I stared at Jack, shocked.

"Go to hell." Brett slammed the door, leaving us behind.

I stood in the middle of the room, not sure who I should be supporting.

Jack grabbed the rest of his stuff. "I have to go. I meant what I said about not wanting to be here when your dad shows up."

"Wait a minute. What was that about? I'd expect something like that from Luke but not you."

"Brett was the one with the problem."

"You both have problems, and I don't understand it." I walked to my bed and started moving pillows around again to help Jack find his phone. "You say you care about me. Well, how about you show it?"

"I'm sorry, okay? I was worried about your dad showing up, and then Brett came in with a big attitude. I'll ease up, but your brother better do the same."

"I'll talk to him." I touched his arm.

"He's not going to say anything to your dad, is he?"

"You're fine."

Jack found his phone under the nightstand, and I followed him down the stairs. I prayed Brett was in his room and Jack wouldn't spot him as he headed out. I followed Jack through the kitchen. I didn't know I'd been holding my breath until Jack was safely away.

www.allmytruths.com

Today's Truth:

**Sometimes it's possible to love someone,
even if those around you hate them.**

I/Brett

grew

to

love /hate

Jack.

I/Brett

loved/hated

Jack's

laughing/taunting

smile/sneer

hands/fist

heart/black core

confidence/ego

promises/threats

touch/jabs

friends/gang

walk/swagger

whispers/insults

attention/vigilance

popularity/reign

Jack

became

everything/nothing

There is a thin line between everything/nothing

A line that can easily bend/curve/twist/bow/crack/
splinter/fracture/break/

c

r

u

m

b

l

e

Posted By: Your Present Self

[Tuesday, October 22, 6:47 PM]

A few days later, I ended up at Ali's house. She'd called me just as I arrived home from school. I threw my book bag on my front step and fished out my keys while I talked to her.

"What are you doing tonight?" she asked.

I unlocked my front door and stepped into an empty hallway. The sun had started to go down earlier as fall approached, and the house was dim with shadows. "That's a hard one," I said. "I have a few choices. There's a dinner party I'm supposed to host with diplomats and that Hollywood premiere I planned on attending . . . I'm at a loss for which to blow off."

"How about both? If you do, you can come to dinner at my house. My dad is making his famous chili, and there's enough to feed a small country."

I weighed the real options of TV dinners, left-overs, or cereal without milk against a night with

Ali's family. My dad was with the team, and Brett had gone paintballing with some old friends.

"I have to check with my publicist, but it should be easy to get out of my plans."

"If it's not too much trouble," Ali said.

Later that night, I sat next to Ali, surrounded by her parents and siblings, fighting to get a word in among everyone's conversations. Ali's brother kept getting yelled at for having his phone out, and her sister pouted when I got the last piece of cornbread. I threw a jab back at her dad, who teased me about Jack. I felt as if I belonged.

It was later, when I stood between Ali and her mom, helping with the dinner dishes that I understood what was happening. My family had shifted.

My world had cracked open when Mom died, but now it felt more whole again. Beacon had given back something missing in my life. Ali, Jack, and Jenna had become my family.

It was my birthday, my sweet sixteen and I'd been kissed, as Jack said when he met me at my locker with a bouquet of roses. Luke joked he got them from the gas station on the way to school. As if I cared.

Jack took me to dinner at a fancy steak house. There was so much food we left enough on our plates for another whole meal. Dad had told the two of us to save room for cake.

When we got home, we gathered around the kitchen table. Brett had invited Julia, probably as a buffer from Jack. Everyone sang "Happy Birthday" off-key, and I blew out the candles on the store-bought lemon cake, a flavor I didn't even like.

Dad gave me the new cell phone I'd been asking for, Brett handed me a card with money in it, and Julia pulled a bag out of her purse and held it out to me. "It's nothing big, but I thought you'd like it."

"You didn't need to get me anything," I said, surprised.

Even though she had been dating my brother for a few weeks now, the two of us had probably only said a few words to each other. Usually Brett picked her up, and the few times she was at our house, Brett ushered her to his room before I had the chance to say anything.

"It's your birthday," she said, pushing it into my hands. "Everyone deserves something on their birthday."

I pulled the tissue paper out of the bag and found a bracelet made of dark red and yellow glass beads. "Oh, wow, I love this."

"I figure it's the colors of Beacon, so you can wear it to a game or something."

"That's great, Julia," Dad said, clapping his hands. "It'll be perfect for when she's cheering for Jack."

"Thanks." I slipped it on my wrist and watched it catch the light. It really was pretty.

"Now let's get into this cake." Dad sliced a big piece for each of us.

Jack dipped a finger into his frosting and winked at me when he tasted it.

The two of us grabbed our plates and slipped away to the living room. I sat down on the couch, and Jack scooted next to me. It was dark, and I lit the candle still stuck in my piece of cake with a box of matches I had grabbed from the kitchen.

"I haven't given you your gift yet." Jack slipped a box out of his pocket.

"No, you haven't." I cupped my hands and let him drop his present into them. I held the box and shook it. "What could this be?"

"Hey, be careful. For all you know, that's made out of fine china."

"Sure, right." I broke off the ribbon, lifted the lid, and pulled out a pair of small gold heart earrings. "Oh, Jack, I love them."

"I remember you talked about the locket your mom gave you when you were a baby. I figured you'd like something to wear with it."

"It's perfect." I fought back tears. Mom should have been there, singing "Happy Birthday" with everyone, getting to know Jack, and laughing with Dad. "Thanks for being with me tonight."

"I wouldn't want to be anywhere else," Jack whispered into my ear.

I bent forward and blew out the candle so we were sitting in nothing but darkness. Jack took my hand and pulled me closer, and we started kissing. I closed my eyes and thought not about what I had lost but what I had gained.

Later that night, I woke to my phone vibrating under my pillow. I grabbed it, thinking it was Jack wishing me one last happy birthday. It had become a joke with him. He'd probably said it at least fifty times that day.

"Kate," Ali whispered loudly into the phone. "I need to talk to you."

"I'm here," I mumbled.

"Are you listening?"

"Yeah. What do you want?"

"No, seriously. Are you really listening or just saying you are? Because what I have to tell you is big."

"I'm listening." I sat up against my pillow. I turned on the lamp next to my bed. I figured she was calling because of my birthday. She'd sent me a text earlier, but I hadn't heard from her since then.

"Promise you won't judge."

"Mm . . ."

"I'm serious."

"I promise," I said, but I would have promised pretty much anything at that point.

"Okay." She took a deep breath. "I slept with Luke tonight."

Now I was awake. "What? Like had sex?"

"No, we just spooned. Yes, sex, Kate, and I know it's soon and we've only been together for a few weeks, but I like him."

"You had *sex* with Luke? Really?"

"Yeah, is that so hard to believe?"

"Sorry. I'm just surprised."

Ali and I were both virgins, and while she had talked about sex, I didn't think it was something she was thinking about doing. She and Luke weren't even a couple.

"Did you plan it?"

"No, his mom went out on a date with some guy, and we were alone, and it, well . . . it happened. First we were making out, then we were in his room, and he had a condom, and I didn't want to say no."

"So it was okay?"

"It didn't feel real good, but I'm glad I did it. It's not as bad as you think it's going to be, and it was special." Her voice broke when she said the word *special*. She started to cry.

"Ali, what's wrong?"

"I'm fine. It's just . . ."

I waited for her to speak again.

"I'm okay. I'm glad I did it. It's okay that I did it."

"Well, if it makes you upset or you need to talk to me again, you can call me."

She was quiet for a minute, and then her tone turned angry. "Why would it upset me?"

"I don't know. I meant—"

"You know, I'm not the only one who should be thinking about sex. What about you and Jack? You can't hold out forever."

I wondered how the conversation had shifted to Jack and me.

"It's something you need to do sooner or later. He's not going to spend all of high school waiting for you to give it up. Not a guy like Jack."

Ali had no right to start talking to me about having sex with Jack. I spoke slowly, trying to keep my voice level. "Sex isn't a problem between us. It hasn't come up."

"Maybe it hasn't, but he's thinking about it. Every guy does. If you want to stay with Jack, you're going to have to put out."

"Okay." I sighed, not wanting to fight with her. Ali had just had sex. There was no way she'd understand why I wasn't ready to sleep with Jack. "I need to go to bed now. Call me if you need me."

I hung up and pulled the covers over my head. I thought about what Ali said. She was right. Sex was becoming an issue between Jack and me. We didn't talk about it, but we didn't need to. It was there every time we made out and his hand slipped under my shirt, pulling off my bra. It was there when he tugged at my jeans, trying to wiggle them free from my body. I'd rest my hand on top of his to stop him. It left a heavy question, and I couldn't keep ignoring it. He wouldn't let me. There was a certain progression of things, and I learned that you could quickly pass each of them up until there was only one place left to go. Jack and I had reached that point, and truthfully I wasn't sure if I was ready to take the last step.

29

The next day in choir Ali never mentioned the phone call. Instead, she focused on Julia.

"I can't believe you spent your birthday with her," Ali said when Julia came rushing into the room right before the bell. "She is so weird."

We were all in choir together, but I hardly ever talked to Julia. She sat on the other side of the room and kept to herself. I wondered how my brother even ended up talking with her.

"Seriously, she's like a freaking cow," Jenna said, scrunching her nose. "I mean, come on. Get off your fat ass once in a while."

Jenna was out of her mind. Julia might not have been stick thin, but she definitely wasn't heavy. I thought she was pretty. She wore her curly blonde hair in a ponytail and always seemed to be smiling. Besides, she was good for Brett. She helped ease the tension between him and Dad, which had put Brett in a better mood these days.

I bit my lip and watched Julia. After Jack had given me my earrings and finished his cake, he'd gone and talked basketball with Dad while Julia helped me wash the dishes. She talked about her younger brothers, and we joked about the frustrations of living with boys. I liked having her over, and I'd told Brett that after she left. Jack even seemed to have a good time with Brett and Julia.

She paused near us and waved.

I started to wave back.

Ali stared at my bracelet. "Oh, God, where did you get that? Please don't tell me Jack picked it out for your birthday."

I touched the bracelet. I'd put it on that morning at the last minute and loved the way it matched my Beacon sweatshirt. "Oh, no, it's not from Jack. Julia gave it to me."

"It's hideous," she said loud enough that I was pretty sure Julia and everyone else in the room could hear. "I know you had to be nice to her last night, but did your dad make you wear it today?"

"Something like that," I said quietly and pushed the bracelet under my sleeve.

"There's a point where being nice is just plain ugly."

"She's not so bad. She gets my brother off my back," I said, but then I slid the bracelet off and into my bag. I pulled the zipper shut and felt a tinge of guilt.

Mrs. Reid started talking about the song we were singing, and I glanced over to Julia's section of singers. I caught her eye and shrugged. I waited for her to nod back or give me some kind of forgiveness, a sign she understood what I'd done. But she didn't, and who could blame her? How could she, when I didn't even understand who I had just become?

Dad knocked on my door a week later as I was getting ready for school.

"Morning, Kate," he said in an unusually cheerful voice.

"Is everything okay?"

He never knocked on the door, let alone came into my room. I swear I usually heard him walk faster by my room in case I decided to open the door and try to have a conversation. I could probably build a bomb in here and he'd never know.

"Everything is fine," he said, rocking on his heels. He was dressed in a suit, hair still wet from his morning shower. "I wanted to make sure you'd be at the game tonight."

It was Beacon's first game of the season. Everyone was going. "Of course. I can't wait."

"Good. I was hoping you'd say that." He clapped, as if he was done talking. I figured he'd turn and walk out, but he paused. "It's been nice seeing you at my practices."

"I like watching the team. I've missed basketball." The words slipped out of my mouth, and I felt as if I had betrayed something by saying it. The play-off game in eighth grade flashed through my mind, but I pushed it aside. The truth was I did like being a part of basketball again.

"Well, then, I guess I'll see you tonight, kiddo."

"I'll be there." I watched him walk down the hall before I turned to my dresser.

I dug around in my top drawer, then pulled out a picture I'd hidden after Mom got sick. The photo was of Mom, Brett, and me crowded around Dad at the end of one of his games. Brett and I wore foam fingers proclaiming Dad's team was number one, and Mom's arm was draped over Dad's shoulder. Instead of the usual sadness I felt looking at it, my body felt warmed. Dad had come and talked to me. He wanted me at his game. Maybe I'd been wrong about giving up basketball. Maybe that's what would bring Dad back to me.

Jack's time was consumed with practices now that the season was starting. Dad required him to weight train in the morning and be ready to run drills in the gym after school. I had no idea how he was getting his work done. The talents Jack had on the basketball court were unmatched in the classroom, so while I took honors level courses, he didn't.

We were both taking a current world issues class, though, at different times during the day. It was a semester-long course all students were required to take. There wasn't a textbook. Instead we read newspapers, magazines, and opinion pieces on current events. I loved the class and the opportunity to not just learn about what went on around me but what other students thought about these issues.

Most of the players, however, loathed the course. They'd complain at lunch, claiming it was biased, only focusing on political issues and not more current things like sports.

"If the class is about world issues, we should look at all the issues," Luke argued.

Ali, Jenna, and I would remind the boys over and over again that which pro player signed with which team probably wasn't an important world issue. But they believed Mrs. Sheridan didn't know what was really important and blew off most of the assignments.

I had a suspicion the real reason the team didn't like the class was that the material was new and they couldn't copy old worksheets and tests. I wasn't sure it was true, but Brett talked about the help the basketball players got. I believed Brett. There was no way Jack could be passing all his classes with the work he put in on the basketball court and the lack of time he put into his schoolwork.

I was in my bedroom trying to finish some reading and questions when Dad called from downstairs.

"Kate, Jack's here."

"Send him up!"

Jack appeared in my doorway and held up two paper coffee cups with steam rising out of them. "I brought hot chocolate and hot chocolate. Which would you like?"

"Geez, so many choices. I think I'll take hot

chocolate." I tilted my face to him, not reaching for the drink but for his lips.

He leaned down and kissed me.

"I wasn't expecting to see you tonight." I cringed as I caught sight of my outfit in the mirror. I wore a yellow Olmstead High T-shirt, complete with holes, and black sweatpants I had cut off at knee length. I'd pulled my hair into a ponytail and wrapped a bandana around it. I was a giant bumblebee.

"Well, don't be so excited to see me," he teased and handed me one of the cups. He used his free hand to yank on my ponytail.

"Of course I'm excited to see you." I pushed my books aside on the bed. "I'm always excited to see you."

"That's what I like to hear. It's a lot better coming over here when I don't have to worry about your dad finding me." He started his usual routine, wandering around my room, looking at the pictures on my bulletin board. I'd hung up the basketball picture I'd pulled out of my top drawer the other day. It was next to a picture of my family on a camping trip for Brett's birthday. He'd begged Mom to be able to rough it for a night, so the four of us drove to a campsite about two hours away and pitched a tent. I was miserable, but Brett loved it. He loved anything to do with the outdoors and survival.

Jack laughed at a new picture of Ali, Jenna, and me, taken late one night at a party. We were trying to make a pyramid, Jenna and Ali on the bottom with me trying to keep my balance on top.

As Jack continued to look at pictures, I searched the room for stray pairs of underwear or other gross things I could hopefully get rid of before he noticed. Luckily, I was safe and my room was relatively clean.

"How was practice?" I took a sip of the hot chocolate, feeling the warmth slide down my throat and into my belly.

"Good. Your dad worked us hard, but I think we'll be ready for Thursday's game against Perry. What are you working on?"

"The current issue questions due tomorrow. They suck." I gestured to the papers and the articles I was researching.

Jack grabbed a page.

"Did you finish them yet?" I asked.

"Man, there are a lot of questions here. I didn't think we had that much to do. I haven't even started." He threw the pages down and fell onto my bed.

I flopped next to him.

His hand found its way up my shirt. "I really don't want to do them, do you?"

I let him kiss me. Of course I didn't want to do the homework, but it was due tomorrow. "I have to finish it."

"No, you don't. I'll get us an extension. Mrs. Sheridan will give me a break. I'll tell her I had a late practice."

"A late practice?"

"Yeah, it's fine. Teachers do it for the team all the time. And if we're lucky, they'll excuse us from the assignment. They understand how hard we work."

"*I've* been working hard on these all night."

"What if," Jack started, rolling over and kissing my neck, "I help you finish the questions by giving you a back rub?" He placed his hands on my back.

I started to lose all desire to do any kind of work. "Something tells me they wouldn't get done if that was the plan," I said, rolling out of his grasp.

"Can we work on this together?" He reached for my hand and rubbed it between his two hands. He was so cute I couldn't resist.

"Let me finish this last question, and then you can have all my attention. Does that work?" I knew if I worked with Jack, we'd never get anything done. Besides, there were a lot of other things I'd rather be doing with him.

"Deal." He grabbed my TV remote, settling on the bed.

I tried to concentrate on the last question, but my eyes kept wandering back to Jack. It wasn't easy to work when he was sitting right there, all hot and sexy. He had a faded Beacon shirt over a blue long-sleeve tee that made his blue-green eyes look amazing. Every couple of minutes he'd grab at me, trying to get me to do anything but the work.

Brett came home just as I finished. He'd probably been out with Julia. He stopped by my room.

Jack looked up from the bed. "Hey, man," he said lazily.

Brett made a face, muttered, and turned to walk away.

"Nice talking to you too," Jack yelled.

Brett's shoulders tensed, and he started to turn around, but then he shut the door.

"Why can't you two just get along?"

"He's the one who doesn't like me."

"It doesn't matter. I just wish you'd figure out how to get along." I put my pen down and shook out my wrist. The answers were two pages, front and back.

"Damn, Kate, that's a lot of writing."

"Yeah, I think you'd better get home and start working on them."

Jack picked up my papers and looked over them. "Can I borrow these?"

"Borrow them?"

"Yeah, you know, just to look at. To help me with my own ideas."

"I guess," I said, but I really wasn't sure I wanted to give them to him.

"Geez, Kate. These aren't some top-secret government papers."

"You promise to bring them to class tomorrow?"

"Don't worry. I'll take good care of them." He rolled the papers up, tucking them in a back pocket.

I bit my lip, wishing he hadn't creased them like that. Would he get them to school in one piece?

He tousled my hair. "Okay, I better go. It's ten. I need to get home, and I don't want your dad thinking

I'm overstaying my welcome."

"You worry about my dad too much. Sorry I was such a nerd tonight," I said, upset that after finishing the homework I didn't get to relax with him. "I'm glad you stopped by. Next time we'll make it a little more interesting."

"I agree," Jack said, kissing me. "We'll make it a lot more interesting." He winked as he walked out of the room.

I groaned at his cheesiness and followed him all the way out the front door. He grabbed my hand, giving it a squeeze, when the cold air hit us. It would soon be snowing.

"Thanks for letting me hang," he said, giving me one final kiss before climbing into his car. "I'll see you in school tomorrow."

I watched his car lights fade away down the dark street.

A few days later, as I pushed my way out of Mrs. Sheridan's class, she stepped in front of me and blocked my exit. "Kate, do you mind stopping by my room at the end of the day? I need to talk to you and a few other people for a couple of minutes."

"Sure." I shrugged and wondered what she needed, but I pushed it out of my mind and tried not to think about it until the end of the day.

When the final bell rang, I headed to her room.

On the way, I ran into Jack, Luke, and Dave, a super tall skinny guy on the team. I waved. "What are you doing? Don't you have practice?"

"Mrs. Sheridan asked us to meet with her," Luke said. "I don't know what the hell she wants, but she better be quick. Your dad's going to be pissed if we're late."

"She wanted to talk to you? She asked me to stop by too. Do you know why?"

Jack shrugged as we all walked in and gathered around her desk.

"Okay," she said as she pulled a stack of papers from her bag and started sifting through them. She pulled out a few sheets and held them up.

I recognized one as my own.

"I'm not sure if you three understood the activity. That's why I wanted to talk to you together."

"What are those?" Luke asked.

"It's the discussion questions you had to do for homework. I started reading some of the answers, and while they were well written, they're all the same."

"What?" I asked.

Mrs. Sheridan looked at all of us over the top of her glasses. "Your responses. You all have similar answers, or at least most of it is the same. Some of you left things out and didn't go into as much detail, but besides that, there isn't a difference."

"I don't understand," I said, reaching for my paper and scanning it. "These are the questions I did, but how are they the same?"

"Mrs. Sheridan, I think it's my fault," Jack said.

"We were at Kate's house going over the articles and answering the questions together. They look the same because they pretty much are. I know you like when we work in groups or with partners to compare ideas, and that's what we were doing. We thought since they were for discussion, it would be a good idea to talk about the topics together." The words fell off his tongue, smoothly forming a tale that almost had me convinced.

Mrs. Sheridan blinked a bunch of times as if she didn't completely believe what he was saying.

"Yeah, it helped to go over the articles together," Luke said.

Dave nodded.

"Okay," she said slowly. "I understand where you could have gotten mixed up. We do go over work a lot as a class, and I guess by calling them discussion questions . . ." She started to nod faster as if the idea was suddenly coming to her. "But I wanted you to do these questions yourself, not in a group. I wanted to see what each of you thought, individually, on the issues."

"We're real sorry," Jack said. "I guess we should've realized that. We'll make sure to do our own work next time, unless you say we can work with partners.

We didn't mean to do it the wrong way."

Mrs. Sheridan was either buying all his crap or using it as a lame excuse to not have to deal with disciplining athletes. It was basketball season. She wouldn't want to accuse three players of cheating.

"Okay, I'll let it go this time, but in the future, don't assume you can turn in the same work unless I say you can. I do want you to think for yourself sometimes." She handed the papers back to us and turned to her desk, signaling the end of the discussion.

The boys made promises, and I stood there amazed.

"Thanks, Mrs. Sheridan," Luke said.

We walked out of the room, the boys flashing their dazzling Beacon boy smiles with duffle bags full of practice equipment bumping against their backs.

It was quiet in the hallway. Most people had left for the day. Bright flyers advertising clubs and band concerts fluttered against the walls in the empty corridor.

The guys started talking about tomorrow's game.

"Jack," I hissed in disbelief. How could he have done this? There was no way I was letting him get away with it. I stopped, and when he turned to me, I motioned for him to stop too. "I need to talk to you."

"I have to go to practice, Kate. We're already going to be ten minutes late. I'll call you tonight."

"We need to talk now." I tried to stand in front of him, but he kept on moving. "I don't understand what just happened. I need you to explain it to me."

"Don't worry. We're good. This isn't an issue anymore."

"Maybe not for you."

He shrugged and continued to follow his friends, farther and farther away.

I threw my bag against a locker.

A girl a few feet down stopped loading books into her bag to stare at me.

"What the hell are you looking at?" I said, angry to have a witness.

"Nothing. I'm sorry," she said and quickly closed her locker. She grabbed her stuff and walked in the same direction Jack had gone.

I picked up my bag and headed down the hallway, angry and alone.

I left Jack a number of messages while he was at practice, but I figured he'd try to avoid me all night. He proved me wrong, though, and called as soon as practice ended.

I was sitting on the couch watching some game show as I stuffed my face with peanut butter–covered graham crackers, my weakness.

"Yes," I said, drawing out the word to show how mad I was.

"Hey, sorry I wasn't able to talk before practice," Jack said casually. "Your dad would've flipped if I was any later than I already was. I didn't want to get him mad, not with a game tomorrow. Thanks for covering for me and the other guys."

"Covering for you?"

"Well, you know what I mean."

"I didn't cover for you. I didn't say a word."

"That's why everything worked out."

"I never gave you the answers so you could pass them around."

"You mean to Dave and Luke? What was I supposed to do? It wasn't fair to keep the homework from them. They would've failed. They were asking about it, and I had it. I didn't give them your copy, though. I kept that one safe."

"Safe from what, Jack? You copied my work and then passed it on to two other people." How could he act as if this was no big deal? How could he talk to me the way he did to Mrs. Sheridan, as if I were dumb enough to fall for his crap?

"I had to help them out. They were struggling. That was a big assignment, and our grades affect the team."

"They struggled because they didn't do the work. You gave them the answers. You helped them cheat."

"Well, if we could have gotten the answers another way, we would have."

"Another way? What about doing your own work?"

"Doing our own work? God, Kate. We have a different kind of work we need to do. You don't think we work our asses off on the court?"

I couldn't speak. It was impossible to get my

thoughts straight. Everything in my head was spinning, and if I opened my mouth, the words wouldn't be nice.

"Don't act like you don't understand how this works. We needed the answers, and I thought you were willing to help us."

"I wasn't planning to let the team cheat off my homework assignment," I said loudly.

"Don't worry. I won't be asking you for favors anymore." His tone had turned cold. "How stupid was I to think my girlfriend would want to help me with some homework?"

"That wasn't help, Jack."

"Maybe it wasn't to you, but believe me, there's plenty more people around here willing to share. It won't be your problem again."

"Sounds like a plan," I said sarcastically and hung up without saying good-bye.

I sat on the couch staring at the TV, not focusing on anything. I wasn't really surprised Jack's friends had used my paper. They were always copying someone's work at lunch or memorizing test questions passed on from someone who had already taken the class.

What surprised me was that Jack had done it too and stood up for them.

www.allmytruths.com

Today's Truth:
Rights aren't always earned; they are expected.

Privilege.

What is it?

It seems to be a phrase thrown around a lot to show entitlement. It's a word that makes people assume what they're doing is allowed, even if it isn't.

To my parents, privilege was something we earned. It was a privilege to watch PG-13 movies with my parents, but if Mom heard Brett or me using any of the swear words from it, we wouldn't be allowed to watch them anymore. It was a privilege to get new clothes, but if I didn't hang them up when I came home, my mom would take anything on the floor out of my room and hide it.

Privilege was something granted and taken away. Privilege had control.

However, I don't view privilege that way anymore.

Those who are truly privileged never doubt its existence can be taken away.

Privilege to some isn't something you earn. It's what one expects.

That's how Beacon views privilege on and off the basketball court.

Those at Beacon who are glorified believe privilege gives them liberties to blow off homework, talk back to teachers, arrive late to school, leave early, not come at all, preview questions on a test, park in spots marked *Faculty*, smoke outside on school grounds, and make a boy who may not be as athletic feel as if he will never fit in. Privilege can make someone either feel invincible or search for a way to feel worth something even when everyone else is telling him he isn't.

Posted By: Your Present Self
[Tuesday, October 29, 9:16 AM]

Jack stayed true to his word and didn't mention his homework again. I don't know how he was getting it done, but it certainly wasn't with help from me. Dad was holding the team captive with endless practices, and if I wanted to see Jack, the basketball court was the best place to catch him.

Today I finished my homework and sat on the bleachers staring at the clock. Jack promised he'd shower and change quickly, but I'd been waiting for at least fifteen minutes. He was worse than a girl getting ready. I had no idea what the heck he was doing for so long in the locker room.

I got up to walk around the gym. I'd been sitting all day, and I was sick of it. I spotted a basketball Dad must have missed behind a wastebasket and picked it up. I intended to set it down by Dad's stuff, but instead I bounced it a few times. It echoed in the empty gym.

The ball felt familiar in my hands, and I thought back to the days when I loved to play the game. I slowly dribbled it on the floor and made my way to the basket to take a shot. The ball swished through the hoop without touching the net, and I pumped my fist in the air.

"She's still got it, folks," I yelled, and an imaginary crowd cheered for me.

"Got what?" a voice said behind me.

I jumped in surprise.

It was Luke, and he picked up the ball and walked over to me.

"My crazy good basketball talent." I stole the ball out of his hands. "And apparently my defensive skills."

"Is that so?" He smirked. "Do you care to try to uphold that title? The results may make you weep."

"I'm not afraid of you. First one to make five shots," I said. "And just to be nice, I'll let you start with possession of the ball."

"Deal." Luke dribbled the ball.

I was ready for him, though, and stole the ball when he tried to go around me.

I sunk a three pointer. "Bam, that's how it's done," I shouted. "Who's the first one to score? Who? Who?"

I loved the feeling I got when I scored first. It was the rush I used to get from competing, and I wanted nothing more than to feel it again.

Luke charged me, and we were playing a real game full of elbows, shoves, and trash talking.

The score was three to one when Jack came out.

"Who's winning?" he asked.

I pointed at Luke. "He is for now, but I'm just saving my best moves for the end. I don't want to beat him too quickly."

"Right," Luke said, dragging the word out.

"Can I help Kate out?"

Luke shrugged, and I threw the ball to Jack. "I don't really need help, but I guess you can if you want to play next to all my glory."

The three of us fell into a game that became a pretty good matchup. Jack and I each scored once, and together we tried to keep Luke from getting any more baskets.

Jack blocked Luke and allowed me to sink the final basket.

"Victory," I shouted and ran over to hug Jack.

The three of us were sweating, and I felt giddy

and high on the reminder of what basketball used to feel like.

I heard clapping behind us and turned with the other two to see Dad standing with his briefcase next to him. "It looks as if Kate gave the two of you a run for your money."

"I went easy on them," I said.

"Yeah, right." Luke laughed.

Dad walked over and slapped Luke on the back. "You may want to put in some more practice time. The two of you are some of my best players, but I think Kate may be a contender for your spot on the team."

"I'll let them keep their varsity positions. I wouldn't want to embarrass anyone." I followed everyone off the court. "Jack and I are going to grab some dinner, if that's okay, Dad."

"Of course, but don't keep him out too late. My boys need to rest up."

"Yeah, yeah, yeah," Jack said. "I'll make sure to get home early. I wouldn't want to lose any beauty sleep."

Jack slung an arm around me, and Luke followed us to the parking lot. I would've thought I'd be jealous of Dad calling Jack and Luke his boys, but I kind of liked the sound of it.

"Tell me you're not having fun," Ali wailed over the phone.

It was the weekend, and Jenna and I were with most of the school heading to a party after the basketball game.

"Seriously, my mom is such a bitch," Ali said.

"We're not having fun, and we promise to keep it that way," I told her.

Jenna held up her case of beer and danced around in a circle. We followed a crowd of people headed down the sidewalk to Jay's house, where the post-game party was being held. Beacon had won their fifth game. They were undefeated and didn't show signs of breaking the streak anytime soon. Jenna and I had cheered the team on until our voices were hoarse. Meanwhile, Ali was at home on lockdown, forced to read because she was failing English.

"This absolutely sucks." There was a bang, as

if Ali had thrown something. I had a feeling it was our current reading assignment, *Of Mice and Men*. "You're going to have fun, aren't you?"

"I'm sure this party will be like all the others." I rolled my eyes.

Jenna faked opening one of her beers and chugging it.

"You won't miss much," I added.

"Says the girl who actually gets to be there. You're lucky. You never have to worry about getting grounded."

"What do you mean?"

"Nothing. Sorry. I'm in a shitty mood. I didn't mean to say that."

"Well, you did." My voice was hard. I knew what Ali meant, even if she wasn't going to admit it. My friends never mentioned Mom, and I didn't bring her up. They thought it was cool Dad was so busy with basketball that I was able to do pretty much whatever I wanted.

"Listen, I gotta go. If my mom finds me on the phone, she'll murder me with it. Call me when you get home."

"I'll try."

"Promise?"

"Yes, yes, whatever." I hung up and turned to Jenna. "Apparently, Ali's life is ending because she missed the game and the party."

"Well, she was the only person in the world who wasn't in the gym tonight."

I couldn't argue with that. The game was a sellout, and it seemed everyone from our school was there. Now we followed most of the crowd to Jay's house. His parents were away at a wedding, and he lived far back from the road, a perfect combination for a party.

Jenna stopped for a minute to put down her beers and tie her shoelace. "So," she said, standing up. "Did you tell her how when Liz was cheering, she shook her ass in front of Luke the entire game?"

"No way. Are you kidding? I'm not saying anything about Liz. Ali would freak."

"Well, maybe it'll finally teach her to stop running after him like a lost puppy."

"I'm staying out of it," I said.

"She's stupid to believe she's the only one Luke is interested in screwing. I mean, really. He's such a creeper. He's always trying to get girls drunk so they forget how slimy he is." Jenna grabbed the bottles off the ground and groaned. "God, these things are heavy."

"Don't you think you should hide those? You know," I said, glancing over my shoulder, "in case of cops."

Jenna waved her free hand. "You think a party this size is a secret? If the police actually gave a crap, they'd have busted it up by now. They don't. We're fine."

"I thought—"

"You thought wrong. Those cops aren't stupid enough to screw around with the team during the season. Besides"—she held up a beer and grinned— "this tastes a lot better than the junk they have inside."

"I didn't realize you were such a beer snob." I quickened my pace. "Come on. I want to find Jack."

Jenna agreed, and the two of us made our way into the house. It was packed, and most of the team had already arrived.

Jenna headed to the kitchen to put her beers in the fridge by bumping her hips into people to make it through the crowded room.

I walked over to a group of players. "Have any of you seen Jack?"

Their hair was still wet from showers after the game, and they were passing around a bottle of whiskey and taking huge sips.

One of the guys, Josh, lowered the bottle and wiped his mouth with the back of his hand. He turned to me. "Yeah, and I'll let you know for a little price." He grabbed himself, and the other guys snickered.

"Get over yourself," I said and flipped him off.

"Oh, feisty," Josh said. "That's what I like."

What an asshole. The way the team acted made me so angry sometimes. "Forget it." I headed out of the room.

"Kate," Mike, a senior on the team, yelled. "I saw him head upstairs a little bit ago."

"Thanks," I told him and shot the rest of them a dirty look.

People were sitting all over the steps, and it was like walking through an obstacle course to get past them. The air was thick with smoke, and my eyes watered. I wanted to find Jack so I could drag him off somewhere we could be alone. Dad had been working the team nonstop this week, so I'd only been able to see Jack at school. I headed down the hallway of Jay's house but had no idea where Jack would be. The house was huge, and there had to be at least eight doors upstairs.

I heard someone coming up the steps and turned as a boy raced straight at me.

"Move it," he shouted, and I pressed myself against the wall.

He ran into the bathroom, leaving the door half open, and doubled over the toilet. I kept walking so I wouldn't have to hear him throw up.

I was almost at the end of the hallway when I saw a light and heard loud, pulsing music coming from behind a door. I hoped this was the room Jack was in. I opened it and saw two people under the covers of a giant bed.

"Um, hello, we're in here," a girl's voice said. The comforter covered most of her, but I knew it was Liz. Her long red hair was unmistakable.

"I'm sorry. I didn't know. I'm looking for Jack." I started to back out of the room.

The comforter moved down, and I saw Luke wrapped around Liz's naked upper body. "Hi, Kate. Wanna join us?" he asked lazily, beckoning me with a finger.

"Uh . . . pass," I snapped at him and left. I

slammed the door for emphasis. "Damn it," I said out loud to myself. Why did Luke have to do that to Ali? He was such an asshole, and I didn't understand why Ali didn't realize that.

I leaned against the wall, feeling sick and angry.

"Kate!" Jack headed up the steps. "Where have you been all my life?"

"Jesus, Jack, I had no idea where you were," I whispered when he wrapped his arms around me.

He reeked of alcohol. "Well, here I am," he said and kissed me on the lips.

I kissed him back for a few minutes until he started tugging at my bra under my shirt. I pushed Jack away and grabbed his hand. "Not here. Let's head downstairs."

"You're right. You don't have a drink. We need to get you a beer," Jack said and followed me.

"No, it's not like that. You wouldn't believe what I walked in on."

We reached the kitchen, and Jack grabbed two beers out of the fridge. He tossed one to me and then cracked open the other. He sucked the foam as it escaped.

Jenna walked in from outside and joined us. She

had a green and white scarf wrapped all around her neck, and she stunk like smoke.

I breathed through my mouth and took a few steps away from her.

"So what did you walk in on?" Jack asked.

"Ohhhh," Jenna said, "did you see something dirty and sexy?"

I wrinkled my nose and played with the tab on my beer. "It was definitely dirty. I was trying to find Jack and found Luke and Liz instead." I shook my head. "I don't think I need to tell you what they were doing."

"I was right," Jenna said, clapping. "I knew she was hot for him."

"The two of them are nothing new," Jack said. "Luke's been screwing her for the last couple of weeks."

I closed my eyes and shook my head. "Seriously, Jack? Why didn't you say anything? You know how Ali feels about him."

"Luke's being Luke. It's what he does. He hooks up. Everyone knows that."

"I'm staying out of this," Jenna said. "I didn't see

anything, so I'm not saying a word."

"Ali would kill me if she found out I knew and didn't say anything."

"She's going to go nuts," Jenna said, her eyes wide.

"Thanks, as if I needed you to remind me." My stomach was all queasy. I put my beer on the counter and pushed it away. "I'm not sure how I'm ever going to get the picture of Liz and Luke out of my mind."

Jack grabbed my beer and pushed it back into my hand. "Drink this, and then I'll show you a few things that'll be sure to make you forget what you saw."

I grabbed Jack with my free hand and pulled him toward me. He could make me forget, and I was ready to lose myself in him for the night.

My phone rang early the next morning. I pulled my pillow over my head and tried to ignore it, but the ringing wouldn't stop. I walked across the room and fished my phone out of my purse.

"Hello?" I said, not bothering to check the caller's name. I hadn't gotten home until late last night, and it hurt to open my eyes to the light streaming through the cracks of my blinds.

"Why didn't you call last night?" a voice demanded.

"Who is this?"

"It's Ali. What the hell happened?"

I crawled back under the covers and put the phone on speaker. "I'm sorry. I didn't get home until late, and I was so tired—"

"You promised you'd call me," she whined.

"I would've, but I wasn't thinking about that."

"No one was thinking about *me*. I was stuck at home while everyone else was having a great time."

"Believe me, it wasn't such a great time."

"Why not? What happened?"

I didn't want to tell her about the nasty hookup I walked in on. She'd flip out, but it wasn't the kind of thing you kept from a friend. I silently cursed Luke for being such an asshole and putting me in this position.

"Oh my God, something did happen. Tell me what happened."

"You're not going to like it," I told her and tugged on my hair. "It's about Luke."

"What about him?"

I stayed quiet, buying time so I could figure out how to tell her.

"Damn it. Just tell me."

"I walked in on him and Liz together in bed. Jack said they've been hooking up for a while now. I'm sorry, Ali." I said it all quickly, as if getting it out fast would make it easier to tell her. When I stopped, Ali was the one who was silent. "Ali? Are you okay?"

"You enjoy this, don't you?"

"Excuse me?"

"You had to try to ruin it, didn't you?"

"Ruin it? I don't know what you're talking about."

I didn't expect her to be happy when she heard the news, but I definitely didn't think she would lash out at me because of it.

"I'm talking about how you couldn't wait to tell me how Luke was hooking up with Liz."

"I didn't want to—"

"You think you're so great because Jack is crazy over you. The whole team loves you, but you don't care. You still have to go and make other people feel bad."

"Get real, Ali. I thought you'd want to know."

"Well, I didn't," she said firmly. "And in the future, stay out of my relationships."

"Oh, don't worry. I will," I snapped, but I wasn't sure if she heard me. She'd hung up, and I was left holding the phone with no one on the other end.

www.allmytruths.com

Today's Truth:

Your reality might not be the truth.

I once heard there are always two sides to every story.

Dad tells a story of Luke that is very different from mine.

In Dad's version, Luke can do no wrong. Luke is perfect. The one who will bring a championship to the school.

In my version, I can see through Luke. I know who he really is.

Dad believes things only one way. He will never understand what he knows is only a warped reflection of what reality is.

Dad's side of the story: "Luke scored twenty-two points in the game last night."

My side: "Luke scored with two girls in one night."

Dad's side of the story: "Luke had to go home today because he looked awful, and I think he's coming down with something. I told him not to worry about his Spanish test. I'd talk to his teacher."

My side: "Luke looks awful because he was out all night partying and getting high. He doesn't give a shit about the Spanish test."

Dad's side of the story: "I really think the tutor is helping Luke bring up his grade in English. I'm glad we won't have to worry about his eligibility."

My side: "Luke's tutor is writing his papers for him and probably half the other guys on the team."

Dad's side of the story: "I talked to Mr. Drew about the fight Luke got in. It turns out the other kid has been threatening Luke for some time. It won't be a problem anymore. The kid is on probation and will get kicked out if he so much as looks sideways at Luke."

My side: "Luke follows this poor boy around and calls him a homo. Luke threw the kid's clothes in the toilet the other day when he was showering after gym class. The kid was at his breaking point and just wanted it to stop."

Dad's side of the story: "Luke hasn't been at practice four times in the last two weeks. It turns out that his mom had to pick up some extra hours at work and Luke was watching his little sister."

My side: "Luke has been going over to the college twenty minutes away and screwing some girl who thinks he's a sophomore at her school."

Dad's side of the story: "The town loves Luke. He started volunteering on the weekends to help build the new community center."

My side: "Luke calls the people in this town reject hillbillies. The only reason he goes to volunteer is that one of the workers there is his hookup for pot."

Dad's side of the story: "Luke already has college recruiters looking at him. He's a phenomenon and the talk of all the big universities in the state."

My side: "Luke told his study hall advisor to screw off when she told him to quiet down and work. He said he didn't need to use the time studying because he was getting a full ride to any college he wanted."

I could have told Dad all my versions of the story, but he'd never comprehend them.

Luke was Dad's star. He could do no wrong.

I had a feeling there was absolutely nothing Luke could do to change Dad's opinion of him.

Not a thing.

Posted By: Your Present Self
[Sunday, November 3, 7:23 PM]

"I need your help," Ali said Monday at school.

I closed my locker door and faced her. "Oh, really? Now you want me in your business?"

"Don't act all dramatic. I'm over it. Or at least I will be if we can get the boys to come over on Friday. They don't have a game, and my mom said you and Jenna can sleep over. I'll snag some alcohol, and we can party in the basement. What do you think?"

I was skeptical. "Why do you need my help?"

She let out a huge sigh as if the answer was obvious. "I need you to get Luke to come over. He will if you invite Jack and tell him to bring everyone. I want to keep Luke away from Liz."

"Sure, okay. I'll talk to Jack about."

Ali jumped and squealed. "Thanks, Kate. I knew I could count on you."

I shook my head. "Sure, but please don't make

that noise again."

Ali slung an arm over my shoulder, and everything was back to normal between us.

The boys agreed to Ali's little party, and we all found ourselves in her basement Friday night. We told her mom we were watching a movie, but the boys were passing around a bottle of vodka and trying to get us to take shots with Ali's mom's lemonade as the chaser.

Ali was working hard to make Luke forget Liz. She was snuggled up to him on the couch, and from the way his hand kept creeping up the back of her shirt, I was pretty sure he wasn't thinking about Liz either.

Dave held up his phone and waved it. "Check your messages, boys. We've got an early Christmas gift."

"What do you mean?" Jack asked. He untangled his hand from mine and sat up to dig his phone out of a back pocket.

"Liz sent us a little something," Dave said, waggling his eyebrows.

"Hell, yeah," Luke said, looking at his phone. "Her little something just gave me a big something." He grabbed his crotch.

Ali swatted his hand away. "What are you talking about?"

"Nothing," Jack said and closed his phone. "It's just some stuff the cheerleaders have been doing for the team."

"Like what?" I moved my hand behind Jack and tried to get his phone out of his pocket. He pushed my hand away.

"Stop it, Jack. I want to see."

"Trust me. You don't."

Jenna grabbed Dave's phone. "You can't mention something and then tell us to ignore it." She looked at the picture for only a second before she threw it on the ground. "Are you serious? Naked pictures?"

Ali jumped up and glanced at the picture. "Freaking sluts."

"You're kidding me." I stood and faced Jack.

"Calm down. It's not a big deal."

"No big deal?" My voice was getting louder, until I was shouting at Jack. "What the hell are the cheerleaders doing sending you naked pictures?"

Luke shrugged. "Well, maybe if you'd loosen up a bit and send Jack something to look at, he wouldn't need these pictures."

"Seriously, Kate," Dave said, giving Luke a high five.

"I think you need to send the man some pictures fast."

"You guys are assholes," Jack said. He turned to me. "I always delete them when I get one."

Jenna tried to change the topic and grabbed the bottle of vodka. She went around filling shot glasses. "Let's forget this and get wasted."

I tried to catch Jack's eye, but he ignored me and picked a shot glass.

Luke raised his high. "To cheerleader skanks who are nowhere near as beautiful as these girls."

"I second that," Ali said. "To dirty, nasty whores."

Reluctantly, I picked up my glass and toasted with the rest of them. I swallowed my shot and tried not to make a face as it went down.

I watched Jack, but he ignored me. I wanted to say something. I wanted to yell at him and make him delete the new pictures, but I couldn't. Not with his friends around; they'd never let me forget it. I didn't want to look like the bitch who tried to control her boyfriend. Jack wouldn't go for that. I'd talk to him later and make sure I gave him a piece of my mind.

Instead, I let Dave fill my glass again and threw back another shot so at least it would look as if I could hang with everyone else. There was no way I'd let Luke and Dave see they had gotten to me. What happened between Jack and me was none of their business.

Two hours later the boys left and Jenna, Ali, and I changed into our pajamas and spread our sleeping bags out on the basement floor. My head was spinning and I knew I'd drunk too much. I wanted to go to sleep and forget about Jack's cell phone.

Ali pulled a camera out of a side table drawer and waved it in front of us. "Let's take some pictures."

"Pictures?" Jenna asked, yawning. I lay on my side and watched the two girls.

"Like the cheerleaders." Ali put her hands behind her, up the back of her shirt. She fumbled around for a couple of seconds and then pulled her bra out. "We'll give them a little competition."

"You're not serious?" Jenna giggled nervously as Ali handed her the camera.

"Of course I'm serious. Do you really think I want Luke to be looking at pictures of those bitches on his phone? I'm going to give him something better to look at." She pulled her shirt off and held it in front of her chest. I marveled at how she did it just like that, as if it were simple to take your top off. Ali threw her shirt at my head. "Okay, I'm ready."

Jenna shrugged and held up the camera. The flash lit the dark basement.

"You're crazy," I told her. "What if Luke sends it to the rest of the team?"

Ali held her hands up and shrugged. "I've got nothing to hide. I'm a lot better looking than nasty-ass Liz. Take a few more."

Jenna snapped pictures as Ali posed. "How many do you want? I don't think we need a whole photo shoot."

"You're right." Ali took the camera. She flipped through the shots. "Luke's going to love these." She put her shirt on and walked over to me.

I knew what she was thinking. "No way."

"Come on. Jack would love you forever. Just let me take one."

"Not a chance." I crossed my hands over my chest as if that would stop her.

"Kate, stop being a baby. You really want the cheerleaders sending your boyfriend naked pics?"

I shook my head, but I thought about what Ali said. After we started taking the shots of vodka together, no one mentioned the pictures again for the rest of the night, but Luke's comments were stuck in my head. Did Jack really think I was uptight? I was pretty sure the boys talked to each other about stuff like that. I wondered if he told the rest of them about how I wouldn't sleep with him. It wouldn't be surprising. Sex was becoming a major issue. Jack was getting more and more aggressive when we were making out, and I knew he wasn't going to wait forever. It had gotten to the point where he'd get angry if I stopped him. He still hadn't said anything, but I could see it in his face. I didn't know why I was acting as if it was such a big deal. I was crazy about Jack, but something didn't seem right. It was times like this I wished I could talk to my mom.

I moved away from Ali. "This isn't going to happen."

"Jack would love it," she said and stuck the camera in my face. "Think about how pumped he'll be when he opens the message from you."

"Oh, yes," Jenna said and clapped. "That would be awesome. Send it to him right before he goes out onto the court."

"I highly doubt a topless picture of me is going to improve Jack's game." I sat on my sleeping bag.

I was ready to end the whole conversation, but Jenna pounced on me. She held me down and pulled up my shirt while Ali took a picture.

"What the hell are you doing?" I pushed Jenna off and reached for the camera. "Give it to me right now."

Ali held on tight and looked at the screen.

Jenna peered over her shoulder, "You look hot, Kate."

Ali turned the camera around so I could look at the picture, and I couldn't argue. My face in the photo was twisted in a look of surprise, but the cheerleaders had nothing on me. I did look pretty damn good. Jack would go nuts over something like this.

"Come on. Let's take a better picture. You can make your face look all sexy."

"One picture?" I asked, feeling my willpower to fight this dissolve.

"Yep." Ali tugged at my shirt. "Let's do this. I want to send mine to Luke. Give him something good to dream about." She grinned wickedly at us.

"One," I repeated and pulled off my top. I held it in front of me and then let it go so Ali could take my picture. I blinked as the flash blinded me.

www.allmytruths.com

Today's Truth:

**A photo allows people to see
only one version of you.**

I face the camera, but I do

not smile.

Click.

Captured is the skin
that seals in my heart from all
that has tried to break it.

Click.

Captured is the line of freckles on my shoulder,

a constellation of brown created by the burning sun.

CANARY

Click.

Captured are my lips,
which seal in words I cannot say to my father.

Click.

Captured are my eyes,
foggy windows hiding a soul that is bruised.

Click.

Captured is the mole on my right breast,
a secret marking no one sees.

Click.

Captured is a scar cut across my forehead
a memory of falling down to the hard earth.

Click.

Captured is my hair
a veil that falls over my face to create
a shadow of what you see.

Click.

This is me.
All of me.

Open.

Exposed.

I stand in front of you with nothing
to hide.

Posted By: Your Present Self
[Saturday, November 9, 11:04 AM]

39

I woke with a start as if I'd been dreaming I was falling. Only, unlike a dream where you wake before you hit the ground, the realization of what I did last night slammed into me harder than any ten-story fall.

This was why I didn't like to drink. Drinking made you do stupid, awful things you regretted in the morning. My head was foggy and I felt sick, but I crawled over to where Ali was still sleeping and shook her. "Where's your camera?"

She rolled over and groaned but didn't answer.

I poked her hard so she'd open her eyes. "Your camera. I need it."

"It's on the table."

I moved toward it.

"But if you want to send your picture to Jack, don't worry. I already did."

I froze. "You're kidding, right?"

"No, I sent it to him before we went to bed. He probably had some pretty hot dreams last night. I bet if you check your phone, you'll have a message from him."

I pulled my phone out from under my pillow and held it. But I couldn't bring myself to look and see what Jack said. I knew he would want the picture, but it wasn't me. I clutched the phone and turned to Ali. "I can't believe you sent my picture. I never told you that you could."

Ali laughed, which made me angrier.

"This isn't funny," I shouted.

Jenna rolled over and opened her eyes. "Shut up," she said, tossing a pillow at me. "Some of us are still sleeping."

I was shaking. I couldn't believe Ali thought this was funny. "You sent Jack a naked picture of me."

"Relax. Calm down. I'm joking. I didn't send the picture."

"You didn't?" I lay on my back and waited for my heart to stop racing.

"I didn't. Geez, you went psycho. It's only a picture."

"Will you erase it? I can't send it to him."

"Yes, relax. I'll get rid of it. Jack will have to be

content with looking at your boobs in real life."

Jenna crawled out of her sleeping bag. "Why are you talking about boobs?"

"Don't worry," Ali said, waving a hand. "It's nothing."

Jenna rolled back over.

I allowed myself to relax. "Ali?"

"Yeah?" She sounded annoyed.

"You promise to get rid of the picture?"

"I promise."

I had no reason not to believe her.

www.allmytruths.com

Today's Truth:

One word can mean more than any other word you have ever said in your life.

Jack has some new favorite words:

Sex

Please

Come on

Want

Need, need, need.

He says these words over and over again like a two-year-old

who wants something

and only knows how to get it by grabbing, taking, and repeating its name.

Jack practices these new words everywhere:

In my bedroom

CANARY

In cryptic messages sent to my cell phone

On the couch in my living room

During conversations whispered late into the night
before we hang up to sleep

Outside against the side of a house at a party

As his hand slides up my back at lunch

In the empty gym when it is pouring out and we wait
for the rain to slow

At the movies in the dark row on the side of the theater

In folded notes he passes to me in the hallway

And everywhere, everywhere, everywhere else.

Jack has become a pro at saying these words,

and I let him practice.

I listen to him say them over and over again,

and I try out words of my own:

Wait

Stop

Not Ready

Go Slow

Scared, scared, scared.

I say my words

over and over

and he says his words

over and over

until we say them so many times they don't feel different.

They become heavy, bloated, saturated,

Unnecessary.

And so, I learn a new word:

Yes.

Posted By: Your Present Self

[Wednesday, November 13, 1:14 AM]

I said yes to Jack the week before Thanksgiving in his basement after a game.

Jack was high on a sixteen-point win. He'd played the entire second period. Dad didn't put any other sophomore in for more than five minutes. The success of the game got people talking about Beacon's chances at going to the play-offs, and everyone was buzzed by the prospect.

Jack wanted to watch the video footage of his time on the court. He claimed it was all a blur to him. Dad, also in a great mood, agreed to let him borrow it. Jack put it in the DVD player, and we settled onto one of the mammoth couches that were so comfy they always made me want to fall asleep.

Jack chewed on his bottom lip as he fast-forwarded to the part in the video where he was called into the game.

"There I am," Jack said softly.

I didn't watch the TV. Instead, I watched Jack's face. He stared at the screen, his eyes wide. I watched as the game played out for him and realized he wasn't watching himself with pride as some of the other players might. It looked like he couldn't believe that was him on the screen.

When the game ended, he turned to me, shaking his head slowly. "I got to play in that."

"Congratulations," I said. "It was pretty cool."

"It's incredible."

It was incredible. All of it: Jack, me, Beacon, what my life had become. Two years ago I'd watched Mom die and Dad shut down. I'd given up basketball. A year ago, if you asked me where I'd be, I wouldn't have believed any of this. I didn't think I could move forward back then, and now, here I was with Jack, the two of us together.

I'm not sure who moved toward the other first, but suddenly we were kissing and not the kissing we usually did where Jack pulled at me, begged me, or tried to take from me. This was slow, almost as if it were the first kiss or maybe the last and we needed to memorize it all.

Jack trailed his hand down the side of my face,

his eyes locked on mine. I didn't look away as I often did, shy and self-conscious. Instead, I took it all in, everything, and when Jack continued to kiss me slowly, moving lower and lower, I didn't stop him. He pulled at my jeans, and I held my hips up slightly so he could slide them off of me. He paused as we lay there and asked if he should keep going. His eyes were clear and honest.

I said yes.

And so he did.

And so we did.

"I want to enlist," my brother Brett announced the next night at dinner, seemingly out of the blue. I later learned the words had been dangling on his lips for months, already spoken to everyone around him: Uncle John, Julia, the guidance counselor, the history teacher, and the recruitment department four blocks from our house. These words had been uttered to everyone. Everyone except Dad and me.

I paused, the spaghetti dangling off my fork, threatening to fall back onto my plate. "Enlist? Enlist for what?"

The six o'clock news continued behind Brett, a brown–haired woman telling the viewers about a massive thunderstorm heading our way, complete with heavy winds and damaging hail.

"I want to enlist in the Army," my brother said, looking Dad straight in the eye.

"The Army . . ." Dad said slowly. He blinked, waiting for Brett to respond.

"You're crazy. They'll ship you off to war." My heart pounded. He couldn't be serious. Why would he want to put himself somewhere dangerous?

"Well, I don't *want* to enlist," Brett said, ignoring me. "I'm *going* to enlist. I've been thinking about it for a long time. Before you made me go to Beacon, the recruiting officer at Olmstead High was helping me."

"When did this ever become an option?" Dad said. "I always thought your interest in the military was just for fun."

"That's where you're wrong, Dad. My interest is what I want to do with my life. I've been talking to Uncle John about it for a while now. He thinks it's a great idea."

"Uncle John? What kind of rubbish has he been filling your head with?"

"It's not rubbish. It's what I want to do. If you weren't so busy with everyone on your team, maybe you would have noticed what your own son was interested in."

Dad wasn't the only one who hadn't been paying attention to Brett. This was all a surprise to me also. Sure, Brett used to beg Uncle John to tell him stories about his days in the Army the minute he walked in our door, and he was always watching those war movies where things blew up all over the place, but I never thought this was something he personally wanted to do. Enlisting was a big deal. The thought surprised me as much as it terrified me.

"You will not enlist," Dad commanded, interrupting my thoughts.

I bit my bottom lip, forcing myself to stay quiet even though I wanted to get up, shake Brett, and yell at him.

Dad gripped his fork, the tines pressed into the table. I don't think he knew what he was doing, because he seemed so angry.

I didn't want to get in the middle of another fight, so I kept my eyes on the radars on the screen, big blobs of green and yellow floating behind the weather woman's body, slowly moving closer and closer to our house.

"I'm eighteen, Dad," Brett said. "I don't need your permission." He looked in Dad's eyes, holding his gaze, but I could tell from the slight shaking of his hands that he was scared.

My leg itched, an intense itching that got worse when I thought about it, but I didn't want to scratch. I didn't want to make any movements that would remind Dad I was still in the room and potentially cause him to tell me to leave.

"We're not having this conversation, Brett. You're not going to enlist in the Army. The Army is a parasite designed to prey on boys who have no other options. You go to Beacon; you have the whole world in front of you."

"What are you talking about? The whole world in front of me?" My brother kept his voice even, calm.

It was obvious nothing Dad said would change his mind, and that scared me. I was horrified at the thought of Brett joining the Army.

"You, Brett, are not the type of person who goes into the Army. The Army is for boys who can't get into college. The Army is for boys who aren't responsible enough to make something of themselves in school, to work hard." Dad was on a roll, spewing out the kind of speech only the privileged could make. A speech for people who would never consider an option like the Army.

Dad's voice only grew louder. "It's a last resort for kids who have spent their whole lives messing up. They fill you with promises to make a man out of you, when what they're really doing is targeting those boys at the bottom. Boys who have messed things up so bad they have no other option."

Brett broke his gaze with Dad and put his head down. When he brought it back up, his voice was strong and steady. "I *am* one of those boys, Dad. You've said yourself I don't have the grades to get into a good college. I don't have any talents or athletic abilities. And every time I start to forget these things, one of your players is more than willing to remind me of what a waste I am. I'm graduating in less than seven months with grades just above failing, a grade point average that's probably not even good enough to get me into a community college, and no one knows where I'm going to go or what I'm going to do after I graduate. If I'm not one of those boys, then who am I?"

When Dad didn't respond, Brett pushed his chair back and left the room.

Brett signed his papers the day Beacon won their thirteenth straight game, a win that had gotten the media talking about championships, attaching Dad's name to all their predictions.

It was an away game, and Brett had promised Dad he'd come watch. They'd had some kind of secret talk the other night in Dad's office, and when they both walked out in good moods, I'd thought I could let go of my fears about Brett enlisting.

It wasn't until I headed back on the team bus with Jack, who was drunk on the win, that I realized Brett had never showed up. I watched Dad at the front of the bus, joking with the assistant coaches, and wondered if he'd also noticed Brett's absence. Dad would be upset he hadn't come. Dad was all about getting us to go to the games to help complete the happy family image he wanted to portray to the Beacon community.

When we got home, the kitchen light was on.

Dad unlocked the door, and in an unusually good mood, continued to talk to me, reliving the glories of the past day.

I followed him into the kitchen, where he looked at the pile of papers on our dinner table, the light illuminating a bright orange Post-it.

"Jesus Christ," he said, his mood shifting abruptly.

"What?" I tried to get a look at the pages Dad was now sifting through. The top one had a date circled in red. "What are those?"

"Your brother signed his papers for the Army."

Dad threw the documents onto the table.

I grabbed them, focusing on the words scrawled on the Post-it: "I'm out celebrating with Julia. You can congratulate me later."

"He signed papers?" I flipped through the documents and tried to make sense of them. I couldn't believe Brett had enlisted without Dad's approval. "Didn't you two make up? I thought you talked him out of it. Why would he do this?"

"Because your brother doesn't think about how dangerous this can be." He slammed a fist on the table. For a man who, a few minutes ago, was celebrating a big win, he looked completely defeated.

"God damn it, doesn't he realize he's going to kill himself over there?" He walked out of the room.

The door to his office banged shut.

I couldn't stop the tears from falling. I sat and tried to read the papers through watery eyes. I wanted to make sense of what was going on, but it was impossible to focus on the page. All I could think about was what Dad said before he left the room. Brett was doing something that could kill him, and now that he'd signed the papers, neither of us could do anything to stop him.

43

Brett came home late that night. The door opened and closed downstairs, and footsteps hurried up the stairs. I waited for Dad to come out and say something to Brett, but the house remained quiet.

I spent the morning in my room staring at the wall, trying to wrap my mind around what Brett had done. My heart started to race every time I let my thoughts settle on everything for a moment, and I was overwhelmed at the thought of how much danger Brett was placing himself in. I didn't move for what felt like hours, watching the sky grow from dim to light. The game yesterday seemed so far away I couldn't even remember being happy and cheering the team on.

I needed to talk to Brett. Things might have sucked between us, but what he had done was major. I couldn't ignore his decision.

I knocked on his door and got no response. All I heard was the low hum of music too quiet to identify.

I pounded.

"Go away," he said.

"Please, Brett, can I talk to you about this?"

"There isn't anything to discuss."

"There are a million things to discuss. Starting with, this isn't a good idea."

"I really don't think you're in any position to tell me what's a good idea and what isn't. You haven't exactly been my biggest supporter lately."

"I don't understand how to support this decision."

"You don't need to. The choice has been made. Just leave me alone."

"That's not fair."

There was movement on the other side of the door, and I thought he was going to let me in.

I was wrong. Music started to blast, and the bass thumped so hard he wouldn't hear me no matter how loud I yelled.

I kicked the door and then headed downstairs.

How had my family gotten here? We were never a family of secrets before, and now it seemed as if we were all hiding things.

I hung out in the family room all day waiting for Brett to finally leave his room, but it never happened. It wasn't until a horn beeped outside that I remembered Jack and I had planned to go to dinner.

Jack continued to beep his horn even when I flashed the front lights to let him know I was coming. When I was close to his car, he laid on the horn so it wouldn't stop.

I yanked open the door. "Jack, cool it. You don't want my dad to come out."

"I can handle your dad. He loves me." Jack pulled me the rest of the way into the car, his hands quickly finding their way up the back of my shirt. "Your dad isn't the only one who loves me."

"Cool it, Jack, you don't have to jump on me the minute I get into the car."

He held on, and I tried to get away. His elbow slammed into the horn, and the blast made us both jump.

"Damn," he said, "what's your problem?"

I opened my mouth to say something, but a huge sob came out. Tears collected in my eyes.

He looked at me, confused. "What's wrong? I was just kidding around."

"No, it's not that. It's Brett. He enlisted in the Army." My eyes stung, and I fought to keep the tears in.

"What?"

"He signed the papers last night. He left them on the table for my dad and me to see."

"Oh, man, that's rough. I wouldn't join now, not when they're sending everyone overseas."

I swiped at my eyes. "I don't know why he's doing this. He's crazy."

Jack wrapped his arms around me again, but this time it was in a hug. "I'm sure it'll be okay. He's just signed the papers, right? It's not like he's leaving right away, and he has to go to boot camp and stuff."

I nodded, warming my hands over the heat blasting from the vents.

"Then I'm sure your dad will talk him out of it. He's not going to let Brett do something so dangerous."

"He can't unsign those papers. He's committed to the Army."

"Your dad will figure it out."

I didn't answer. I let myself lean against Jack as he held me. I listened to the music on the radio change from one song to another and tried to forget what Brett had done.

Finally, I pulled away. "I need to get out of here. Away from the house. I don't want Dad to come out."

"Okay," Jack said. "Let's go." He backed the car out of the driveway.

I fished around my purse for some tissues and pulled down the mirror. I looked terrible. My eyeliner had left dark smudges above the streaks from my mascara. I tried to get it off. I tried to fix everything so at least I seemed okay on the outside.

Inside was a different story. I was trying to understand. Why would someone purposely put himself in danger? It didn't make sense.

Jack slowed and stopped at a red light. "I told Luke we'd stop over at his house. He invited a bunch of people to hang out."

"Luke's house? You said we were going to get dinner and spend the night together."

"We can, but I wanted to hang with everyone else too. Luke ordered some pizzas. What's the big deal?"

"There isn't." I didn't want to start fighting with Jack too. "Let's go over."

"You'll have a good time. It'll take your mind off things."

I stared out the window, thinking about Brett. All I knew about the Army had to do with the Middle East and the war. I thought of all the images that seemed familiar from movies or the news: images of sandy deserts, rolling tanks, crumbled cities, and snaps of gunfire.

"We don't have to stay all night," Jack said as he pulled in to Luke's driveway. "If you want to leave, let me know."

"Thanks," I said, climbing out of the car.

"It'll be okay."

I nodded, although I didn't really know how Jack could promise that.

Luke's basement was full of guys from the team playing cards around a big table.

I grabbed Jack's hand and pulled him back before the guys could see us. "Are you kidding me?"

"What?" he asked, annoyed.

"I didn't expect to spend the night with half the team."

"I told you we were going to Luke's."

"Yeah, but you didn't say I'd be the only girl."

"Relax, Kate. It's fine. You know everyone." Before I was able to answer, Jack walked into the circle of guys sitting around a table playing cards. I followed, feeling horribly out of place. This was not where I wanted to be.

"Jack, Kate. Take a seat," Luke said. He had a joint in one hand and a beer in the other.

I wondered where his parents were.

"We're about to start another game if you want to get in on it," Luke added.

Jack grabbed an unopened beer from the table. "I'm in."

"Just a warning," Luke said. "I'm stealing money from every one of you assholes." He dealt cards to the other guys who, like Luke, were drinking beer or smoking pot. The whole room was hazy and stinky.

I sat on the edge of one of the couches while Jack pulled up a chair beside the other boys. Every once in a while one of them would offer me a beer, but for the most part they were in a world of their own. I found a magazine on the floor and picked it up to pass the time. I threw it back down when I saw it was *Playboy*.

Luke turned to me between games. "Hey, Kate,

why don't you play this next one with us?"

"No, thanks. I'm okay."

"You're just sitting there," Dave chimed in. "That doesn't look too fun."

"Nah, it's okay," Jack said. "She's fine. She's had a hard day."

"Then you need to be drinking." Luke tossed me a beer.

I missed, and it rolled across the floor. I got up to follow it and heard Jack talking as I bent under the table to grab it.

"Seriously, her brother enlisted in the Army."

I froze. Did Jack really say that to everyone? Luke laughed, and for the second time that night, I fought back tears.

"You have to be shitting me," Luke said. "Brett? Fighting?"

"Don't worry," Brad, a junior, said. "At least he'll be safe. Everyone will lay off him because they'll feel sorry for the little guy."

The room exploded in laughter, and I stood up from under the table, knocking my head. I grabbed the spot I'd hurt and didn't bother to keep the tears in.

"Let's go," I demanded.

Jack looked away from his friends and at me. "Oh, shit, Kate. Sorry. They were just joking."

"Now," I said, not looking at anyone else in the room. I grabbed my purse and started for the steps.

"Busted," I heard someone say.

Luke said something quietly, and everyone laughed again.

I kept going, moving fast. I heard Jack following me, but I didn't stop. I walked through the house and outside. I stood beside Jack's car, waiting for him to unlock it.

"Kate, I said I was sorry." He unlocked the doors.

I slid inside. It was impossible to look at him. "Was that before or after you laughed with everyone?"

"You know I didn't mean it."

"Then why the hell didn't you stop it?"

"I really am sorry. I shouldn't have told everyone."

"You're right. It wasn't your business to tell. Do you think any of those guys care about my brother?" I took a deep breath and glanced at him.

He reached toward my cheek and leaned over to kiss me.

I pulled away.

"I didn't mean to hurt you."

I sighed and reached out to squeeze his hand. It was ridiculous to fight right now. I needed him to help me deal with this, but I couldn't shake what had happened.

Ali pulled me into the bathroom as soon as I got to school the next morning. "Jack told me what happened. Why didn't you tell me?"

"What are you talking about?" I asked.

"How Brett is going off to fight in the war. That sucks."

"Are you kidding me?" I slipped my backpack off my shoulder and looked around the bathroom, wondering if anyone else was listening. No one was. All the stalls were empty. The last thing I wanted was to have the whole school talking about Brett's decision. "Why would Jack tell you that?"

"He was worried. He called me last night after he dropped you off."

"He called you?" Jack and Ali had been talking about me? I imagined what the conversation might have been like. Jack had probably joked about Brett the way he had with the other guys. I was sure Ali wouldn't have been able to wait to get off the phone with him so she could call Jenna to spread the latest gossip. I shoved one of the stall doors and watched it swing back and forth.

"Yeah, but it was only because he cares—"

"You don't know how Jack feels."

"What? He wanted to make sure you were okay. He thought I could help."

"It's not his business. It's not yours. You guys have no right to be talking about me behind my back."

"He was worried."

"So am I." My words echoed off the bathroom walls. "Don't you think I'm worried too? But I'm allowed to be worried. He's my brother."

"Of course you are. He's going to war. I'm sure you're scared. We all are."

"Don't say that. He isn't going to war. All he's done is sign the papers. And don't suddenly act like Brett is important to you." I stared at the tiles on the floor and picked at a hangnail. I didn't believe I could cry any more than I had, but I proved myself wrong. "Nobody ever cared about him before." My voice broke, and then my whole body shook with sobs.

Ali wrapped her arms around me. "I'm sorry."

I wanted to fight her. I wanted to push and shove and get away from her and everyone else, but I allowed myself to relax in her hug. It was only for a moment, but then I broke away. "Don't be sorry. What the hell are you apologizing for? You don't understand anything." I pushed past her and headed out the door.

I walked down the hall and ignored the first bell. I headed outside, fighting against students who were racing inside, trying to make it to their classes before the late bell rang. I kept walking down the steps and away from everyone who would no doubt be talking about Brett. If Jack told Ali, I was sure he'd told other people. And if he hadn't, I was sure Luke would.

I couldn't handle it. I didn't want to face anyone, so I didn't. Instead, I trudged farther and farther away from Beacon and the people who didn't understand what was happening to Brett, to me, and to our family.

45

Ali apologized the next day with a box of cup-cakes. Six chocolate ones with white buttercream frosting and pink sprinkles. She held them up when I approached my locker in the morning. No one had said anything about me skipping school, but I didn't want to press my luck and stay home another day.

I pointed at the cupcakes. "Are those for me?"

"I'm sorry," she said.

I shook my head. "No, I was a bitch. You were only trying to help."

"But it wasn't my place. I should have waited for you to talk to me."

I pulled the wrapper off a cupcake and took a big bite. "It's such a shock. He just signed the papers and I can't stop thinking about how stupid he is for wanting to do something so dangerous. I really wasn't ready to start talking about it yesterday."

"I'm glad we're talking now," Ali said. She

reached for a cupcake. "You know you can tell me these things, right?"

I nodded.

"I'm here for you. Don't ever feel like you can't talk to me."

I licked some frosting off my finger. "And when I don't want to talk, you can bring cupcakes."

"Perfect."

I closed the lid on the box and turned to Ali. "Let's take the rest of these to the boys."

"I think that's a great idea."

I followed her down the hall and hoped she really would listen if I tried to talk.

Brett waited until dinner that night to finally talk to us about the papers he signed.

Dad knocked on my door. "We're eating together. I picked up pizza."

I headed to the kitchen, dread filling my stomach. The last time Dad organized a family dinner was when he told us about Beacon, and that didn't go well.

We sat at the same table we'd used my whole life. It showed its age in the shiny dark wood, smooth in some places and bumpy in other spots where a pen had pressed too hard or a fork had gouged the surface to punctuate a point during a heated argument.

The table where Mom told me she was sick, where Brett announced his intention to enlist in the Army, and where his signed papers from the recruiters were left for Dad.

We sat with Brett and passed out plates and napkins as if nothing was wrong. For a little bit, it seemed like a typical meal. No one talking, our pizza moving methodically from our mouths to the plates, the newsman on the TV the only real noise.

Halfway through dinner, Brett started to talk, his voice rising. "I know you're both mad about what I did, but it's what I want to do. It's important to me. I'm going to request special training in bomb disarmament. I want to go to the Middle East."

I stared at him. "Are you kidding me?"

Brett shook his head slowly. "No, I'm not. I want to help, and I can help over there."

I waited for Dad to rage, as he usually did, but he just sat there staring at his plate.

I spoke for him. "Brett, that's the dumbest thing I've ever heard. You're going to get killed." My words were shrill, hurried, as if I could push the words out that would change his mind.

"I'm aware of the risks. I know I can get killed. But it'll be okay. I'm going to help end the fighting, not be a part of it."

"How?" I said. "I see the news. They're always mentioning soldiers who get blown up or shot and killed. I know what goes on over there."

"Kate, the war you see on TV isn't what it's really

like over there. Not everyone is the enemy."

"You're going to die," I repeated, because it was what my mind instantly went to when I thought about war. "Die. Just like Mom."

Dad finally spoke up, his voice loud and clear. "Enough, both of you. Enough."

Brett and I sat still, waiting for him to say more. Dad closed his eyes and kept them shut.

"Dad," Brett said. "It's going to be okay. This is a good thing."

"How?" he started. "How the hell can you say this is a good thing?"

"Because it is, Dad. What I'm doing is going to help people, whether or not you want to believe it."

Dad stood, looming over the two of us. His jaw twitched, and I knew he was angry. I was afraid of what he might do. "I didn't say anything when you enlisted against my wishes. I tried to grasp why you'd do something so foolish, but this . . . This I can't understand, and I refuse to try. This is not what I expected out of my son."

"Well, Dad," Brett started. "This is who I am now. You need to figure out how to accept it, or you're going to lose me too."

"I've already lost you. You openly defied me, Brett, and I don't know how I can call you my son anymore. Not after what you've done."

"Don't worry," Brett shouted, kicking the chair next to him.

I jumped back, frightened, and hit my knee on the table. I bit the side of my mouth as pain shot through me.

"You don't need to bother with your son, because he's moving out. I won't be your problem anymore." Brett pushed back his chair and stood to walk out, but Dad walked out faster.

"Make sure you leave your key," Dad demanded, slamming his office door.

"Brett," I said and reached out to him, "you don't need to do this. Dad's just mad. He doesn't mean what he's saying."

"Oh, now you're on my side? It's a lot easier to offer help when your friends aren't around to see, isn't it?"

"I've always been on your side."

"Right. Sure your were. You're as bad as Dad."

"I'm nothing like Dad."

"Look in a mirror. I think you'd be surprised how much you've become like him."

I opened my mouth to respond, but Brett's back was turned to me as he walked away.

I sat alone at the table. If I did look in the mirror, would I be able to recognize myself?

www.allmytruths.com

Today's Truth:
Read between the lines.

Brett told us he wants to fight in the war at dinner tonight, but I won't let myself believe it. His sentences came out fractured and broken.

I tried to pick up the jagged shards around me, but I could only hold on to a few.

All I heard were the words that flew out of his mouth, slapping me awake with their wicked connotations, speaking the truth, the truth he didn't want us to hear . . .

Middle East

Bomb

Risks

Killed

War

Violence

Hate

Enemy

His words echo in my head over and over and over again . . .

Middle East, bomb, risks, killed, war, violence, hate, enemy, Middle East, bomb, risks, killed, war, violence, hate, enemy, Middle East, bomb, risks, killed, war, violence, hate, enemy, Middle East, bomb, risks, killed, war, violence, hate, enemy, Middle East, bomb, risks, killed, war, violence, hate, enemy, Middle East, bomb, risks, killed, war, violence, hate, enemy, Middle East, bomb, risks, killed, war, violence, hate, enemy, Middle East, bomb, risks, killed, war, violence, hate, enemy, Middle East, bomb, risks, killed, war, violence, hate, enemy, Middle East, bomb, risks, killed, war, violence, hate, enemy, Middle East, bomb, risks, killed, war, violence, hate, enemy, Middle East, bomb, risks, killed, war, violence, hate, enemy, Middle East, bomb, risks, killed, war, violence, hate, enemy.

Posted By: Your Present Self

[Tuesday, November 19, 8:53 PM]

Brett left before sunup. I watched through my window as he carried his bags down the front steps. He got in the car with Julia and drove away. I stood with one palm against the window, perhaps a wave or a sign for him to stop, and I imagined he saw me.

Dad never came out of his room. He didn't try to get him to stay.

Brett left before sunup. That's all I can say.

What more can you add to that?

Brett left.

He was gone.

Brett might have moved out, but he was still going to Beacon. I saw him Friday sitting next to Julia, and I waited until the bell rang and he stood to leave.

"We miss you," I said, blocking his way.

"I highly doubt that." He shifted his book bag on his shoulder and tried to move around me.

"Talk to Dad. He'll listen and understand. He'll forgive you, and you can move back into the house."

"Forgive me?" he asked, glancing about at the ceiling and shaking his head.

"He's just busy with the team and coaching. You need to talk to him. It'll be okay."

"Do you hear yourself?"

"What?"

"Making excuses for Dad. Acting like he's allowed to be like this, to treat his kids like we're second rate. Wake up, Kate. He doesn't care. He's choosing the team over us. He always has and always will."

"That's not true. Dad loves us." I moved closer to him as bodies leaving the cafeteria pressed against us. I tried to stand my ground, but the movement around us made me unsteady on my feet.

"You're just like everyone else here, believing the team is God. When are you going to understand they're using us—you, Dad, everyone—and we're just playing their game? Talking to Dad is the last thing I want to do, and until you figure out how corrupt this whole school is I'm also done talking with you."

"We don't need to pick sides here," I said, lowering my voice, seeing people watching us.

"You're right. We don't need to pick sides, because you already have."

I let his words pour over me. Luke and some other guys on the team walked toward us. Something flew and hit Brett in the face.

"You have to be kidding me," Brett said, swiping his cheek.

"Oh, sorry, man. We were trying to find the trash can. Didn't mean to confuse it with you," Luke said loudly, and the rest of the guys slapped him on the back.

"Screw you," Brett spat at them. He turned to me,

"Yeah, Dad is real busy with the team. It's nice to be reminded of the important work he's doing."

"Brett—"

"*Brett*," Luke mimicked in a high falsetto.

Brett pushed his shoulders back and stared me down. "Do me a favor. Leave me alone. It looks like you and Dad are fine without me." He walked away.

It wasn't until Brett was gone that I realized I was standing alongside the team, just like Dad.

www.allmytruths.com

Today's Truth:
Be careful what you wish for.

I used to think being compared to Dad was a compliment.

I grew up watching him slay my dragons.

He was my prince, saving me from the dangers that lurked under my bed in the dark.

Now I understand the danger of exalting someone.

The privilege, the favors, the special treatment.

How you have to choose to worship the gods or get stepped on by the followers.

My friends, my boyfriend, the past months at Beacon.

I know about these privileges, the favors, the special treatment,

and I never say anything.

Instead, I use it to my benefit.

I walk over those below me.

I finally am like Dad.

And I'm not sure I like who I have become.

Posted By: Your Present Self

[Friday, November 22, 4:58 PM]

49

Our family was an official mess, and I seemed to be left to deal with it by myself.

I didn't tell Dad about my conversation with Brett in the cafeteria. I tried not to think about what Brett had said. Was being like Dad really so bad?

I shook the thought out of my head. I needed to try to fix my family. If Brett wasn't willing to talk to Dad, maybe I could convince Dad to talk to Brett.

I waited until we were seated for dinner to say anything. The two of us had been moving around the house in relative peace these last few days. I didn't want to upset things, but I needed to get this out.

"Do you worry Brett is okay?" I asked while I pounded the bottom of the ketchup bottle, trying to get the stubborn stuff to come out.

"That's a ridiculous question. Of course he's okay," he responded and picked up the TV remote to turn the volume up so high that I'd have to yell if I wanted to continue the conversation.

He had answered so quickly, without thinking, and I wondered *what* was ridiculous. Was it ridiculous because Brett was somewhere safe right now? Or was it because he would be safe when he joined the Army? Or because he wouldn't be? Did he just feel it was ridiculous to ask questions about Brett at all? I stared at Dad, willing him to look at me, to see that I wanted to keep talking, but he kept his eyes fixed on the TV. He ate his hot dog slowly, not putting it down between bites, apparently so he wouldn't have to move his gaze and risk connecting with mine.

"Do you even know where he is? Don't you care about any of this?"

"Your brother is fine. He's staying with your uncle John. You don't need to worry."

"Do you think about him, Dad?" This time I knew the question was ridiculous. "I mean, not just about him but about what he did? Do you think about him dying? That we might lose him over there?"

Dad remained silent. The image on the TV had shifted, and now the newscaster talked about the desert, the war, and the soldiers.

I strained my neck, squinting at the screen,

picturing Brett in one of the faces of the soldiers. "Why can't we talk about this?" I slammed a hand on the table. A coffee mug swayed on the edge before I grabbed it.

The story about the soldiers ran for ten more seconds, and then the newscaster started a story about a group of kids recycling. Dad turned the TV off, the image disappearing into a black screen.

I kept talking. "I can't stop worrying. I don't know how to stop."

"Not now, Kate. I can't focus on this now. I have way too much to do before the game to talk about this."

"You never want to talk about it," I yelled and pushed my hand across the table, sending the coffee mug flying. It cracked on the floor, the pieces scattering, but even that wasn't enough to get Dad to listen.

Ali stopped and grabbed my hand while were walking to lunch. "Guess what. I got my parents to agree to let us use the cabin." She grinned.

Her family had a place on a lake two hours out of town. She'd always called it her family's weekend cabin, and I'd pictured something like the tiny place my family had rented for two nights one summer when I was young. But when I saw pictures of Ali's cabin, I learned I was very mistaken.

It was huge, full of guest rooms decorated in rustic themes with beds covered in flannel blankets and handmade quilts. There was a giant family room with a fireplace two stories tall and a loft. The back deck overlooked the lake, and she had picture after picture of her family racing around on their boat. Ali might have said she was going to the family cabin, but I joked that she was going to the family resort.

I was dying to go to Ali's family's cabin. I had bugged her all the time to invite me, but now I wasn't sure if I'd be able to hold myself together for an entire weekend.

When I didn't answer, she snapped at me. "Well, don't act all excited. I thought you wanted go to the cabin. I even got my parents to agree to let us go there without them."

"I did want to go," I said, feeling bad about my response. "But it's different now. I've kind of been in a bad mood."

"That's why I figured you'd like the trip. To get your mind off things, to remind you that you can still have fun."

"Fun is the last thing on my mind right now," I snapped, irritated she was trying to tell me how to feel when she had no idea what I was going through.

"I'm not trying to make you mad. I thought this would be a good time. We all did. I invited the boys, including Dave, so we can try to hook him up with Jenna. My parents made me swear up and down I wouldn't invite anyone except you, but they're going to be so busy this weekend with my brothers' games and Heather's gymnastics meet that they won't have time to check on us. It's perfect, and it's going to be so much fun."

"You talked to Jack?"

Ali nodded.

"Before asking me?"

"God, it's not like you own him. I can talk to him."

"What did you tell him? That I needed some cheering up so we should have a pity party for me?"

"No one thinks this is for you. It's a fun weekend together to help you get your mind off things. You can have fun with your friends who are missing you."

She was doing this to be nice.

"Okay, I'll try. I just need to convince Dad it's a good idea."

"That'll be easy. The hard part was convincing you."

51

Ali was right. Dad didn't give the weekend trip a second thought, and I soon found myself heading to the cabin.

I sat next to Jack in his truck as we followed Ali's car, which was packed full of suitcases, food, Jenna, Dave, and Luke. We'd met in the parking lot at Beacon so Ali's parents didn't know the weekend plans involved more than the two of us.

Jack drove for over an hour on the highway and then took an exit that led us to tree-lined, twisting roads where the branches were so low they slapped the windows as if trying to get our attention. Jack kept up a constant stream of conversation with me or the others via his cell phone.

He turned to me and winked. "I think we should sneak away when it's dark and explore the woods."

I rolled my eyes. I knew what he wanted to explore, and it wasn't the woods. "It's freezing cold outside."

"I guess we'll just have to make sure we keep

each other warm inside."

We arrived a little after two and unloaded the packed car. We were only staying for a night, but based on the food, drinks, sleeping bags, clothes, iPod, speakers, and other random items jammed into the car, it seemed we were planning to move in permanently.

"So remind me again what you left at home," Luke joked, pulling out a suitcase on wheels.

Ali said, "You never know what you want to wear until it's time to put it on. What if I hadn't packed the one outfit I wanted? This stuff is important."

"Oh, yes, real important." Luke pulled out a tennis racket. "It's December. We're not playing tennis. Was there anything you didn't pack?"

"For your information, that isn't *my* racket. It's my brother's. He probably left it in there after practice. Geez, give me a break." She dragged a bag into the house.

The afternoon and early evening were low-key. We made a fire, cooked a huge pot of spaghetti, and mixed our Kool-Aid with vodka, turning our drinks thick and sugary. I tried to stay focused on Jack, on being with him and my friends, and the fact that I was having fun.

After dinner we all sat around the fire in the great room. I'd changed into black stretch pants and a Beacon sweatshirt, but even with my heavier clothes and the fire I was cold. I pressed up against Jack, stealing his heat as we sat clutching plastic blue cups of Kool-Aid. I drank slowly. The sugar made me feel sick, and I didn't want to drink too much vodka.

Jack wrapped his arms around my shoulders and gave me a giant hug. I tried to squirm away, but he held tighter. "I'm glad we're here," he whispered.

It wasn't hard to agree. I *was* glad I was there.

"Let's play a game," Ali suggested.

"Strip poker?" Luke yelled.

All the girls groaned while the boys cheered.

"That could be fun," Ali said, giving Luke a look that made it clear they would play that game later. "But I was thinking more like a drinking game. Something with questions or dares."

"Ugh, not truth or dare," I said. "It's too cold, and we always have to do stupid things like kiss another girl or something."

Luke let out a whoop of delight.

I shot him a dirty look.

"What about never have I ever?" Jenna said. She was sitting next to Dave, but so far nothing seemed to be happening between the two of them. Ali and I joked in private that Jenna was more interested in the drawings she sketched than anyone in real life. "We go around taking turns asking questions, and if you have done it or can answer yes, then you take a sip."

"Oh, I like it," Jack said, squeezing me closer to him. "I'm sure there's a bunch of dirt I still don't know about Kate."

I rolled my eyes. "Yeah, so true. My life was full of scandal before I came to Beacon."

"Okay, bring it on," Ali said. She'd been drinking steadily since dinner, and by the way she slurred, it was obvious she needed to slow down. If not, she'd be waking up to her own scandalous stories. "I'll go first, since it's my house. Never have I ever stolen anything."

"You're not starting out easy are you?" Jenna said as she raised her cup to her lips.

Jack, Luke, and Dave did the same.

I sat merely holding my glass.

"Kate, you're honestly telling me you've never

stolen anything before?" Dave asked.

"Um, not that I know of," I said, already uncomfortable with the game and the idea that some of us were using it to judge each other.

"I don't believe that," Dave pressed. "What about answers to tests or a report or questions someone else had written?"

"What? That's not stealing," Luke interrupted. "That's called smart losers giving you help."

The boys high fived each other.

I frowned. I thought about how Jack had passed my history questions around.

"Okay, I have one," Luke said. "Never have I ever made out with a girl."

"Oh, yes, hot," Dave rooted and all the boys chugged quickly so as not to miss which of us girls would take a sip.

Ali shrugged as if to apologize for not being able to drink, and I shook my head. Jenna, however, drank from her cup with a sly grin. When pressed by the boys to say who, she pretended to take a key and lock her lips.

We went through all the typical questions, then

those that bordered on outrageous, the boys trying to get information out of Jenna, Ali, and me.

Jenna said some funny ones, such as, "Never ever have I peed in the shower," to which we all slowly took sips and cracked up when we realized everyone had.

I kept my questions pretty tame, asking things like if people ever cut class or thought certain teachers were cute.

We played for a while, filling our glasses for a second time and coming to the bottom of them when the questions started to turn more serious.

"Never have I ever thought I was better than everyone else on the basketball team," Jack said, looking straight at Luke. We all stopped our talking, our cups frozen in our hands.

Jenna raised her eyebrows at me.

I shrugged. I had no idea what was going on.

"Yeah, that's a no," Ali said, trying to break the tension that had developed.

We remained still, watching Jack and Luke stare each other down. The two of them had been clashing lately on the court, battling for playing time, but from what I saw from the stands it was usually resolved by the end of practice.

Jenna hiccupped, and we all laughed nervously.

Jack continued to stare Luke down, as if daring him to take a sip.

"What do you want, man?" Luke asked. "What kind of question is that? I'm not going to take a sip."

"Okay, if that's the way you want to play," Jack said. "But I thought we were supposed to tell the truth."

Luke glared at him. "Never have I ever," he started and paused, not taking his eyes off of Jack. "Never have I ever said, and I quote, 'I hope Kate's loser brother Brett doesn't come back from Iraq.'"

My eyes widened.

"Wow, Luke, that's harsh," Jenna said quietly, letting her breath come out slowly as she shook her head.

"What kind of question is that? What are you talking about?" I asked, confused. I moved my gaze from Luke to Jack. The vodka made me a bit light-headed, and it was hard for me to understand what was going on.

"Why don't you tell her, Jack?" Luke gestured toward me.

Ali stood up and grabbed Luke's hand, trying to

pull him away.

Dave and Jenna stared, watching everything.

"Come on. Let's put this fire out and head to bed," Ali started.

Jack interrupted. "No, wait a minute. What kind of bullshit thing was that to say?" He balled his hands into fists.

"Yeah, what did you mean?" I stood, my voice rising. I looked at Luke and then at Jack. "Jack, did you say that?"

He took his cup and dumped it into the fireplace as if finishing it would be like taking a sip and agreeing to Luke's statement. He took a step in Luke's direction.

Luke let go of Ali's hand, moving closer to Jack.

"I'll tell you what it is," Luke said. "It's the same type of bullshit you keep trying to spread about me thinking I'm better than everyone else on the team. I know you believe that."

"I'm going to be sick." I broke away from everyone and ran out of the room.

Jenna and Ali tried to follow me, banging on the door of the bathroom after I locked it.

I heard Jack on the other side too. "Let me talk to her alone."

"I doubt she wants to talk to you right now," Ali shot back.

"Shut up and just go somewhere else."

I didn't want to talk to anyone. I wanted them to leave me alone, to go away so I didn't have to try to understand what Jack said or see Jenna with that look of pity on her face. Large, hot tears burned their way down my cheeks as I tried to erase what Luke had said about Brett. I stared at the shower stall.

At some point Jack fought the girls off, and they left after promising me they'd come back if I wanted to talk. It was now only Jack and me.

"Kate, come on. Open the door. I want to explain."

"Explain?" Fresh tears ran from my eyes. "Is there something to explain?"

"How can you think that? What happened out there was stupid. Luke is jealous. Let me in. I want to talk with you."

"How do I know you're not saying things about Brett?" I asked, my tone harsh.

"You know I wouldn't say something like that."

I wanted to talk to him, but everything had been turned upside down lately. I leaned against the door. I heard his body shift on the other side and realized we were sitting back to back.

"Then what happened out there?" I finally asked.

"Nothing. Luke was being an asshole. He's trying to make me mad."

"But why would he say that?" I needed to know.

"Some people know how to hurt other people, I guess."

"You hurt me. If what Luke said is true, you—"

"It's not true. I never meant to hurt you. You know that, right?"

"It's just . . ." I tried to find the courage to go on.

"It's just what?"

"You don't understand. I try to talk about Brett, and you never want to listen. No one cares about what I'm trying to deal with."

"I'm sorry. I'll try to listen more. If that will help, I'll do that for you."

"You shouldn't have to," I said. "You should want to."

I didn't try to talk to Jack anymore. Instead, I rested my head against the door, feeling the hard wood behind it. I hoped he was telling the truth. I hoped he would try to listen more. I fell asleep in that position, too tired to try to figure out if what Luke said was a lie or the truth. I was glad Jack didn't try to get me to come out and even more glad when, in the morning, I opened the door and he was still there, sleeping against the other side.

www.allmytruths.com

Today's Truth:
It's easy to hide things you
don't want people to see.

At first, it's as if I have two faces.

One I wear to school, around Jack, my friends, Dad, and one I have when I go home and am alone.

My first face is the one you see in magazines like *Seventeen* or *CosmoGirl*. The smiling girl advertising clear skin products or lash-extending mascara.

You can page through my life and see fashion pictorials that look like a normal teenage girl.

You will see me in the pep rally spread. Photos of me helping decorate, hanging red and gold streamers from the bleachers and signs proclaiming our intended victories.

I'm at the game, in Jack's warm-up jersey with pom-poms in my hands as I cheer on the team.

I'm there in Jack's varsity jacket after the game, his arm around me as we walk out of the gym to his car. I'm smiling as people stop and congratulate Jack on a game well played.

You can see me dancing at a house party, surrounded by basketball players and their girlfriends as we celebrate another win.

I create images all around me, enough to fill pages of magazines, pretending to be as happy and normal as everyone thinks I am.

The school year and my life move forward without stopping. But as each day starts and ends, it is harder and harder for me to keep moving with it.

I put on my mask and wear it to school. I try to forget

about the wide, dark hole that grows between Dad, Brett, and me, but it doesn't last.

Slowly, as the days march on, my mask starts to crack like nail polish that's been on for days. Small bits flake off, giving people glimpses of what lies underneath, how broken I really am.

Posted By: Your Present Self

[Tuesday, November 27, 7:12 PM]

52

All anyone talked about was the game. Conversations revolved around what team the boys were playing, who was starting, and where parties were after. I half listened to their plans and gave vague answers to questions without really hearing them. I just couldn't concentrate.

Brett still sat across the cafeteria with Julia, and it made me so mad that he could be happy with Julia but ignore me.

I watched Julia during choir. She was the only one Brett would talk to, and I wanted to reach out to her, try to grab onto a piece of what she had to offer, a part of my brother who was crumbling away from me. I didn't have any right to, not after the way I ignored her, but she was my last connection to Brett.

I wondered how she'd reacted when Brett first told her he wanted to enlist. While Dad had forbidden it and I'd begged him not to, had she supported him? Had she let him slip through her hands when she was the one who could have held onto him tighter than any of us?

I hadn't tried to talk to Brett after we fought at school. If the two of us found ourselves in the same hallway, he'd turn and go the other way.

The longer Brett was gone, the more things changed back to how I felt after Mom died. He might not have left for the Army yet, but the hole he'd left in our house made it seem as if he had gone far away. Life got heavy, and when I came across items of his in our house, like a piece of mail addressed to him or an old military magazine, they startled me as if they didn't belong there.

The days after Mom died, I had walked circles around my house touching things, reminding myself of what they were. What I was supposed to do with them. *Here is my toothbrush. Here is the water; turn it on. Here is the toothpaste; unscrew the top, put it on the brush, and pull the brush across your teeth, back and forth.*

Brett's decision to enlist had the same effect on me. I was in a world that kept moving without a single thought to the fear that now invaded my body. Brett was going into the Army, and it shocked me that it didn't affect everyone around me. I wanted to talk to my friends about it, to let everyone know of his decision, of the threats and dangers, but they were too busy making plans for basketball games and weekend parties. No one even asked about him.

Brett and Julia stood and navigated around the cafeteria tables.

I held my breath as they neared me, hoping they'd stop to talk. "Not a word," I said when they continued past me.

"What?" Jenna asked. She had lined up a pack of Skittles by color and was eating them one by one.

I grabbed a green one and tried to act normal. "Oh, sorry. It's nothing. Just talking to myself."

Jenna rolled her eyes at Ali and continued to pop Skittles into her mouth.

Ali started talking loudly. "We'll get our nails done on Thursday, so we can have school colors for the game Friday. I think I want to have Luke's jersey number airbrushed on."

"Perfect," said Jenna. "Kate, do you need us to pick you up for the game?"

"What?" I asked, twirling a piece of spaghetti on my fork.

"The game. Do you need a ride?" Jenna repeated.

"Oh, I don't know. I haven't even thought about it."

"Well, we can swing by and pick you up," Ali said. "If you want to bring your overnight stuff, you can crash at my place after the party."

"Party?" I asked. "Whose party?"

"Geez, Kate," Jenna complained. "Pay attention."

"Yeah, sorry. I'm just tired," I told her and tried to make myself focus, but I really didn't care.

Ali tapped me on the arm with her carrot stick. "Hello. Where have you been? Just pack your overnight stuff and we'll get you at six thirty Friday. It'll be simple. You won't have to think about anything."

"Where have I been?" I asked, frustrated. It was as if I couldn't do anything right for anyone. "You know what's going on right now, Ali. I've got more important stuff on my mind than nails."

"Right. You do, but you don't have to blow off your friends."

"I'm not trying to. I just have a lot going on."

"If you don't want to go on Friday . . ."

I knew that wasn't the answer. "No, no, I'll be there. It sounds good." I turned back to picking at my lunch. I was pissing everyone off lately. I thought about the fight I had with Dad the other day. He hadn't mentioned Brett since, but there really wasn't a chance since he was doing everything he could to avoid me. The only time I seemed to see him was if I went to watch basketball practice or a game.

I stood up from the table. "I'm heading out."

Ali checked her watch. "We still have ten minutes."

"I know, but I want to stop at the library and check something on the computers."

Ali shrugged and fell back into conversation with Jenna.

I headed out of the cafeteria. How could they act as if nothing was wrong? It seemed impossible. Because in my world, nothing felt right.

www.allmytruths.com

Today's Truth:

You have to keep moving forward or you'll realize what you've left behind.

The days after Mom died were filled with movement. People entered the house, carrying casseroles, flowers, and words of sympathy. Our bodies climbed in and out of cars, going from one place to another, where we sat and waited until we moved again. The world pushed us forward, so we didn't have to think about what we'd left behind.

Not until weeks after did I hear the silence. People went back home, our fridge became a mismash of rotting food, and our car sat idle in the garage because everywhere we went reminded us of her.

I had no time to ease into Brett's absence. He signed the papers and walked out of our house. There was no warning or grace period as with Mom.

The silence roars around me.

I have not been okay since Brett signed those papers and left our family.

A cord was cut, the thin line that connected me to earth was gone, and I am now spinning, turning, twirling my way through space, into a deep midnight blue of nothing as I wait for Brett to return.

And I worry that, like Mom, he might never come back.

Posted By: Your Present Self
[Wednesday, December 3, 12:31 PM]

53

Our choir teacher, Mrs. Reid, gave us a free day once a month. She said we got this gift because we worked our voices so much we needed to rest them once in a while. It was a day meant for us to catch up on school-work, but usually people talked in small groups or watched the TV in the corner that was supposed to be used for announcements.

Mrs. Reid didn't do a good job fooling any of us, the boys included. She sat during these days with a cup of steaming tea, shifting positions and rubbing her eyes a lot. We knew she really wasn't giving us a day to rest our voices but was dealing with a bad case of cramps.

"I wish I was able to have voice rest days when I got my period," Ali complained, surrounded by papers. She was trying to study for a test in chemistry.

"It would be nice," I said. "Especially since Dad freaks out when I mention anything that has to do with cramps. I'd stay home all day in my bed with junk food and my laptop."

Today the TV ran the latest episode of a court divorce show, the only thing everyone seemed to be able to agree on. Mrs. Reid sat at her desk and told us she had e-mails to write, but she was probably shopping online. We were on to all her tricks.

The TV switched from the show to a commercial for the local lunchtime news. It was short, a ten-second teaser for the actual news. Most of these teasers claimed silly threats or promises: restaurant investigations where employees didn't wash their hands or a gas station giving away gas for free. The stations usually held these segments until the end of the show, capturing the viewer and then offering little or no payoff for sticking around, the actual story something completely different. Brett and I always seemed to fall for them, no matter how many times we'd been duped.

Today, however, the news promo was different. It didn't offer false claims, miracles, or shocking revelations. There was nothing far-fetched about the woman who spoke solemnly on the screen: "Today on Channel 3 lunchtime news, a local soldier who headed off to war will not return."

It was a short statement, just one sentence, but

it felt as if everyone in the room was gone and it was only me and the television. I forced myself to breathe, wishing someone would turn off the TV.

The court show ended, and the news started. It was the lead story. "A family mourns the news that their son, twenty-year-old Ken Wilson, died in a roadside bomb explosion two days ago. Ken, who leaves behind his wife, Molly, and their eight-month-old daughter, loved his country. His mother told reporters that joining the Army had been his dream since he was little."

I jumped up and ran my fingers through my hair. I couldn't listen to this anymore. I started to gather my stuff.

"Are you okay?" Ali asked.

"I'm fine. I just need to go to the bathroom."

"You're not thinking about Brett, are you?" She'd been watching the television too. "Brett is still here. He hasn't gone anywhere."

"Are you serious? You really can't see why I'm upset?" I wanted to shake her. How could she think this was nothing? "I need to get out of here."

"Wait. I'll go with you." She closed her book and stuffed it in her bag.

"No, don't come." I left the room before she could follow, not bothering to tell Mrs. Reid.

I pushed open the door to the restroom and walked to the sink, turning on the cold water and running it over my hands. I was the only one there, so I didn't wipe away my tears. I gripped the front of the sink, water dripping from my hands to puddle on the floor. I tried to look at myself in the mirror, but everything was blurry.

"It's insane, isn't it?"

I wiped my eyes with the back of my hand and turned.

Julia stood holding the door to the bathroom. She let it swing shut and walked toward me. "Brett enlisting. It seems like a bad dream."

"Please tell me how I can wake up," I whispered.

"At first I didn't believe him," Julia said. "I thought it was a joke. He'd bring up the Army and your uncle John, and I'd just listen to his stories and nod. But then I realized he was serious."

"I wish you would've stopped him," I said softly, even though it wasn't fair. "I wish you would've said something to him so he realized what a mistake this is."

Julia moved to the window. It looked out over

the soccer field. She slid down against the wall until she was sitting. "I tried. When I realized he was serious, I begged him over and over again not to sign the papers."

"I already lost my mom. I can't lose Brett."

"I can't lose him either."

I looked at Julia, and my entire body relaxed. She understood.

I didn't tell anyone about the conversation with Julia in the bathroom or that we'd been texting back and forth since then. She understood what no one else did.

Instead, I tried to maintain the appearance of a perfect Beacon girlfriend.

Tonight I blended in the eyeliner below my eyes and stepped away from the mirror to take a final look at myself. My hair was tied back with a maroon ribbon. I had on a yellow, long-sleeved shirt under Jack's warm-up jersey, and my jeans fell over black flats. I looked full of Beacon pride, the happy fan, but inside I didn't feel any of the excitement that had been buzzing through school all day.

Beacon was playing another undefeated team, Brookline, and I didn't want to go.

I had to admit my lack of enthusiasm wasn't just from what was going on with Brett; it was the team too. I was sick of the way Jack, Luke, and the other boys acted. It was all getting old.

I didn't think I could fake the pep tonight, but I had no excuse good enough to get out of going to the game.

Ali's brother had agreed to drive us. I watched from my living room window and saw his car pull in. I grabbed my purse and took a deep breath, trying to prepare myself for the next couple of hours.

It was dusk, and the quick orange glow of cigarettes in the backseat sparked, bursts of light like airplanes flashing in the sky.

Jenna stuck her head out of the window and yelled, "Hey, girl, you ready for tonight?"

I pulled open the car door. The music pounded; the air was thick with smoke twisting around the girls' perfume. Ali and Jenna squeezed in the back along with a friend of Ali's brother's. Another of his friends lit up a bowl in the front seat. My stomach rolled from the mix of smells.

I tried to find a space for myself, sitting sideways so I was able to close the door.

"You look cute tonight," Ali said.

I smoothed my top. "Thanks."

"What do you think of my outfit? Luke finally let

me wear his jersey."

"It looks good," I said and tried to think of something else to say. I knew I was being lame, and Ali and Jenna would be able to see right through me if I didn't figure out how to sound interested.

"Yeah, I know. I might not give it back." Ali stroked the jersey and hugged her arms around herself as if Luke was the one wearing it. "I can't wait to watch Beacon kill Brookline. Luke's excited about this game."

"Blah, blah, blah. All you talk about is Luke," Jenna said and stuck her finger in her mouth, pretending to gag.

The guy in the passenger seat held up his pipe and lighter. "Anyone want a hit?"

"No, thanks," Jenna said. "In case you forgot, tonight's game is huge; we don't want to be all spaced out for it." She dug around in her bag and pulled out a water bottle. "I do have something to drink, though. Some fancy rum I stole from my parents that they'll never notice is missing."

She took a sip and held the bottle toward me, but I waved it away.

The bottle went from front to back, among the hands of everyone in the car. They joked about what would happen at the game, how much they would drink after, and who would probably end up screwing who.

Jenna took a drag on her cigarette and blew smoke out the window. "Hey, Kate, I bet your dad is ready for this game."

"He's a bit obsessed at the moment."

"Can you blame him?" Ali's brother said, looking at my reflection in the rearview mirror. "The whole school is counting on him to bring home a championship this year."

"Believe me, he knows."

The door handle dug into my hip. I turned toward the window, watching the houses flash by, the world muted as the sun ended its daily cycle. Everyone smoked, drank, and tried to speak louder than each other. I wished they'd stop. My stomach hurt. This all seemed so stupid. I couldn't concentrate on their pointless conversations. It was the same old stuff, every day, every weekend.

Julia was home tonight watching a movie with her parents. She'd invited me over, and I wished I was there instead of heading to the game.

I felt suffocated in the car, stuck between people who didn't give a shit about things that really mattered, and I needed to get out. "Take me home," I said quietly.

So quietly I wasn't sure anyone heard me.

"What?" Ali asked.

"Take me home," I said more firmly.

Jenna narrowed her eyes and looked at me. "What the hell? Why would you want to go home?"

"Turn around."

Ali and Jenna gave each other a look, and then Jenna leaned in between the seats to talk to her brother. "Take her home. What's it matter if she's going to mope all night? We'll still make the start of the game."

No one tried to argue with me. Ali's brother turned in to a gas station so he could turn around and headed back to my house.

"I'm sorry," I told them.

"Whatever," Ali said.

Everybody else stayed silent, letting the music throb against the sides of the car. I felt the pulse of my heart. I closed my eyes until the car stopped.

"Get out. We're here," Ali's brother said.

"Thanks," I told everyone and closed the door.

No one said good-bye. The car backed down the driveway before I moved. I heard them laughing as they sped away.

55

Brett spent a lot of time with the recruiters during lunch. I'd see him in their office or sitting at the table in the cafeteria. I used the time to my advantage and sat with Julia on the days Brett wasn't around. I hoped he'd see the two of us together and decide to join us. I could show him I didn't just care about my Beacon friends. I wanted him to see how important he was also.

I knew my friends talked about me hanging out with Julia. I made excuses, claimed she and I had something to talk about or some work to do. They were weak explanations that didn't fool them, but I convinced myself it was okay.

When I ate lunch with Julia, I didn't have to act happy or fill the time with gossip about people who weren't like us. I didn't have to deal with their stupid, superficial conversations. Conversations that used to be easy. With Julia, I could talk quietly about the things that kept us up late at night, the things we couldn't tell other people.

Julia welcomed me quickly. I was surprised how open and nice she was, especially after the way I'd treated her. I tried apologizing to her the first time I sat with her at lunch, but she dismissed my apologies with a wave of her hand. She refused to talk about anything that may have happened in the past, and I knew enough not to push it.

I liked the way Julia calmed me down. I tried to get out of eating lunch with my friends once or twice a week, but they had started giving me a hard time about eating with Julia.

"Whoa, Kate, nice of you to join us," Ali commented when I slid into the seat next to Jack.

"Yeah, I didn't know you still went to Beacon," Luke said and stole one of Ali's fries.

"I know, I know. I haven't been around much. Sorry, guys."

"It's nothing to apologize for. It's a choice you made," Ali said and turned to Luke to whisper something in his ear.

I stared at her, hurt that she'd turned against me too. "Julia's my friend too. It's not as if I'm choosing between the two of you."

Jack broke in before Ali could say more. "We're talking about the Rocky River Academy game during Christmas break. We're thinking of staying after at the ski resort nearby. What do you think? We could rent a condo pretty cheap if we got a bunch of people." Jack looked at me expectantly. I was thankful he was changing the subject, but I wished he'd spoken up sooner.

"That does sound fun, but do you think we'd be able to get a condo?" I said.

"I'm sure my dad could get us something," Luke said. "He knows people who own places there, so maybe we could even stay for free. Are you in?" He looked at me.

The rest of them waited for my response.

"I don't know. I'll have to make sure I don't have anything else planned." I tried to stall and think of an excuse that sounded plausible. There was no way I was going after what had happened at Ali's cabin.

"What could you have planned? Your dad is the coach of the team. He's going to be at the game," Ali said.

"Yeah, you're right." It was obvious Ali was waging some personal attack on me, and I figured it had to do with ditching out on the game the other night. "I still have to check to make sure."

"Right, okay. Well, hopefully you can make it," Jenna said and started to draw circles on her paper napkin.

"If you don't want to go, say so," Ali blurted. "We're all getting a little sick of hearing what your excuse of the day will be. We're not stupid."

"Ali," Jenna said, trying to silence her.

"Oh, really, guys. Stop acting like she's going to do things with us. We know she won't. We're honored you decided to join us today, but you didn't have to."

"I know I didn't have to," I said, narrowing my eyes. "I wanted to eat lunch with you. Maybe I don't sit with you all the time because you treat me like this."

"Why *do* you keep hanging out with Julia?" Ali asked.

"What do you mean?" I asked, not letting her scare me. "I hang out with Julia for the same reason I hang out with any of you guys. Why do I need to have a reason?"

"You *know* what I mean," Ali said and sighed as if this discussion was a waste of her time.

"No, I *don't know* what you mean," I said, emphasizing my words the same way she did. "Fill me in, because I don't have a problem hanging out with Julia, so I'm confused about why you do."

"She's weird, Kate."

"Weird? That's the best explanation you've got? Half the world is weird. You could call me weird because I drink my milk at room temperature." But I knew that wasn't the kind of weird she was talking about.

"You know what I mean. She's not one of us."

"One of us?" I asked, my voice turning to ice. I looked around the table to see if everyone was buying it, but no one would make eye contact with me. "She's my friend, and she's dating my brother."

"Julia's not even a part of Beacon." Ali said as if it were fact. "She only goes to our school because her mom teaches math. Otherwise, she wouldn't be able to afford Beacon."

I ran my fingers through my hair out of frustration. "Do you remember the only reason I'm at Beacon is because my dad works for the school?"

"It's not the same. Your dad is a different part of Beacon. You're a different part of Beacon. I don't understand why you'd want to hang out with her."

The reasons perched on the tip of my tongue, and I wanted to spit every one of them at her. Was she really telling me she didn't think I should be friends with Julia? "Sure, you're right," I said, but my patronizing tone went over her head. "I'm completely different, just like my brother."

"Come on. You know what I mean."

"I do know what you mean, and I don't like it one bit. You talk about Beacon as if it were a piece of property you were buying. I'm friends with Julia now, and that's not going to change."

"Hang out with her. I don't care."

"Good. That's what I plan to do." It was true. I wasn't going to let Ali tell me who I should hang out with.

"Whatever." Ali pushed back her chair and picked up her tray, ignoring the incredulous looks on the faces of everyone else at the table. "Stay as long as you want to, since it'll probably be weeks until you decide to sit with us again."

I watched Ali walk away and waited for someone to say something. When they didn't, I giggled nervously. "I don't know why Ali thinks I need to choose sides. I can be friends with everyone. I'm not sure what's gotten into her. I'll go find her and talk to her after lunch."

Dave gave me a weak smile, and Jenna turned away. Jack shrugged as if he wanted nothing to do with it.

I ate silently. Even though Ali and her accusations were gone, I still didn't feel like part of the group.

I spent the next few days trying to avoid Ali and Jenna. I continued to sit with Julia at lunch and skipped watching Jack practice after school. It was so much easier to run out when the bell rang than to sit with everyone at practice and deal with Ali getting on my case about hanging out with Julia.

Today, however, Ali didn't let me escape so easily. She was waiting outside my classroom door when I left at the end of the day. She linked her elbow in mine. "I'm taking you with me."

I let her steer me around the students heading out of school. She pulled me down the hallway, and I had to walk quickly to keep up. I held my books tightly, afraid they'd slip out as we dodged other students. She spoke loudly so her voice could be heard above the shouts of the rest of our classmates in the hallway. "We're going to meet Jenna in the gym and watch the boys practice. You haven't been there all week, and I'm not letting you run straight home again."

The girl was impossible to predict. One day she was about to blow up at me for not hanging out with them, and the next she was acting as if nothing was wrong.

I shook out of her grasp. "Okay, I'm coming. I promise. You don't need to drag me there."

"I will if I have to," she said. "This is ridiculous. We miss you, and I'm sure Jack would like to see you in the stands."

I followed her into the gym. The boys were already on the floor taking practice shots, while Dad paced the sidelines with a clipboard in his hand. We sat next to Jenna and a few other girls who had boyfriends on the team or wished they did. There were a lot more people watching now that we were getting closer to securing a spot in the play-offs.

Jenna placed her hand on her chest. "Whoa. Long time no see, Kate. I forgot what you looked like."

I whacked her lightly on the arm with my notebook. "Shut up. It's only been a few days."

"If I were dating Jack, I'd be here watching him every day," said Amanda, a freshman sitting behind us.

"Jack understands," I said, even though I didn't know why I was explaining myself to a freshman.

"We don't always have to be together."

"Really?" Ali asked. "Are you sure he under-stands?" And just like that, she morphed back into the Ali I'd gotten used to these past couple of weeks.

"What do you mean?"

"I'm just saying. I'd think you'd want to support your boyfriend. Not ditch out on him all the time."

"I don't ditch out on him," I said, trying to keep my voice calm.

"Don't get mad at me, but maybe we should talk about things." Ali gave me her full attention.

"Usually when someone starts a sentence with the words 'don't get mad at me,' you can expect to get mad at that person." I joked, feeling a bit uncomfortable.

"No, it's nothing bad. It's more of an observation."

"An observation?"

"Yeah, it's not a huge deal, but maybe Amanda is right about Jack."

"Are you serious?" I asked, crossing my arms.

"It just seems as if you're trying to avoid him or something. And when you two are together, you're never happy. Maybe you should listen to Amanda."

"Are you kidding me? Are we really having this conversation?"

"I think we need to have this conversation. It's the truth. You're so hung up on your brother that you're forgetting everyone else around you."

"My brother enlisted in the Army in the middle of a war. I think I'm allowed to get *hung up* on him."

"You are, but aren't you afraid Jack is going to break up with you? Do you even like him anymore?"

"Jack and I are fine."

"I'm not trying to make you mad. I like you and Jack. I want the two of you to stay together. I'm trying to help."

"Are you trying to tell me Jack is planning to break up with me? Is that what people are saying?"

Ali paused, as if thinking about the idea. "No, it's not that. It's just that people have started to notice you're hardly around anymore, and when you are, you're never happy. I don't want something to happen to the two of you; that's all."

I closed my eyes and rested my head in my hands. I wondered if Ali was telling the truth. Were people really talking about us? Was I as close as she said to losing Jack? I bit my bottom lip and tried to imagine not having Jack in my life. It seemed impossible. Unlike Ali, who often seemed more interested in the attention she was getting from boys than in our friendship, Jack really knew me. He knew about Mom and listened when I missed her. Jack understood if I got upset about Dad or Brett. I didn't know what I'd do if he wasn't around anymore.

I thought about Ali getting into my business with Jack, as if she even understood what was going on. I hated that she acted like an expert and talked to me about something that had nothing to do with her. I was mad that she saw I was scared about Brett and, instead of trying to help me, told me I needed to change. It wasn't as if I could suddenly be happy again and stop worrying about my brother. She didn't understand.

Ali put a hand on my shoulder. "You're not mad at me, are you? I'm only trying to fix things before they get bad."

"No, don't worry. I'm fine."

"Okay, good."

I didn't want to hear anything else Ali had to say. I leaned forward and acted as if I was into watching the boys play. My dad had set up a scrimmage, and Jack was guarding a senior who was six inches taller than him. Jack stole the ball and passed it to a teammate waiting to the right of him. I let out a cheer, and Jack looked up. He smiled at me before he turned back to the court.

Dad blew his whistle after fifteen minutes of scrimmaging. "Okay, guys, grab yourselves some water and get back on the court."

Jack, Luke, and a few other boys picked up their plastic bottles and walked over to where we were sitting.

"Hi, girls," Jack said and sat next to me. He kissed my cheek. "Glad you made it today."

"Yeah, Kate," Luke said slowly. "We've missed you at our practices." He squirted his water bottle at me.

"Oh my God, Luke. What the hell?" I jumped up and tried to wipe the water off my shirt.

"Wet T-shirt contest," he said and aimed his bottle at another girl on the bleachers. Before he could douse her, though, Dad blew his whistle.

The boys ran back onto the court.

Ali looked at me. "Oh my God, Luke," she said, mocking me and fluttering her eyelashes. She turned to the other girls. "I'm going to grab a drink from the vending machine. Does anyone want anything?"

Jenna got up to go with her.

I watched the two of them walk out of the gym, confused again and wondering if Ali was my friend or my enemy.

Jack came over the next day when I was working on my homework, or at least that's what I was trying to do. I'd get engrossed in a problem, but it was never enough. Soon my thoughts would leave the questions and drift back to Brett. It had been weeks since he moved out, and Dad didn't even seem to miss him. I'd tried to get Brett to talk to me. I'd even asked Julia to talk to him for me, but nothing seemed to work. Brett was refusing to speak with either of us. It was as if he was already gone.

When Jack called and asked if he could come over, I agreed and told myself maybe he could help get my mind off things. I refused to believe anything Ali had said to me. The two of us were fine.

Jack brought his work, but as usual, it was abandoned. He lay on my bed and played with my ponytail.

I pushed his hand away. "I really need to get this done."

"Forget homework." He inched closer to me. "I

have something more exciting to talk about. My parents are going to be out of town this weekend for some Christmas party thing. I told a bunch of the guys on the team I'd have a party."

"A party?"

"Yeah, at my house on Saturday," Jack said. "Do you think you could find an opening in your busy schedule to fit me in?" He waited for me to answer, as if this was an important question, something I should be considering as heavily as he was.

"I didn't know you were having a party," I said, choosing to ignore the way Jack was acting about it.

He stood up. "You know, you're really starting to piss me off."

"I'm what?" I put down my pen and closed my book. "What are you talking about?"

"It's everything, Kate." Jack frowned. "You've changed. You used to be fun. You used to want to have fun. It's almost Christmas, the basketball team is undefeated, and all you can focus on are depressing things no one wants to think about."

"How can you say that? My brother enlisted in the Army. I have a right to be scared."

"Yeah, we all know about this big, bad war."

Jack shook his head and walked away from the bed. "Forget it, you wouldn't understand."

"Understand what?" I picked up a pillow and hugged it to me, my fingers clenching the fabric.

This was the point where I should have pulled back, stepped out of the fight, but instead I pushed, and I pushed hard. How dare he bring up my brother and act as if this wasn't important.

"I think you're the one who doesn't understand." I started, aware but not caring that my voice was getting louder and I should probably quiet down. "You don't know anything about what's going on with Brett and my dad right now. You have your family. You have parents who love you and can come to cheer you on at games. You have no idea what it's like to lose a parent. And now Brett won't even talk to me. My dad's doing nothing to fix things, and I'm scared that I'm going to lose someone else I love. Don't tell me I don't understand."

I refused to cry. I wanted to at least appear strong.

I waited for Jack to snap back, but he didn't. Instead, he wrapped his arms around me so tight I could hardly move. He stroked my hair. "I'm sorry. You're right. I understand," he said, repeating it over and over until I believed he really did.

www.allmytruths.com

Today's Truth:

**The desire to belong is stronger
than the need to break free.**

When Mom died, we lost our identities.

We were no longer ourselves:

stripped down to our shells, empty inside,

exposed as we felt around in the dark,

groping for something to light us again.

When you experience a loss so big,

you need to redefine yourself as someone without
the other.

A reinvention of who you knew yourself as.

Dad and Brett carelessly threw away their old skin

and climbed into something new, shiny, unfamiliar.

I found myself lost,

floating between who I used to be and who I could

no longer be.

I wandered around, sticking out,

my pieces not quite fitting in the smooth edge of the world

where I once existed so effortlessly.

When I found Jack, my world began to meld back together.

He gave me meaning, a construction.

He filled in the hazy lines of the empty self Mom's death had left.

He brought me back to life,

revived me, and allowed me to crawl into his world and stand tall,

towering over my past as I clung to the security he granted.

And as long as I was with Jack,

I had a place, a self defined.

My world is shifting again with Brett gone.

Pieces are becoming loose,

and I feel as if my seams are weakening.

I need to hold tight to Jack before I lose myself again.

Jack's world does not revolve around this fear of loss.

But for now, his hand is anchoring mine,

and the desire to stay in his world

is stronger than the need to break free.

Posted By: Your Present Self

[Wednesday, December 11, 11:07 PM]

I agreed to go to Jack's party because I wanted to be there, not because of Ali's warnings. Things felt normal again between Jack and me. He hadn't brought up our fight and seemed a little more understanding about my worries for Brett.

Ali texted and asked if I needed a ride, so I accepted her offer as a truce. She picked me up, excited that I was finally dragging myself out of the house. The two of us had packed overnight bags and told our parents we were staying at each other's house. A lie like that usually didn't work so smoothly, but Dad was out of town watching a team Beacon would be playing in two weeks, and Ali's parents had taken her siblings to an indoor water park for the night.

We waited to arrive until after the party started, because Ali wanted to make an entrance. Jack's driveway was already full of cars, and lights blazed from every room. We could hear music and shouting as we walked up the driveway. The door was cracked open, and Ali pushed it the rest of the way with her foot.

"Now the party can begin," Jack announced when he saw me, a sloppy grin on his face and a wet spot on the front of his shirt. "Let's all raise a glass to the sexiest girlfriend in the world."

A large part of the basketball team was in the room, and everyone lifted plastic cups and bottles to toast my arrival.

"Here's to a night of partying," Jack yelled.

"We need to put our stuff down, and we'll be back," Ali told the group.

I followed her up the steps, dumping my stuff in Jack's room.

Ali turned to me so the doorway was blocked. "Let's have a good time, okay? No worries tonight. Let it all loose."

I agreed. I'd forget everything else and have fun. A break from the regular world was exactly what I needed. We headed back down the stairs and I forced a smile, trying to convince myself of my own thoughts.

Jack handed me a beer when I found him, and I took a bigger sip than usual, glad to be doing something a little bad for a change. Tonight was all about letting go.

"That's my girl," Jack said. He wrapped me in his arms and pushed me against the wall. "I'm glad you're here."

"Me too." I grinned at him and realized I was glad to be out with everyone. It felt good to feel normal again.

Jack started kissing me, and I let myself relax. His hands ran up my back, under my shirt, and I pressed myself against him. This was the Jack I hadn't seen in so long, the Jack I had been fighting away, and for tonight, I didn't want to fight. I remembered how good it could be. I knew he was thinking the same thing I was.

"Hey, you two, save it for later," Ali said. "You have the whole night to take each other's clothes off. I want to borrow Kate for a while."

Jack let go of me but whispered in my ear, "I like Ali's idea. I'll be looking forward to doing just that."

I swatted him in mock protest but winked before I allowed Ali to pull me into the kitchen. She opened a brown bag on the counter and turned to me. "Okay, I have lemons, sugar, and some cheap vodka."

I turned the plastic vodka bottle around in my hand. "This looks really classy."

"Nothing says getting shit-faced like cheap-ass vodka."

She took two shot glasses and sloshed a bunch of vodka in them. She set one in front of me.

"Thanks, but I'm going to pass." I pushed it back at her, but she picked it up and jammed it into my hand. A little bit spilled, wetting my shirt sleeve.

"Calm down. It's only one shot. You can stop when I start pushing the fifth or sixth glass at you. Which, by the way, I fully intend to do before we go back to the rest of the party."

"You don't take things slow, do you?"

"Nope, and neither should you. Most of the people here are wasted. We need to catch up." She handed me a lemon wedge covered in sugar and, with the other hand, jiggled her glass. "Take one shot. It's not going to kill you."

"It's never just one shot with you."

"I promise. Now toast with me. Here's to the boys we love. Here's to the boys who love us . . ."

I looked from Ali to the glass and thought back to the way Jack wrapped his arms around me and called me his girl. I wanted to be the Kate he was crazy about, so I picked up the shot and joined in the toast with her. "And if the boys we love don't love us, then screw the boys and here's to us."

The two of us knocked glasses and threw back the vodka.

"Damn," I said. "This tastes like crap."

Ali held out another shot, "Well, you know what they say. The drunker you are, the easier it goes down."

The music blasted around me, vibrating the floor under my feet. I took a deep breath. The world slipped out from under me. For tonight, instead of letting the uncertainty pull me down and paralyze me, I welcomed the warmth from the alcohol that crept into my veins. I didn't care about anything except that I was having fun with Jack and Ali.

Later that night I settled onto Jack's lap in the hot tub and pulled my hair into a wet ponytail. I'd finished my beer and, along with the shot I had taken with Ali, the alcohol was making me sleepy in the steamy water. I rested my head against Jack's chest and closed my eyes, listening to everyone talk.

Someone pressed something cold against my neck, and I jumped in surprise, jamming my elbow into Jack.

A guy on the team waved a bottle of white wine in front of my face. "I swiped this from my parents. They keep all the good stuff locked up in the basement. Have you ever gotten wasted on a three-hundred-dollar bottle of wine?"

"No, thanks," I said and leaned back against Jack.

"Come on," he said. "Lighten up and have some."

"Lighten up?" I raised my eyebrows and squinted at him. "I'm sorry. I didn't know I had to drink the wine you stole from your parents to lighten up."

"Hey, I'm only trying to help my man Jack out. You're always so uptight. It would be nice for you to relax."

"Are you for real?" I looked at Jack for help, but he just shrugged.

"It's not going to kill you to have a little."

"Where is this coming from?" I didn't know what was making me madder: the fact that the team thought I was uptight or that Jack wasn't standing up for me.

"We were having a good night," Jack said. "Now you're doing the goddamn judging thing. I'm so sick of this shit."

"You know," I said, dropping my hand into the water. "A good boyfriend would support his girl-friend instead of going all crazy on her."

"Crazy is right."

"Go to hell," I shot back. It was quiet around us. We now had everyone's attention, which made me even angrier.

"You're making a fool of yourself," Jack said. "Get yourself together." He shifted, pushing me off him and into the water.

His friends laughed.

I sank for a moment and wished I could stay under and hide from all of them. Instead, I stood up. "Whatever. I'm gone. I don't want to be here with you." I climbed out of the hot tub.

Jack didn't say anything. He'd already turned back to the group.

My body tensed in anger, but I didn't want to give him the satisfaction of seeing I cared. I walked toward the steps without bothering to look at him again.

I held onto the railing, not caring that my bare feet were crunching in the snow. I stopped in the empty kitchen and leaned against the sticky counter covered with cups, alcohol bottles, lemon wedges, and sugar.

Luke wandered into the room, a cigarette burning in his hand. He stopped and watched, his gaze moving over me from the bottom to the top.

My face got hot, and I crossed my arms over my chest.

"Sexy outfit," he said and winked.

My bikini dripped water all over the floor. "Screw you."

"Damn, what's wrong?"

I shook my head. I wasn't about to spill my feelings to Luke.

He held up his hands, a long piece of ash falling off the cigarette. "Fine. Don't tell me, but don't waste a perfectly good party being pissed off. You need another drink."

He dropped the cigarette on the counter and opened the fridge.

"No, the last thing I need is a drink."

"Believe me," he said, popping the tab on a beer and walking to the cupboard to grab a glass. "It'll help. You drink enough of this and you'll forget whatever it is that's making you mad."

He turned his back to me and poured the drink into a glass. I watched the cigarette smoke curl up from the counter.

It was the word *forget* that convinced me. "I don't need a glass. The bottle is fine."

"No way. You, my dear, are a classy woman and should drink from a glass."

I took the drink when he offered it and gulped it. I coughed, and a bit escaped out of my mouth onto my bathing suit.

I wiped my lips with the back of my hand. "Oh, shit, this beer is nasty."

"But it works."

I tried to get the rest of the drink down without throwing up.

Ali walked in and looked at the two of us suspiciously. "What are you up to in here?"

"Dirty and naughty things," Luke said and slid up against Ali. "Do you want to be bad with us?"

"Luke got me a beer. That's all," I said, not wanting to start another fight. The drink sloshed around in my stomach, and instead of making me feel better, it made me feel worse. "Do you want to finish it? I've had enough."

I held out the glass, but Luke stepped between us. "Here, Ali. You can have mine. I just opened it." Luke pushed his drink at her before she could grab my cup. He pointed at my cup. You're not going to waste that, are you?"

He was staring hard at me. It creeped me out, so I finished it off just to satisfy him. I slammed the cup upside down when I was done.

"I guess that answers whether or not Kate swallows." Luke laughed.

I slapped his arm hard. I should have known better than to hang out with someone as skeezy as Luke.

"Do you want me to answer that question too?" Ali said loudly and, with her hip, shoved me against the counter. She giggled so hard some of her drink splashed out. "Damn, that's a whole sip I lost."

Luke and I watched as she bent and licked it off the sticky surface.

Luke placed a hand on my lower back. "Maybe both you girls could show me your talents," he said, sliding his fingertips down till they grazed the top of my bikini bottom.

Ali grabbed my other hand and pulled me forward, and I slipped in the puddle that had gathered around my feet. "Kate has something she needs to do with her *boyfriend*." She narrowed her eyes at me. I knew she thought I was flirting with Luke, which was an absolutely disgusting thought.

She took me out of the room and back toward the hot tub. "How about you go find Jack?"

"I need to lie down." Suddenly it felt as if everything was off-center. "I don't feel too good."

"Seriously? You're such a lightweight. What did you have, two whole beers tonight?"

"And that shot." I clutched my stomach and groaned.

Ali was right. I hadn't drunk a lot. I shouldn't have felt like that. I tried to remember what I'd eaten or determine if I was coming down with something.

"Just don't puke on yourself. That would be nasty." She walked with me to the steps and left me at the bottom. "You can make it upstairs yourself, right? I want to go grab Luke before he leaves."

I nodded and headed to Jack's room. I tripped on the first few steps and gave up walking. I crawled instead. My stomach churned, and all I wanted to do was close my eyes and sleep.

I pushed open the door and climbed into Jack's bed. He had an old comforter spread out, flannel on one side, and I wrapped myself into it. My swimsuit was probably getting his sheets damp, but I didn't care.

I stared at the ceiling and let the room spin around and around, pulling me out of control so I slipped away faster and faster. Everything was cloudy, and the edges went soft. I let the dark creep in and closed my eyes.

I must have passed out, because when I woke the clock next to Jack's bed flashed 3:27 a.m. My mouth was dry, and I craved a glass of water. People were still awake somewhere in the house, their voices rising and falling in conversation, muffled music playing from the distance.

The bedroom door was open now, light coming in. Someone was standing in the doorway.

"Jack?" I tried to lift my arms, but they didn't budge. I couldn't move and felt tangled in the sheets.

The door opened wider to let him in and then shut again, leaving the two of us in the dark. He sat on the edge of the bed, and my stomach heaved as the mattress bounced slightly.

"I'm sorry about earlier," I mumbled, my words sliding together.

He pulled the sheets back and ran his fingers down my arm with slow, gentle pressure.

Goose bumps spread all over, a familiar tingle traveling throughout my body. "I'm so cold," I told him, trying to welcome him in.

The bed shifted, and he was beneath the sheets.

I pressed my body against his warmth, trying to still myself and stop everything in the room from moving.

He smelled different, of smoke and beer and a mix of something new, but I didn't care. Jack was here with me. Jack was next to me, and it all felt okay again. At least it did for a moment. My stomach heaved, and I sat up.

"Wait. I think I may need to go to the bathroom. I don't feel so well." I tried to sit up, certain I was going to be sick.

He put his hands above my chest and pushed me back down roughly.

I gasped.

He pulled at my bikini top and struggled to get the back untied.

It seemed impossible to do anything. It was too hard to move. I lay still as he took off my top and then yanked off my bottoms.

I was sick and dizzy, but I wanted Jack. I wanted

to know he wasn't mad at me anymore. As his mouth fell over mine and his hands moved everywhere, I wished for the room to stop moving, for my life to stop spinning.

He kissed me again, and I yelped when he bit at my lip. Jack wasn't usually this forceful, but my nausea clouded any more thoughts.

I stayed still, unable to kiss him back. His hands explored me. It felt different. It was as if it wasn't me; it wasn't as if it was him.

I kept my eyes shut, forgetting where we were, who we were, and tried to pretend we were someone else. We were Jack and Kate but the Jack and Kate from months ago. The Jack and Kate who met outside a hotel, who stayed there until the sun came up; the Jack and Kate who kissed for the first time on a driveway in the middle of a crowded party; the Jack and Kate who first showed each other how they felt when it really did seem it was all about love and each other. I closed my eyes and pretended he was that Jack and I was that Kate. I let myself remember and remember and remember in order to forget, forget, forget.

"Jack," I whispered as he moved over me and nodded.

He was breathing heavy, a funny noise that sounded as if he had a cold.

He started to unwrap something, and as he shifted, I realized it was a condom.

I grabbed at his wrist to stop him and opened my eyes, everything clear for a moment. It was then I realized what was wrong. Why Jack felt different.

"Luke," I whispered.

"Hey, baby," he drawled lazily and held me against the mattress, his hand pressed against the sore spot on my chest where he had pushed me down.

"Stop." My voice came out tiny and weak. I needed to stop him. He was moving over me.

"Just enjoy this," Luke said, his breath hot and wet against my ear.

"Jack," I called out for help.

Luke laughed.

My mind told me to punch him, hit him, kick him, but it was impossible. My body seemed to be made out of rubber.

"Hey, I'm up for playing games if you want to call me Jack."

"No," I screamed, and I felt my voice coming

from deep inside.

Luke put his hand over my mouth, and I bit him as hard as I could.

He slapped me. "You bitch."

I kept on screaming. This was not going to happen. I would not let it. I screamed and screamed until the room was once again flooded in light.

This time, Jack really did appear.

"What the hell? Can't a person even get laid in peace?" Luke hissed, pushing me away roughly and covering his eyes with the hand I'd bitten. "Close the goddamn door."

"Kate?" Jack asked sharply, as if he were scolding someone. He walked in. Right up to the bed where I was lying with Luke.

"I hate to break it to you, man, but she was begging for it," Luke said.

"Go to hell," Jack said. He was so close to the bed that if I reached farther, my fingers could brush against his skin.

Luke shifted, and then he was sitting up. He laughed softly.

I wanted to shout out and tell Jack that Luke was lying. That I had fought him off and I would never do something like that to him, but my mouth seemed full of cotton. Before I could explain anything, Jack left me. He walked out. He slammed the door and turned everything dark again.

The bed bounced up and down as Luke got up. He got dressed and then kicked at the side of the bed. "Forget this," he said. "I'm going to find Ali."

I gripped the sheets tightly around me until he left the room, and then I threw up over the side of the bed.

I stumbled to the door and locked it. I wasn't sure what kind of protection it could offer, but I needed to do something to at least pretend I might be safe. I found the bag of clothes Ali and I had dropped in Jack's room earlier and put my pajamas on. I didn't want to wear anything that reminded me of the earlier part of the night. I lifted a leg to put on my pants and stumbled. I sat against the wall to pull them up. My body was vibrating, and standing was not working in my favor. I welcomed the warm flannel pants and sweatshirt, glad I hadn't let Ali talk me into bringing the sexy lace tank top she'd volunteered to pack for me. I fished my cell phone out of my purse and typed, AT JACK'S. NEED U TO GET ME.

I only hesitated for a second before I sent the message.

Brett replied almost immediately, BE THERE ASAP.

I let out the breath I'd been holding. Brett was

still here for me. I wasn't so sure he would be after everything that had happened, but he was coming. I closed my eyes and welcomed the way my brain started to fade and everything disappeared. I was losing consciousness again, but this time I didn't fight it. It was a relief.

I didn't open my eyes again until I heard a pounding on the door.

I thought the worst. I pictured Luke outside coming back to finish what he had started or Jack wanting to break up with me or Ali ready to fight me. I curled into the fetal position, wound tight and protected. I prayed whoever was outside would leave me alone.

"Kate? Are you in there?"

It was Brett.

"Are you alone?" I asked.

"Yeah, everyone in the house is asleep. Are you okay? Open the door."

I crawled to the door and unlocked it. I couldn't look Brett in the eye when he walked in. Instead, I looked around the room that only hours earlier had felt as safe to me as my own. Jack's basketball trophies lined a shelf over his bed, his framed picture with LeBron was on his desk, and a pile of clothes fought their way out of his laundry basket next to the window. When I had been in here before with Jack, I'd felt protected and loved, but now it terrified me. There was nothing comforting about Jack's bedroom.

"What's wrong? Why are you in here alone?" Brett stood over me.

I wanted to curl back into a ball.

"Did Jack do something to you?"

My voice came out low and gravelly. "Just take me home."

Brett stooped down to my level. His hands were fists, and the muscles in his neck strained. "What the hell did that bastard do? I'll kill him."

I closed my eyes and shook my head.

"Damn it, Kate. Tell me what happened." Brett walked to Jack's bookcase and picked up one of the many trophies. He threw it at the window and shattered the glass. Cold air flooded the room.

I buried my face in my arms. "Jack didn't do anything," I said, and it hurt how true those words really were.

Brett walked over the broken glass, the pieces cracking under his shoes.

"I need to leave. Please. People probably heard you, and I don't want to face anyone."

Brett wrapped his arms around me and helped me up. I leaned against him and allowed him to maneuver me down the steps. Brett was moving fast, and I knew he didn't want to see anyone just as much as I didn't want to run into them.

He was silent until he'd driven us away. "Can you tell me what happened?"

"No," I whispered. I wouldn't let my mind go there. I kept my eyes focused on where we were heading, not where we had been.

The streets were empty, a quiet dark. We moved down side roads without streetlights. In one house, I saw a light flash on for a minute and then turn off again. I wondered why it had come on. Was it a child who'd had a bad dream? Someone who needed to use the bathroom? A late-night phone call or maybe someone in love, watching their partner sleep.

I used to do that with Jack.

When we were in the movie theater, I'd look at him out of the corner of my eye. I'd watch as the screen lit up his face, watch him react to whatever was happening with the actors, and I'd smile because

I was sitting next to him.

He'd catch me staring at him across the room at a party, give me a wave, and come over.

In the beginning, it seemed we were never far away from each other.

And some nights, when we had his house or mine to ourselves for a few hours, I would watch him when we were kissing, his eyes closed. I'd keep mine open and think, *This is what it is to be loved; this is what it is to be lucky.*

I laughed at how stupid I had been.

Lucky? What did I have to feel lucky about now?

I thought about how Jack had reacted when he walked into the room. He didn't yell or fight Luke. He didn't wrap me up in his arms or even listen to me. Instead, he walked out.

"He just left me there."

I said it so quietly Brett didn't even hear me. He kept staring forward as we drove home in the dark, and my words disappeared into the air.

www.allmytruths.com

Today's Truth:

Those who once made you feel everything can make you feel like nothing.

I AM

> what's under the rocks outside in our garden,
>
> the ones we played with when we were young,
>
> daring each other to lift to see what was underneath.

> Outside, I may look normal.
>
> I blend in.

> Below the surface, I'm different.
>
> I'm dark.

I AM

> the moist dirt that, when the rain pours, becomes mud.

Thick, black, and

nothing but a mess.

Posted By: Your Present Self

[Saturday, December 14, 4:37 AM]

64

Brett put the car into park on our driveway but left the engine on.

"Dad's not here," I said. "You don't have to run out of here as if he's going to chase you down."

"Do you want me to come inside?"

I shrugged. The only thing I wanted at the moment was for Jack to show up. Or maybe for Luke to drop dead. I'd take either.

"How about you tell me what happened? I know it wasn't just about you having a few too many drinks."

"I didn't drink a lot."

He raised one eyebrow.

I spoke loudly, practically shouting, "It's the truth."

Brett shrugged, and I knew he didn't believe me. "It doesn't matter," he said. "I told you I wouldn't judge. I'm just glad you called me."

"Thanks for coming to get me. I know it's late." I touched his arm lightly, which felt weird and out of place for our family, but I needed to make some kind of safe connection with someone.

"Nah, it was late when you first called. Now that it's almost five. It's early morning. I've got a good start to my day."

"And I need to sleep." I looked at our house and thought about my warm bed in there. I wanted nothing more than to crawl under the covers and never come out.

"Kate," Brett said, turning all serious. "Do you know by not telling me what's wrong, I'm imagining the worst?"

I knew what he was saying was true. It wasn't fair to not say anything after Brett had come in the middle of the night to get me, but I couldn't tell him. He'd go nuts. He'd want to protect me. It was as simple as that.

Once, when our cousin had taken a marker and drawn all over my favorite doll, Brett went after her Barbies. She went home with a bagful of bald Barbies, crying.

If I told Brett, I wasn't sure Luke would make it out alive.

"I'll be fine," I told him and stepped out of the car. I grabbed the door handle, still feeling a bit shaky.

I stopped and considered telling him the truth. Brett would understand. He would listen.

But the truth shamed me. I was the one who had let Luke come into the bed. I had let it happen.

There was no way I could tell the truth, so I stayed quiet.

I felt like a robot walking toward the house. My insides were nothing; my body was a machine working to keep me moving. It took one foot slowly in front of the other to get me to the front door.

The house was quiet and dark when I walked inside. I flashed the front lights at Brett and watched him drive away. Dad had left a Post-it on the microwave: *"There's leftover pizza in the fridge. Be back tomorrow afternoon. Hope you had fun at Ali's house."* I ripped down the note and crumpled it, thinking about all the fun I had.

I went directly to my room and called Jack. I left a message trying to explain, asking him to call, wanting him to forgive and help.

I waited. I didn't sleep; I didn't think; I didn't anything. I just lay there, my mind blank, waiting for Jack to tell me everything was going to be okay.

I hid in my room all the next day and stared at my phone. I called Jack again and told him I needed to talk. After, I expected his name to flash across the front of my phone and his voice to say my name. I needed him to fill the rest of the space with words that would make everything better.

I held the phone in my hand, looking at the screen, willing it to light up, to ring, to vibrate. To do anything but be silent. I held it in my palm when it was wet with my sweat. I carried it to the bathroom with me in case I missed his call. I gripped it tight during fits of tears and the moments when they stopped and I tried to catch my breath and wipe my clouded eyes.

I didn't shower, because I didn't want to miss his call. I smelled of smoke, vomit, and the stink of last night. It all seeped so far down into my skin that I wasn't sure if I'd be able to wash it out. I ached to erase the night, but I also needed to fix things with Jack.

I held my phone secure in my clenched fist as exhaustion finally took over, pulling me into a weak, thin sleep. I woke over and over again, relishing the first moments when I'd forgotten what had happened, those two, three, four seconds when things stayed okay, right before the world slammed back into me, the heavy wooden stake of memory too close to my scarred heart.

I dragged myself into the shower when I heard Dad leave the house Monday morning. I was supposed to be at school, but he hadn't bothered to check on me yesterday, so I figured I'd also be left alone this morning. I wouldn't go to Beacon and face everyone. I could only imagine what they were saying about Jack's party.

I left my phone on the sink so I could hear it ring. I had eight missed texts from Ali, but I couldn't read them. I wasn't ready to talk to anyone but Jack.

I undressed and stepped into the shower. I sat, curled into a ball as the bathroom filled with steam, the hot water turning me pink and then red. Mom used to yell at me for taking such long showers, and sometimes when she and Dad wanted to mess with me, they'd turn off the hot water. I'd come out screaming, and the two of them would laugh and laugh. Now I could sit in here for hours, and no one would say a word.

After, I stood dripping in front of the mirror. I couldn't see myself, and I didn't want to. Instead, I drew a new me. I traced a silhouette into the steam, making myself skinny and tiny. I put *X*s over my eyes and a straight line for my mouth. I was all lines and angles. There was nothing inside of me. You could crack me in half if I was bent too far.

I stared at the image until the steam evaporated and I was looking into my own eyes. My whole body was there, clear, in front of the bathroom light. I saw myself, but nothing in my reflection looked familiar. I was a stranger, someone I might pass on the street and not even notice.

Right above my left breast, where it was soft and fatty, three bruises lined up one after the other. Three faint lines that weren't there two days ago, before Jack's party. I remembered Luke pushing me down on the bed. I shuddered when I remembered Luke pressing his fingers into me so hard they left marks. He was disgusting, and I hated him for what he had done. He'd done this to me.

I stared at the mirror and told myself I wasn't to blame.

He had forced himself on me.

But I had accepted him so easily and welcomed him into the bed. Shouldn't I have known he wasn't Jack?

I shook my head at my reflection.

"No," I said. "This isn't your fault. Luke did this to you."

I pressed my fingers into the bruises. The skin was still tender, and I sucked in my breath. I pressed harder to feel the pain. I let my fingers move between the bruises and dig into them, as if I could get the bruises to join and make the mark of my mistake bigger. I turned off the light and continued to push my fingers into the wound. I wanted it to be dark so I couldn't sense anything but the pain.

When someone knocked on my bedroom door, I assumed it was Dad, finally coming in to check on me.

I pulled myself out from under the covers. "I'm sleeping," I said and hoped it would keep him out.

The knocking continued, and I heard a familiar voice. "It's Ali. Let me in."

I stared at the door in horror. I wasn't ready to face Ali. Unlike Jack, she'd been calling nonstop, and I'd been too afraid to pick up the phone. I didn't want to talk to her or listen to her messages. There was no doubt in my mind she had some version of what had happened the other night. Jack was the only one I'd wanted to talk to, but Ali was the one who crowded up my voice mail.

She pounded on the door and shouted, "You need to open up now."

Dad yelled something from downstairs, and I knew I had to deal with Ali or he'd come up.

I crawled out of bed and unlocked the door.

Before I could open it all the way, Ali pushed through.

"Why haven't you answered my calls?"

I sat back on my bed. "I haven't been feeling well."

Ali laughed bitterly. "Feeling well? Did this sickness happen before or after you screwed my boyfriend?"

Her words sliced right through me.

"He's not your boyfriend," I said and immediately regretted the words.

"You bitch."

"I didn't sleep with Luke," I told her, but I knew from the revolted look on her face she didn't believe me.

"Oh, really? Are you saying Jack and Luke are liars?"

"Jack's telling everyone I slept with Luke?"

"He said he walked in on the two of you going at it."

I grabbed a pillow and held it against my chest. I dug my fingers into it to keep myself from jumping up and shaking Ali. I was desperate to make her see I hadn't wanted this to happen. "It wasn't like that. Jack didn't understand what was going on."

"So you did have sex with him?" Ali crossed her arms. "God, Kate, you're ridiculous."

"No, I stopped him. I thought he was Jack, but then I realized he wasn't." Even I knew how lame those words sounded.

"Right," Ali said slowly. "Sure. You thought he was Jack."

"You really think I'd sleep with Luke?"

"Of course you would. You're so obvious when you flirt with him."

"I'd *never* do something like that." I wanted to laugh at how unbelievable Ali was. There was no way in hell I'd ever consider Luke attractive. I thought about how much Jenna and I joked about his nastiness, but that confession wouldn't go over well with Ali.

"Well, you proved yourself wrong, because you did." She grabbed a framed picture of Jack and me together after a basketball game. She looked at it for a second and then threw it on the ground.

The glass broke, and I gritted my teeth, steeling myself not to react.

She walked to me so she was right in my face. "You stupid slut."

"I *didn't* sleep with him. He tried to rape me."
The word fell out of my mouth, slicing my tongue like
a razor. I hadn't allowed myself to think about that
word for longer than a second. When it had started
to creep into my head, I'd pushed it into the darkness because it seemed like something so awful. But
that's what had happened. I *hadn't* wanted Luke. I
hadn't flirted with him or told him in any way it was
okay to have sex with me. Luke had tried to rape me.
The truth was there, hanging between Ali and me.

She took a step back. "Are you kidding me? *Rape*
you? You're certifiable."

"That's what happened," I said, trying to keep my
voice calm, even though I was shaking all over.

"I think I'd know if I were sleeping with a rapist."

"Luke is not a good person."

"Get real. You knew *exactly* what you were doing
with him, and now you regret it because you got
caught."

I tried to plead with her, to get her to listen. "I
had no idea what was going on. I was confused and
sick. None of it makes sense. I must have had too
much to drink."

"People get wasted and hook up all the time, and

they don't go calling it rape. Just because you regret it when you're sober doesn't mean you didn't want it when you were drunk. Besides, I saw how little you drank. You were playing the goody-goody all night."

She was right, but how else could I explain that night? Nothing about it, how I felt and what Luke tried to do, connected. "He told me he was Jack; it was dark, and I felt so—"

"Shut up," she screamed. "I don't want to hear it. No one's going to believe that."

"It's the truth"

"Who do you think everyone is going to listen to, a whore like you or Jack and Luke? You don't have a chance."

"It's not my fault."

"I will destroy you," she hissed.

She slammed my bedroom door so hard Dad called to me again from downstairs.

I dug my fingers into my bruises and winced. I let my mind focus on that night and remembered what I had done to ruin everything.

www.allmytruths.com

Today's Truth:

The people you want to forget always come back in the end.

Just one moment	destroys it all
A single action	breaks me and you
Can we find	again what he took
Knowing makes	forgetting impossible

Posted By: Your Present Self

[Monday, December 16, 7:58 PM]

I stayed home from school the next two days. I knew it made it look as if I was giving in and letting Luke win, but Ali had made it totally clear I was the loser in this fight. Dad never even noticed me missing from his morning routine, and I wondered if anyone else at school did either.

My room became my refuge, my cave in which to withdraw. My covers held me in my bed, layers of them, their heavy heat soaking up my tears.

When I did get up, I sat Indian style, staring in the mirror, trying to make eye contact with myself. I wore a tank top and forced myself to look at the bruise, which had turned angry shades of yellow in the middle and dark blues and purples on the outside. I continued to push with my fingers to make the reminder of my mistake grow larger and larger.

I left my window cracked to feel something, even if it was just cold air. I let in whispers of wind that danced with the quietly clacking blinds. At first, I turned the radio on, but even the pop songs hurt. They all sang of love, not of loss and betrayal. Instead, I found an old box fan and kept it on for noise.

I called Jack. I hadn't heard from him, and I needed to talk to him. I called him four, five, six times in a row. I left messages trying to explain myself, trying to find words to describe something I couldn't understand.

"Jack, it's Kate. Please call me. I need to talk about what happened."

"Jack, it wasn't what you thought it was. What you saw in the bedroom."

"Jack, I thought it was you in the bed. I need to explain."

"Jack, please pick up. I need you to listen. Talk to me."

"Jack, this isn't the way it's supposed to be. Nothing is. It's all wrong. Talk to me. What you walked in on; it's not what you saw."

"Jack, Luke did this. He pretended to be you. I thought I was with you."

"Jack, it's Kate. Please."

I called him constantly. Sometimes I left a

message, and sometimes I remained silent, knowing he'd see my name in his missed calls. I hoped I could get him to say something to me, anything.

After staying in my room for four days straight, the door opened with a sudden purpose.

Dad stood illuminated by a halo of light from the hallway.

"The school called. They said you haven't been going to class. You've missed the last three days. Is that true?"

I met Dad's gaze with swelled, red-rimmed eyes, dirty, knotted hair, and pajamas at five in the afternoon. It was obvious things weren't right. "I haven't been feeling well."

"You're sick?" he asked, confused. "Is there anything I can do?"

I wanted to tell him everything that had happened. The words hung there, ready to spill over, but he was already glancing back down the hallway. I heard some kind of game on the television and knew he was anxious to get back to it.

I shook my head. He didn't want to hear about this. Not now. Not ever.

He walked to my bed and put his hand on my forehead. "I had no idea. I've been so busy trying to get the team into the play-offs . . ."

"Is it okay if I stay home tomorrow? I still don't feel good."

"One more day is okay," he said. "I told the school you were sick. I didn't want them to think I didn't know what was going on with my own daughter." He laughed and walked to the door.

I felt nauseated at the thought of what he didn't know.

"You should have told me you weren't feeling well."

My head throbbed, and I fought back tears. *You should have asked.*

He averted his gaze and talked to the ceiling. "I told them there's no reason to worry. I'm glad there isn't. I'm glad you're feeling better. Good," he said and pulled the door shut, closing out the light until it was a thin thread fighting to stay lit against my world of darkness.

www.allmytruths.com

Today's Truth:

Sometimes anything is better than nothing.

"We need to talk."

"It's not you; it's me."

"I think we're better as just friends."

"I'm not into you."

"I need something more."

"I need to find myself."

"It's bad timing."

"We are both at different places in our lives."

"I don't see myself with you."

"I don't want to be in a relationship right now."

"We grew apart."

"We are different people with different needs."

"Maybe if I had met you ten years down the road."

"I am entering the witness protection program."

"I need to focus all my time on basketball this season."

"I want to see what else is out there."

"I need to work on myself. I can't love you until I learn to love myself."

"I need a break to figure things out."

"This is moving too fast for me."

"I'm not good enough for you. You need to be with someone who will treat you right."

Any of these excuses would be better, even the bad ones that sound made up, because at least I would have a reason.

Any reason would be better than the silence that screams in my ears when Jack doesn't even try to understand what happened that night at his party.

When he doesn't want to fight for me.

When he doesn't want to acknowledge what he saw.

When he acts as if he never knew who I was.

When he moves on with his life, while I float by as a ghost.

His smell, so familiar, and mine, haunting me as he blows away, the thin wispy vapors of our relationship evaporating behind him.

Posted By: Your Present Self

[Wednesday, December 18, 7:37 PM]

Dad followed through with the deal made during our conversation. He let me stay home one more day and then told me I had to go back to Beacon. The ironic thing was that, after pretending for almost a week, I really was sick this morning.

I was terrified of running into Luke and threw up while getting ready, which made everything worse.

I waited to go inside Beacon until the warning bell rang. I checked my phone one last time. Jack still hadn't called.

I felt as if the whole world was watching me as I walked into the hallway. I kept my head down. Every whisper I heard I assumed was about me. I was sure by now they all knew a version of the story that was nothing like what had really happened.

Jack was the only one I wanted to see. There wasn't a question whether I'd run into him; it was a certainty. I'd stolen a hall pass from Dad's briefcase.

He had a ton and would never miss it. Jack would see it and believe Dad was asking him to come to his office during lunch. Dad wouldn't be there—he ate lunch with the other coaches in the athletic office—but I would be. It was devious and could totally backfire, but I needed to talk to Jack. I wasn't going to sit around and wait for him to finally decide to pick up the phone. He'd made it clear that wasn't going to happen.

I spotted an office aid and handed her the pass.

"Coach Franklin needs to get this to Jack Blane. Can you deliver it?"

"No problem," the girl said, grabbing my pass and glancing at me before heading down the hallway. I wondered if she knew what had happened, if she believed what everyone was saying. I moved through the hallway with my head down, slipped between bodies, and pretended I was invisible. It was easier to think I could just disappear, because I imagined they were as disgusted with me as I was.

I hurried to Dad's office when the bell rang before lunch. I sighed in relief when I saw Jack wasn't there yet. I sat on the couch and picked at its loose threads.

I didn't have to wait long.

Jack entered without knocking and walked right past me, not even seeing me on the couch.

"Jack." I stood and blocked the door. It was a pathetic thing to do, but I was desperate. I needed to make him listen.

"What are you doing here?"

"I need to talk to you."

"Talk?"

"You haven't answered any of my messages, and I had to get you to listen."

"What could you possibly say that you didn't the other night in bed with Luke? What?" He yelled the last word with so much force that spit flew onto my face.

I didn't wipe it off. I didn't move. "I need to explain."

Jack stood there, wearing the gray hooded sweatshirt he'd let me borrow so many times, the one with the small hole in the left sleeve I used to poke my finger through.

"You don't," he said.

"I don't?"

"You don't need to explain. I don't give a shit what

you have to say. I'm done, Kate. With everything. You told me exactly how you felt when you were in my bed with Luke."

Jack pushed past me, my shoulder banging into the door. Pain shot up my arm, but I was too busy feeling a different kind of pain, the kind that enveloped me, saturated me, and dripped into every single part of me.

It was as simple as that. The breaking apart. A quick crack with his words, and we were no longer together.

www.allmytruths.com

Today's Truth:
It is possible to lose everything.

I make a list of things I found . . .

Jack

Ali

Beacon

Friends

Happiness

Noise

Life

Smiles

I then make a list of things I have lost . . .

Jack

Ali

Beacon

Popularity

Friends

Happiness

Noise

Smiles
Laughter
My mother
My father
My brother

When I compare the list
I see that the things I have lost
are more than the things I have found,
leaving
me
with
negative zero.
Less

than

nothing.

Posted By: Your Present Self
[Thursday, December 19, 3:10 PM]

Julia cornered me in choir. It was one of Mrs. Reid's voice rest days, and I was sitting next to three boys who were laughing at some lame Japanese comic book they had. I'd been trying my hardest to ignore Ali at the top of the choir risers. She was talking loudly about some party she was planning on going to with Luke. She looked pointedly at me, and I knew she wanted me to know she was still with him. It made me sick that she still wanted to be with him after what had happened.

I tried to look busy, as if my math homework was the most exciting thing in the world, but Julia wasn't buying it. She sat behind me and whispered in my ear, "Why are you avoiding me?"

"I'm not. I really haven't talked to anyone."

"Brett's really worried about you, and so am I. What's going on?"

I glanced toward Ali.

Ali caught my eye and whispered loudly, "Slut."

A few of the girls laughed.

"I'm sure the rumors have reached you too," I said.

"I've heard what people are saying, and I know none of it's true. What happened, Kate?"

I started to shake. This was so unfair. Ali sat up there as if she was perfect, judging me like I was a piece of trash.

I turned to face Julia and pretended it was only the two of us in the room. I shut out all the noise around me and started to talk. "Jack did find Luke and me together. But it wasn't the way everyone is saying it happened."

"I never thought it was," she said.

I hated myself for keeping this from her. Of course she wouldn't have believed Luke and Ali. She'd listen to the truth.

She sat quietly as I relived what happened two weeks ago at Jack's party.

When I finished, she hugged me and asked, "Why didn't you tell me when it happened?"

"I didn't want to lose you too. I was afraid of what you'd think."

"I'll tell you what I think. Luke is an asshole. He's

worthless, and the last thing you should do is keep this inside."

I twisted my hair around my fingers and let it go. "It made me feel so dirty to think about what he tried to do. It's next to impossible to speak the words out loud."

"You need to tell someone," Julia said firmly. "He can't get away with this."

"No one would believe me. Why would they? Ali is right. It'd be my story against everyone else's version."

Julia leaned forward, looking me straight in the eye. "He tried to rape you, Kate. You've got to go to the police."

I ground the pencil I was holding into my math note-book. The thought made me feel sick. "There's no way."

"They *would* believe you. You also need to talk to your dad."

"My dad would not be able to handle this. He treats the team as if they're his own kids."

"This isn't something you can ignore. You need to speak up or they're going to keep doing the same thing."

"Who?"

"The basketball players," Julia said. "They can't

get away with this."

"It's not their fault. It's Luke's."

"Are you kidding me? You cannot still be supporting them."

"I'm not."

"You are. And they need to be punished. All of them. They've been getting away with things like this forever."

"Everyone thinks they can't do anything wrong. Including my dad." I drew circles around and around in my math book so I wouldn't have to look Julia in the eye.

"People only believe it because no one will stand up against them."

"Maybe nobody has said anything because they're afraid."

"What do you mean?"

"If someone were to speak up loud enough that people had to take notice, how do you think that person would be treated? The town loves the basketball players. They act as if they're gods."

"You need to try. You need to do something, or it's going to keep happening."

"I'm not strong enough," I whispered. "I can't do this."

"You're wrong. Think about all you and Brett have been through during these last two years. You're tough, and you'll do the right thing."

"No one is going to believe me," I repeated, but I also knew I couldn't let Luke get away with it. I wasn't that kind of person. I refused to be weak anymore.

The bell rang, and everyone started packing up their stuff.

Mrs. Reid made some lame comment about us being ready for class tomorrow now that our voices were good and rested.

"I believe you. And your dad will believe you. Talk to him."

I shoved my books in my bag and stood with Julia. "I'm not sure that will help. My dad hasn't listened to me in years."

"He'll listen," Julia said.

I sighed, wishing I was as sure as she was.

I didn't have to wait long for the opportunity to talk to Dad. He found me sitting in my room in the dark. I was looking out the windows facing the pool, staring outside, trying to figure out what to do. It was too cold to swim, but somehow seeing the pool made me feel a little better.

"Kate," he said, exercising his talent of avoiding my gaze. "Jack said something at practice today that didn't seem quite right."

My gaze shot up at the mention of Jack's name, and my stomach turned at the thought that he'd talked to my dad about me. I looked down when I saw not concern or sympathy on Dad's face but anger.

"His games have been off. He hasn't been playing well. I've been on him, asking if he's not been sleeping enough, worrying about school, or having problems with you."

"Dad," I said hoarsely. "No, don't ask about us.

We aren't together."

"I know. Jack said you're the reason his game is off."

"He did?"

"You need to stop being the problem. We have a real shot at making the play-offs, and I'm not about to let anything or *anyone* screw that up. He said he broke up with you last week, but you won't leave him alone."

I turned away.

"Have you been calling him? Texting? Following him around school?" Dad went on talking, not waiting for me to respond. "Don't make yourself into a fool, Kate. Leave him alone."

I opened my mouth to argue. I wanted to tell him how it was over forever with Jack, but he wouldn't understand unless I told him everything. My stomach turned around and around, an angry black hole. My body felt like wet, dripping cotton, dragging me so low I didn't know if I could stop falling.

"Something happened," I whispered.

"What?" Dad asked, his voice still loud and angry.

I spoke louder, matching his volume. "Something happened last weekend at Jack's house. I wasn't sick this week; I didn't want to go to school."

"What do you mean?"

"You're not going to like what I have to say."

"You're not making sense."

"I went to a party. I was sleeping, and I thought it was Jack, but it was Luke, and he . . ." I couldn't go on. I glanced out the window at the pool, my vision blurred by tears. I imagined Mom out there swimming. I pretended she was still strong, healthy, and would get out and come upstairs and wrap her arms around me.

"And he what?"

I shook my head. I couldn't say this, not to Dad. What kind of person would he think I was?

"He what, Kate?" Dad walked to me and put a hand on my shoulder. "Are you okay?"

I leaned against Dad. I liked the way his touch felt, safe and strong. Ever since Mom had died, he didn't hug me anymore. Right now, his hand on my shoulder, standing next to me, he cared.

I took a deep breath and let the words fall out. "Luke tried to rape me."

Dad pulled his hand off my shoulder as if he'd

been burned. He stepped away and now, instead of standing with me and offering support, he towered over me. "What are you talking about?"

"I was sick. I went to sleep in Jack's room." I spoke quickly, trying to get him to understand what had happened. "When I woke up, I thought it was Jack, but it wasn't. It was Luke. But I stopped him. I stopped him." The words came out disjointed, broken. They crackled off my tongue, the meaning in each confession full of electricity that shocked me.

"No," Dad said.

"What do you mean, no?"

"You can't talk like this. The team. The play-offs. My job."

"Your job?"

Dad paced the room. He ran his fingers through his hair, and I knew what he was thinking and it wasn't about me. I felt sick. He had the disheveled look he got when he was working through plays for the team. He stopped abruptly and grabbed my shoulders. "Who have you told this to?"

I let out a cry of surprise. He acted as if he was going to shake me, but he didn't. He dropped his hands. He was scaring me. How could he even think about the team right now?

"You, Julia, and Ali. I tried to tell Jack, but he wouldn't listen." I started sobbing as I said Jack's name and had to push the rest of the words out. "Jack walked in on the two of us." I wiped at my swollen eyes. My whole body ached as if I had run a race barefoot over sticks and pebbles that were still stuck in my feet.

"This didn't happen," Dad said firmly.

"It did, Dad."

He took a step toward me. "God damn it, Kate."

I cowered and he backed away.

He walked to the window and yanked the cord on the blinds. They fell with a loud clatter.

I jumped. "It wasn't my fault." I pleaded with him to listen to me.

His face shifted so he looked less angry. He knelt next to me. "Listen. Do you understand what would happen if you told people about this? It would be worse for you than anyone else. You'd have to tell your story to everyone. Do you really want to talk about it again? Especially in front of Luke?"

"Not at all. That's what I told Julia when she said I needed to tell someone."

"You're right, honey. It would be awful. Let's think about this for a minute. I'm only trying to protect you."

Dad sat on an arm of the chair and stroked my hair. His closeness reminded me of the night after Mom had died, when he wrapped me in his arms and held me as if I was a little kid again. He hadn't been this close to me physically since, and it felt nice.

"Not only would you have to tell your story over and over again, but think about the team. It would destroy them. We're so close to the play-offs. Do you really want to ruin everything?"

I shook my head. Basketball was what brought Dad back to me. I didn't want to lose him again.

"You shouldn't have to go through this. It's awful, and I don't want you to hurt any more than you have to."

"I just want it to disappear."

"Tell you what. I'll take care of this, okay?" Dad continued to stroke my hair.

I closed my eyes, pretending it was the way it used to be and we would leave the room together to watch a basketball game downstairs.

"I'll make sure Luke knows what he did was wrong."

"You will?"

"Of course. I'll make everything okay," he said and stood up. "Let me deal with it. You don't have to think about it anymore."

I nodded. I should've felt lighter for telling him what had happened, but as I watched him walk out of the door and pull his cell phone out of his pocket, I felt a sense of unease. If Dad said he was going to take care of things, shouldn't I feel safe now?

71

Eight days later the final bell sounded, and my class-mates rushed out the doors, eager to escape and start Christmas break. For the last few days everyone had been talking about vacation plans, trips to tropical climates or skiing in the mountains, vacations that involved planes or boats to get away. I looked forward to my own escape much closer to home, one that involved my room and the option of not having to see, talk to, or interact with anyone. A trip away from the walls of Beacon.

I'd stayed quiet as Dad had asked me to, but I didn't see what good it was doing. Luke seemed to purposely seek me out, winking or licking his lips every time he saw me. Ali made vulgar comments whenever she could, and Jenna just looked on with pity. I tried to avoid them, but Beacon was a small school and they seemed to have made it their mission to remind me of what had happened that night.

Dad had been acting weird ever since I told him

about the night at Jack's party. He avoided the house even more than usual, and when he was home, he constantly asked me how I was feeling. It was as if he was waiting for me to do or say something. I kept thinking he'd tell me about what he'd done to Luke, but he hadn't mentioned it.

Julia knew I'd talked to Dad, but I refused to say anything more about it. She wouldn't be happy with what she heard, and I was beginning to wonder if I'd done the right thing by agreeing to Dad's request to stay silent.

I was away from school on break, but it sure didn't feel like the holidays. Dad hadn't put up a Christmas tree yet, and I didn't say anything. At first I thought he was busy with the team and didn't have time to put it up during Thanksgiving break. It had been a tradition in my family to go and cut down a tree the day after Thanksgiving, bundling up in warm clothes and heading to a farm about an hour away. Everyone would sweat in the car the whole drive but freeze once we started our trek into the woods. Brett and Dad would suggest cutting every tree we saw within reasonable size, but Mom and I would search for the perfect one. The two of us would pull every-one deeper and deeper into the woods and make the whole experience last a lot longer than it had to. We'd emerge from the forest with the best tree, though. Brett and Dad would act all proud as if they had found it when they pulled it out on a sled to be paid for and tied up.

Last Christmas, our first after Mom died, my aunt decorated the house. She brought over a tree and boxes of decorations to create a false Christmas wonderland in a house that didn't feel very festive. Dad complained about the needles for weeks after. He'd yell when he stepped on a forgotten stray one and it stuck in his big toe or sock, and he swore off real trees. Brett and I didn't remind him that our trees had always had needles and they'd never bothered him before. Instead, we accepted that real trees were something else we lost along with our mother. The list of these things had grown larger and larger, the hole she left not only the loss of a person but increasingly the loss of what we knew as a family.

I picked up my phone and dialed Brett's number. I figured he'd answer when he saw it was me. I was right.

"You okay?" he asked.

"As good as I can be," I told him, thinking about Jack, Luke, and everything that sucked about life right now.

"I get worried when you call."

I thought about how messed up that was. My own brother shouldn't think the worst when I just want to call.

"Dad hasn't put the tree up."

"The tree?"

"The Christmas tree. Our house is the same as it always is."

"Cold and without love?"

"Brett."

"Hey, I'm just telling it like it is."

"Why don't you come home for Christmas?"

He sighed. "You know I can't do that."

"Why not? This is your house. You can come back."

"Sure, after a long lecture about what a loser I am and how I've destroyed my life. I'm not going to be somewhere I'm not wanted. You don't see the way Dad looks at me. It's as if I've betrayed him in the worst way possible."

I considered telling Brett that I *did* know what he was talking about. I thought about how angry Dad was when I first told him about Luke. How he wasn't worried about me but about what my accusations might do to the team. I understood exactly, but I knew telling him would only make his feelings toward Dad worse.

"I wouldn't look at you that way," I said.

"I can't pretend to be someone I'm not for Dad."

"Just promise you'll think about it."

"I'll think about it," he said but without much conviction.

"Thanks," I said, even though I knew it was a long shot.

After I hung up, I went into the attic to find the boxes with all the Christmas stuff. I walked around the house decorating as much as I could. I left a Post-it for Dad: *We need to cut down a tree! Let me know when, and I'll pack the hot chocolate in a thermos!*

I waited for Dad to mention the decorations or my note, but when he still hadn't said anything on Christmas Eve, I realized there was one way he was a lot like Brett. Holiday cheer and fa la las were not on the top of their lists.

72

I carried Dad's and Brett's gifts downstairs Christmas morning. I still held out hope Brett would return home. I couldn't imagine him staying away today. It didn't seem right to spend Christmas without your family.

I got Brett a documentary about fighter pilots. He used to watch shows like that over and over again, and I figured it would be a peace offering, something to get us to start talking about the Army. Jack had helped me pick out Dad's gift. It was an old Pistons jersey from the seventies. We found it over two months ago when we drove an hour away to catch a college basketball scrimmage. We'd stopped at a sports memorabilia store that had a bunch of old team jerseys hanging in the window. It was the perfect present, even if it did remind me of Jack.

I left the gifts on the table, unsure of where to put them without a tree. Dad would love the jersey. Despite everything that had been going on during the last few weeks, I was excited for him to open it.

"Merry Christmas," I said and shoved the bag at him when he walked into the kitchen.

He looked up dazed, as if he'd forgotten it was Christmas, and for a fleeting moment, I wondered if he had. "Oh, Merry Christmas, honey." He took the present and turned it over and over in his hands. "This was nice of you. To get me a gift, I mean."

"Open it."

He pulled off the paper, lifting the jersey out of the box.

"Do you like it?"

He held it against his chest and turned to me. "It's great, Kate. Really great." He put the jersey back in the box and headed to the fridge. He pulled out a carton of milk. "I have something for you too. It's on my dresser." He poured himself some cereal and sat at the table.

Really? This was his great reaction to my gift? When I realized he wasn't going to say anything more, I headed to his room. I tried to remember what he'd gotten me in the past: pink-and-green tennis shoes he'd had to special order, a basketball autographed by the Pistons, tickets to a play for Mom and me, a pearl necklace with my initials on the clasp. His gifts always had to do with something important to me, so I looked forward to opening them.

I found this year's gift right away. There was an envelope with my name on it. I ripped it open and pulled out a card with a Christmas tree on the front. I wondered if it was Dad's replacement for the one he hadn't put up. "Merry Christmas," he had scrawled inside, not even signing it. A plastic card slid out.

A three-hundred-dollar gift card to the mall.

I turned it over and over in my hands as if checking to see if it was real. I thought it was a joke and half expected Dad and Brett to jump out laughing. But I was wrong. It wasn't a prank. Dad had given me a gift card for Christmas. The most generic, impersonal gift there was.

I took it to my room, shaking. I picked up my scissors, the sharp pair with the orange handles, and sliced the card into small pieces, watching the pointy plastic fall to my floor.

Brett never showed up on Christmas or the days after. On New Year's Eve, my phone rang. It was the song I'd programmed to play when Jack called. My heart pounded as I looked and saw his name. I cleared my throat. "Hello?"

Loud music played on the other end, but Jack didn't answer.

"Jack? I can't hear you. Are you there?"

"Luke is lonely," a muffled voice said.

"What?"

"Luke is lonely. He's wondering if you'll come over and help him ring in the New Year with a bang."

There was a bunch of laughing, and the phone went dead.

My hands shook as I jabbed at the End button.

My cell rang seven more times with Jack's number. I didn't have to pick up to know it wasn't him. I ignored the incoming calls and hid it under my pillow so I wouldn't have to look at it. My fingers rubbed over the bruise on my chest, harder and harder. It was now the size of a small apple and a mess of sick, violent colors.

The eighth time my phone rang, I pulled it out and silenced it. I dialed Julia. She answered right away.

"Kate?"

"Hey," I said, then stopped, unsure of what to say next.

"Is everything okay?"

"Not really. Someone keeps calling me on Jack's cell phone and saying awful stuff."

"Didn't your dad take care of things?"

"He told me he would," I said, but I knew now there was a fine line between saying you were going to do something and actually doing it.

Julia must have heard the doubt in my voice. "Did he?"

I started to sweat. "He said he would."

"But he hasn't," she finished, and I imagined the disappointment in her face.

"Maybe he still will," I told her, but it had been

almost two weeks since I'd talked to him. People who are serious about things don't take two weeks to do it. I knew I was now just pretending something was going to get done. But isn't that better? How do you face a truth like that?

"Do you want to come over? We're watching movies and waiting for the New Year to start."

"Is Brett with you?"

"Yep, he's on the couch stuffing his face with popcorn."

"Does he know about Luke?"

"I would never tell him something like that without your permission, but he worries about you."

"Thanks for not saying anything."

"I won't, but maybe you should."

"Not right now."

She didn't press me any further.

"Thanks for the offer to come over and hang, but I'm going to stay here. Can you tell Brett I said hi?"

"Of course. And, Kate, happy New Year."

"Yeah," I said. "Same to you."

I hung up and stared at my blank TV. I couldn't

bring myself to turn it on. I didn't want to see the images of crowded streets of people smiling, their arms around each other, counting down to a New Year.

My phone rang late in the evening, when I had drifted into sleep. It was Jack's number again, and the voice mail message beeped not long after. I dialed my mailbox and heard nothing but a bunch of people laughing into the phone. I deleted it before the message was over. I didn't need words. I understood what they were trying to say.

www.allmytruths.com

Today's Truth:

Beacon does not welcome you anymore.

I am a fish.

I swim around in a giant fishbowl while everyone watches through the glass.

Their eyes are huge and bulging, warped by the water, faces distorted like fun house characters in mirrors.

Bodies blocking the hallway, faces laughing.

Fingers pointing.

Eyes locked on me.

Everyone watches as I walk through the halls.

Alone.

I'm scared for class to end.

For the bell to shriek my inevitable doom.

I sit in class willing the minute hand to slow down.

But it never does.

Isn't that how it works?

The moment you dread is right in front of you before you know it.

The halls are the worst.

I keep my head down so I don't see anyone as I swim down the hallways.

But I can still hear them.

The words tug at my ears.

Whispers dance around me at night, blowing their harsh winds into my dreams.

Closing my eyes at night only invites their words to visit me in sleep.

The boys press against me in the halls.

Pretending to stumble and grab me from behind as I push through them.

It makes me sick.

Their hot breath against my ear:

"Now that Jack's done with you, and Luke's used you, let's see how the coach's daughter can play off the courts . . ."

And the girls.

Standing against their lockers.

Identical Barbies stepping back from me with disgust.

Ali and Jenna looking at me with revulsion.

Perfect on the outside, but I can see the fear inside.

Afraid.

Afraid to speak up because they may be the new victims.

The one singled out for the next attack.

I want to scream.

I want to stand in the middle of the room and shout at the top of my lungs,

"You don't scare me. I'm stronger than that. Look at me. Look at me for who I am."

But I don't.

Because they won't.

My mouth opens and closes. Silent bubbles float up with words I wish I could say.

And I lower my head and continue down the hallway as the thunder roars around me in silence.

In silence.

In silence . . .

Posted By: Your Present Self

[Thursday, January 2, 7:31 AM]

Beacon welcomed everyone back from winter break with a pep rally. The boys stood in front of the cheering school, and Dad talked about how great they all were. I swear I saw their heads swelling with each word that came out of his mouth.

"Thank you for your enthusiasm," Dad said and grinned in front of the microphone. "We all appreciate it, especially my boys here."

He gestured toward the team, and everyone went crazy. Stomps shook the bleachers, and shrill whistles and catcalls pierced the air. I was standing next to Julia, who had met me at my locker so we could walk to the gym together. The pep rally was mandatory, but how do you force someone to have pep? I had no doubt Brett skipped out on it; he'd take any punishment before he'd support the team. I wished I had made the same choice.

The crowd quieted, and Dad started speaking again.

"We're more than halfway through the season, and no one can stop us yet. If I made a guess, I'd say no one will be able to beat us this season. Now I'd like to celebrate some of the statistics from your Beacon basketball team."

Dad started to list points earned, free throws made, rebounds, and a bunch of other accolades that made everyone cheer and cheer for the team. Luke grinned when his name was called. The students around me screamed and clapped for him, and when Dad placed his hand on Luke's shoulder and beamed at him, I knew for sure Dad had placed the basketball team over me.

I couldn't decide what made me sicker: what Luke had tried to do to me or what Dad had chosen to do about it.

75

Julia was my savior at Beacon. She welcomed me back to the usual table, and we talked about everything but what had happened. Brett sometimes sat with us, and I liked that. The two of us didn't push each other to talk, and it was okay. It was easy to see things through Brett's eyes now. I understood why he hated Beacon so much, and I did everything possible to remove myself as well.

I started to slip into the bathroom between periods and arrive to class right when the bell rang. That way I didn't need to listen to the whispered comments directed at me and learn exactly how nasty they all thought I was. I'd stand in front of the bathroom mirrors with the top of my shirt pulled down, staring at my bruise, which had become a giant blob, ugly and bold on my chest, ensuring I'd never forget.

Today, the door to the bathroom swung open, and I let go of my shirt. It was Jenna. I pulled it up quickly so the bruise was covered.

"Hey," I said, figuring it was better to acknowledge her than not saying anything. I reached for the faucet. I turned the right knob and stuck my hands under the water as if everything was perfectly normal.

She didn't turn on her water. Instead, she met my eyes in the mirror. "I shouldn't be talking to you. Ali would kill me."

Jenna's words stung, but I didn't doubt what she was saying. Ali was a bitch. She probably would go after her if she saw the two of us together.

I stared at a piece of paper towel that clung to the edge of the sink and thought about how unfair it was that Ali controlled Jenna too. She was my friend, and I hadn't done anything to hurt her.

"I understand why Ali's mad at me, but why are you a part of it?" I said.

"I can't be on both sides."

"Why not? Why can't you make your own choices?"

Jenna ignored my question and leaned close to me. "I'm going to tell you something, but if you ask me to repeat it, I'll deny it. Okay?"

I nodded, wondering what I was agreeing to.

"Ali is my friend, and we're going to stay friends. But what happened with Luke was messed up." She paused as if waiting for me to say something.

I didn't.

What Luke did was beyond messed up. I already knew that, and why should I care what she thought, if she was going to ignore me as soon as we stepped outside?

I pumped the soap dispenser slowly: one, two, three, four, willing her to stop. To disappear. I focused on the sudsy mess in my hands.

"It wasn't your fault," Jenna said as she reached over for the same soap dispenser. "What happened to you. I know you didn't do it."

"Of course I didn't," I told her and laughed. "Why would I ever do something like that?"

I knew she was trying to meet my eyes again as she moved away from the sink and yanked out papers towels. I scrubbed my hands under the water. It was hot. Too hot. My hands turned red, but I didn't turn it off. I didn't want to silence the rush of water blocking out the roaring in my ears.

I tried to ignore her, but she wouldn't let me.

I turned off the water. She thrust some towels in

my hands, forcing me to look into her face.

"How did you feel that night?" she asked.

It didn't take a rocket scientist to figure out what she was getting at, and I wasn't about to play into this sick game she and Ali had concocted. "Whatever Ali's saying about how drunk I was is a lie."

"That's not what I'm asking."

I shrugged. "You want to know how I felt? Messed up. But I wasn't. There was no way."

"What did you drink?"

I closed my eyes and held them shut for a moment before opening them. "I can't do this. I'm done with this conversation. I don't need you to interrogate me."

"Was Luke ever around you when you were drinking?"

"What does that have to do with anything?"

"I think Luke put something in your drink."

"No," I said, but I wasn't so sure.

"I heard him talking about the stuff a few weeks ago. He was asking Nick Sateen about getting him some weird shit called liquid ecstasy. Nick just laughed, so I figured it never happened."

I remembered the beer Luke had given me, the

one he'd insisted on pouring into a glass, and my whole body shuddered. "What the hell, Jenna? Why wouldn't you say something?"

"I didn't know he was going to toss it into your drink. I figured it was some nasty habit he did by himself. But then I started thinking about everything, and I don't know; it kind of makes sense."

"It makes complete sense," I told her. I remembered how sick I'd felt after the beer from Luke and the haze and heaviness that followed. I wasn't stupid. I'd learned about drugs like that in health class. My teacher tried to scare us away from drinking with stories about date rape drugs. "That bastard."

"We always knew he was a creep," Jenna said, and for a minute it was like it used to be, when the two of us were friends.

"Why are you telling me this?" I asked, reminding myself we weren't friends. Jenna had ignored me like everyone else. She supported Ali, and I knew if it came down to it, she'd do whatever she had to to step up to Ali's defense.

"I just couldn't believe you'd hook up with Luke."

"Thanks," I said, relieved Jenna believed me.

We both jumped as the door swung open and a

girl talking on her cell phone walked in.

"I need to go," Jenna said. "It sucks what happened. Luke is a pig."

I started to follow her out, but she stopped.

"This doesn't change things. I'm on Ali's side," she said. "She's my friend. She's been my friend for-ever. I'm not going to ruin that. I just thought you should know about Luke."

She pushed the door open and headed into the hallway. Jenna had been right about one thing: the lines were being drawn, and she'd made her choice very clear.

I leaned against the sink and looked at my reflection.

Luke had known what he was going to do to me.

Maybe I wasn't the specific target he had in mind, but I'd certainly let myself become the easiest. He gave me that drink with the purpose of finding me later to have sex. He planned everything, and I'd given in to Dad's pleas for my silence and let him protect Luke. I pushed open the door to a stall and threw up in the toilet.

I moved through the school for the rest of the day with a warped kind of confidence. I didn't do anything wrong that night, and Jenna's speculations destroyed any doubt I had about my role in what Luke tried to do to me. What had happened wasn't my fault. I wasn't to blame.

www.allmytruths.com

Today's Truth:

**You can only keep things inside
for so long before they start to**

destroy you.

In history class we learned how canaries were used in coal mines to warn miners of dangerous gases.

A canary was lowered into the deep, dark bowels of the mines. If a bird was pulled back up alive, the miners knew it was safe to go down.

If it died, the bird was sacrificed, an early warning saving the lives of the miners.

The miners also brought the birds with them. A canary sang and sang, and if the bird stopped singing, the miners would evacuate. The bird was more sensitive to the harmful gases, and the miners would have enough time to get out safely. The bird, however, usually didn't.

I imagine the birds doing what was natural and

having that used against them. Their tiny lungs that sang were what ultimately destroyed them.

I think about the canaries and how their purpose for the miners was to breathe in the air until it got too toxic and killed them.

I think about this as I replay Dad's words in my head.

I have been silent, as Dad demanded of me. Each night before I go to bed, I think about what Luke did and what Dad didn't do. I think about how Jack hasn't cared, how he moved on without a second thought of me. I think about all these things, and I stay quiet. I push it deep down inside, and for now I'm still alive.

But I wonder how many dirty fumes I'll continue to ingest before I sing my last song, before I can't go down any deeper with the secrets I know.

Posted by: Your Present Self

[Tuesday, January 7, 8:03 PM]

I started to do whatever I could to avoid going home. I'd catch the bus and ride it around the city until night filled the sky. Some afternoons I'd end up at the library, sitting in the stacks on the third floor away from everyone. Other days I'd wander around the mall a few towns over, a mall far enough away that I wouldn't run into people from Beacon.

Today I got off the bus four blocks from the hospice where Mom stayed. The weather was cold, and the sky loomed gray above it. We had only known the place when it was warm and sunny. Today, with the windows sealed shut and the grounds muddy from melted snow, it reminded me of somewhere a person would go to die.

I went through a back fence, pulling myself over it to get to the path I used to walk with Mom. I followed it deep into the woods until I got to the lake she had loved. Parts of it were frozen, while other sections broke off in jagged holes, and I could see water glistening under it. I found a rock and sat, the wet earth soaking through my jeans.

I wondered how Mom would have reacted if I told her about Luke. I imagined her clenching her jaw and closing her eyes, taking a deep breath before she opened them again. That's what she used to do when the pain got too bad. She thought she hid it from Brett and me, but we knew. I pictured her doing the same thing when I told her about Luke; she'd react different from Dad. When she spoke, she wouldn't ask me to stay quiet. She wouldn't fill me with lies about how she'd handle everything and make me feel as if it would all be safe and okay. She'd make sure Luke would never do anything to me again. She'd fight for me and make sure everyone knew how I'd been hurt. She would have done what was right.

I thought about her reaction, and I vowed to do what she would have done.

I wouldn't let Luke get away with this.

And I certainly wouldn't let Dad get away with it either.

RACHELE ALPINE

www.allmytruths.com

Today's Truth:

**Sometimes no matter how loud
you talk, no one can hear you.**

Dad doesn't care about	how
you hurt me, just that I spoke the truth	loud.
He doesn't want to	do
anything to help me. He protects	you
over me. He ignores how you	have
destroyed me. I want	to yell
and shout my pain	until
I can force the world to listen. Until	they
have no choice but to stop and	hear
how my life has been destroyed by	you.

**Posted By: Your Present Self
[Thursday, January 9, 5:23 PM]**

The next day in class, Mrs. Reynolds called me up to her desk. "Do you mind running these papers to your dad?"

I bit my bottom lip. I wanted to say no, but how do you tell a teacher you don't want to take papers to your own dad?

"Sure." I took the stack and walked slowly to his office. I prayed he'd be in a meeting. Somehow, luck was on my side. When I arrived, his door was open but his seat was empty. I slipped in and put everything on his desk. I was about to leave when I heard someone come in.

Whoever it was came up behind me before I could turn around, and I felt breath hot on the back of my neck, tickling my ear. "What a surprise. I came in here to find Coach and got you instead."

I spun around.

A hand grabbed my hip.

It was Luke.

"Hey," he said. "Long time, no see."

I wiggled myself out of his grasp and tried to go around him, but he moved in front of me.

"What? Are you too good to talk to me?"

I wished Dad would show up.

"I hear you're saying bad things about me."

I bit my lip to keep quiet. He was scaring me. Should I scream? Someone would come quickly, wouldn't they?

He licked his lips and smirked at me. "People are saying you're talking about how I tried to rape you. I told them they were wrong. You asked for it so bad that night."

"No," I said, but my voice was shaky and small. I spoke louder. "I didn't want that."

He put his fingers on my shoulder and let them trail down my arm slowly. "It sure seemed like you wanted it."

I couldn't do this. It was impossible to talk to Luke and stay okay.

His fingers stopped and wrapped around my wrist. "I think you might want to think about telling the truth instead of spreading lies."

"You wanted me to pass out." I pulled my arm out of his grip, my fingernails scratching him. "You put something in my drink." I spat the words at him.

Luke paused, and for a second, a brief moment before his face twisted back into its usual slimy mask, I saw panic.

And I knew what Jenna had told me was true.

"You think I drugged you? Come on, Kate. Do you really think I need to resort to something like that to get ass? You're little friend Ali spread her legs for me the instant I glanced at her."

"You're a disgusting pig."

Luke shrugged. "Hey, say what you want. But I wonder who people would believe if they saw the picture Ali sent me."

The room felt like it was spinning. I grabbed the edge of Dad's desk for support. "What are you talking about?" I asked, but I already knew what picture he meant.

He winked at me. "It seems our little Kate gets a thrill out of showing people her tits. But I already found that out. You were all about me seeing them at Jack's."

Bile rose in my throat, and I swallowed it down.

"Please, Luke, please delete the picture."

"What was that?" he asked and moved so close I could feel his breath against the side of my face. "Do I hear you begging me? Just like you begged for it at Jack's house?"

"Go to hell," I said.

I bolted. I ran out the door and down the hallway. I ran and ran and didn't feel like I'd ever be able to get far enough away from Luke.

www.allmytruths.com

Today's Truth:

**You need to know how to
act in an emergency.**

TIMELINE TO DISASTER:

10:10 a.m.

Realize you can't hide from Luke in the bathroom all day. Go to your next class when you hear the bell ring. Keep your eyes down. There is no one you want to see and everyone you want to avoid.

10:13 a.m.

Hurry into third period and pass two basketball players, panic because they are staring straight at you. They're smiling. You feel like a rabbit caught between two lions. Avert your gaze and convince yourself this isn't about what Luke mentioned. Try to act normal and pretend you're okay.

10:37 a.m.

Notice the whispers and glances. Watch as they pull out their phones and check them, then lean over to their neighbors who also look at their phones. Hear your own phone vibrating in your bag but leave it there. You're too busy focusing on your desk, pretending you are invisible as more heads turn toward you.

11:09 a.m.

Rush out of class when it ends. Run down the hall because you know something is wrong. People are looking, people are laughing, people are pointing at you.

11:10 a.m.

Put your hand in your bag and feel the shape of your phone. Tell yourself to check your message. It's probably a text from Julia that has you scared for nothing. Tell yourself you'll laugh when you find out it's not a big deal. Talk yourself into believing that, but still don't open your phone.

11:11 a.m.

See Jack coming toward you in the hall. He's with Amanda. They are holding hands, and you hate him for it. Turn and walk the other way.

11:14 a.m.

Take your seat in art, a different seat for the last few

weeks, away from the table of friends you used to sit with. Work on a picture of dark browns, reds, and black, blobs that bleed together but make no images.

11:56 a.m.

Create a sudden jagged line across your paper as a note is thrust in front of you. Unfold it and read, "Nice boobs." Tear the note up until it's tiny pieces of confetti. Push them off your desk and watch as they flutter to the ground.

11:58 a.m.

Open your cell phone to the picture of yourself that you never wanted Jack to see. Hear the room erupt in catcalls and applause. You're open and exposed. There is nothing you can do to hide.

Posted By: Your Present Self

[Tuesday, January 14, 10:47 AM]

Art wasn't over, but I grabbed my bag and walked out the door. I couldn't sit in class acting as if everything was okay, because it wasn't. Everyone had seen the picture of me and watched for my reaction when I pulled out my phone. The same awful picture I never wanted Jack to see was now on every single person's phone in the school.

I headed to the competition gym, the last place I figured anyone would find me. I knew it would be empty; I'd memorized Jack's schedule months ago. I took a seat on the bottom bleacher and stared at the court, trying not to remember all the times I'd sat and cheered Jack on. In my head, I heard the ball bouncing across the floor, the squeaking of sneakers and shouts between team members. I shut my eyes and tried to picture Dad's games that Brett and I used to go to with Mom. I saw it vividly, all of us together, a family still.

I held on to the image of the four of us until a bell rang, signaling the end of class. I jumped up and ran into the hallway before someone found me alone. I slipped between everyone else pushing their way to class and kept my head down.

"Skank," a voice said, and an elbow jabbed me.

I skidded a little and dropped my blue tote bag. My books and other items spilled out all over. I bent to pick things up, grabbing the copy of *The Great Gatsby* I was reading for English, scooping up pens and papers, trying not to see who was walking around me, afraid of who I'd make eye contact with. I reached for a notebook that had slid away from me and a foot went flying in front of me, kicking it down the hall. I lost sight of most of the remaining items as they were passed from person to person, a makeshift soccer game, as people laughed and whispered from all around me.

The bell rang, and everyone cleared.

I picked up what I could find, shoving it all in my bag, not caring if I crumpled things.

I stood and locked gazes with Ali, who was striding down the hallway, talking with Jenna, ignoring the fact that the bell had already rung.

I froze as they continued straight toward me.

"Hi, Kate," Ali said when they reached me.

I stood quickly. I tried to back away but hit a locker.

Jenna smirked, "Sexy pic. I had no clue you were into that stuff."

"So," Ali said. "I hear you're still pretending you didn't throw yourself at Luke."

"I didn't do anything," I said and clenched my teeth.

Jenna walked around me slowly. "You're nothing but a nasty slut," she said, shoving me into the locker.

I winced and looked at her incredulously. How could she shift from the girl she was in the bathroom to who she was now? Had I been so wrong about the people I once called my friends?

"None of this is my fault," I said.

"Get real," Ali started. "After that picture you sent out, no one is going to believe you."

"I didn't send the picture out." My voice rose in a frenzy.

"Right," Ali said, drawing out the word. "Just like you didn't screw Luke."

"It's the truth," I said, trying to sound firm, even though it was taking every ounce of my strength to not break down.

I ducked to the left, shooting around the girls

before they could stop me.

"You're nothing. You blew it with us. Now you don't matter to anyone," Ali shouted after me.

Jenna laughed.

I ran, my bag slapping my side, threatening to spill open again as Ali yelled louder and louder.

I ran as heads poked out of classroom doors and teachers looked to see what all the noise was about.

I ran when they saw who was in the hallway and why and did nothing to stop it.

80

I left Beacon, and I didn't care if I ever went back again. My tennis shoes slipped on ice as I walked down the hill from school. Big fat flakes fell from the sky, and I wished I could lie in the snow. I imagined myself falling asleep, letting the flakes layer on top of me until I was nothing but a pile of white. I'd become a frozen piece of myself, with a hard ice shell to keep everyone from getting too close.

At my house, I wrapped myself in Mom's old quilts and sat looking out at the pool. The wind whipped and bent the tree branches. I stared at the gray sky, trying to figure out what to do. There was no way I could show my face at Beacon again. Not with that picture all over the place. It was only a matter of time until Dad found out about the picture too. He hadn't believed me when I'd told him Luke tried to rape me, and the picture would only confirm his thoughts that what happened was my fault.

Julia seemed to think it was so simple to stand up to Luke and the rest of the players, but it wasn't. They were everything to the school, to the community, to Dad.

I focused on the pool outside. It made me think of a different pool, one from when I was younger. A community pool Brett and I would beg Mom to take us to because our friends hung out there. She always protested that we had our own pool and it was silly to go somewhere else to do something we could do in our own backyard. But usually Mom would agree and pack a cooler full of snacks that cost a lot less than the ones they sold at the pool, though the pool snacks always tasted better. We'd throw our towels and sunscreen into a wagon and take turns pulling it.

Brett's friends were wild boys who did cannonballs off the side of the pool, soaking the girls who were lying on towels. They ran along the side of the pool and made the guards blow their whistles, reminding them to slow down and walk. My friends were girls I knew from school, girls I'd sit and giggle with on blankets, jumping into the shallow sections when we got too hot, and watching everyone through our sunglasses and talking about them. The boys had their side of the turf; we had ours.

The pool had been my favorite place to go until the day Dad came along.

Mom was usually the one to take us since Dad

worked basketball camps during the week, but it was a Sunday and the four of us were stir-crazy, ready to get out of the house. We all walked there together, separating when we arrived, Mom and Dad in chairs under an umbrella and Brett and I with our friends.

I was lying with my friends, eating junk food and watching the little kids splash each other in the baby pool, when a shadow fell over our towels.

"Kate, how about you and Brett jump off the high dive with me?"

My friends and I looked up, holding our hands to our eyes against the glaring sun, to see Dad staring down.

I shrugged, my lips salty from eating chips out of a can and hands greasy from sunscreen. "Sure, Dad, I'll jump, but I don't know about Brett. He doesn't like the high dive."

Dad acted as if he hadn't heard me and headed over to Brett and his friends. I followed, knowing he wouldn't be able to convince Brett.

Heights were Brett's weakness. For as long as I could remember, Brett was terrified of high places. Otherwise, he wasn't afraid of anything. He would go into the woods at night, watch scary movies where people got hacked up with chainsaws, and taunt the big dog two houses down, but he refused to have anything to do with heights.

Brett was pretty good at keeping his fear hidden. I could see what he was doing each time we went to the pool, running around with his friends or staying in line at the slide, avoiding the diving area.

"Brett," Dad said, reaching him and his friends. "I want to see you jump off the high dive. Kate and I are heading over there."

"The whistle's going to blow soon for rest period. I don't think we have time."

"You're not going to let your sister show you up, are you?"

"What? No way," he answered quickly in case anyone suspected this might be true.

A bee buzzed around our heads in lazy, dizzying circles. It flew past me, and I swatted it away. I missed, and Brett ducked, jumping back as the bee buzzed around for a second time.

"Then let's go," Dad said.

At this point, he had an audience. Brett's friends had gathered around and everyone watched him.

"They're about to blow the whistle for a rest

period," he protested once more.

"We still have five minutes. It's more than enough time."

The line for the high dive was long, and I hoped Brett could play out the clock and wait for the rest period whistle.

Brett's friends and a few of mine gathered around the fence separating the jumpers from the spectators.

The line moved fast, too fast, and we were now at the front of the line, climbing the wet metal steps. Dad went first, and as he jumped, I turned to Brett and said, "You don't have to do this, you know. Walk away. Explain it to Dad. He'll understand."

"No, he won't," Brett said bluntly. "I have to jump."

I was at the top looking ahead at the long white diving board that jiggled slightly from Dad's jump. I turned, taking one last look at Brett's terrified face, ran, and plunged into the pool.

The cold water shocked me. I swam to the ladder where Dad was. The two of us clung to the side, watching Brett reach the top of the diving board.

Brett made eye contact with us, and Dad waved in a pushing motion, as if he could lead him onto the board from below. Brett's legs were shaking, and it didn't take a rocket scientist to know he was scared. I clenched my teeth and dug my fingers into my palms. Why did Dad have to make him do this?

Brett took a tentative step out. At first, he held onto the rails that rounded up from the step, but then had to let go to keep moving. He took another step, and he now stood at the edge of the board, staring down.

I heard a single whistle and then multiple whistles answering back. "Rest period," yelled the lifeguards in unison. Around me, the pool erupted into the groans of unwilling kids who reluctantly pulled themselves out and raced toward the concession stand to be the first in a line that would soon wrap around the eating area.

"You need to jump and get out," a voice called from the side of the pool. I spotted a red-suited lifeguard staring Brett down, her hair in two braided pigtails, the straps of her suit pulled down over her arms to avoid tan lines. She hollered the message again, making a funnel shape with her hands to increase her volume in case everyone else now watching didn't hear the first time. "You need to jump. It's rest period."

"Come on, Brett," Dad said quietly, staring at him, expressionless. "Jump."

"You need to get off the diving board," the guard bellowed a third time, and I wondered if she got in trouble if she left people in the pool too long after the rest period whistle was blown.

"Jump, jump, jump," the boys along the fence started to chant, grabbing the lifeguard's word and shaking it over and over like my grandma's dog used to do when he had a stuffed animal in his mouth. "Jump, jump, jump."

My heart seemed to speed with their beat, and I willed Brett to jump. I wanted him to prove to Dad he was strong.

I wanted him to jump.

But he didn't.

Brett slowly backed up, and once his foot touched the top of the ladder he grabbed the rails and pulled himself backward, tripping a little as he stepped down. His eyes shined with tears as the chant seamlessly shifted to, "Wimp, wimp, wimp."

Brett burst out of the diving pool, flying past all the blurred faces, avoiding Dad.

As he ran and the chant picked up, I hated Dad for trying to force Brett to jump when he wasn't ready.

After all these years, I realized Dad hadn't

changed. But Brett had. The Brett I knew was nothing like that boy Dad had taunted. Brett had found the courage to stand up to Dad, to all of those who doubted him, and the strength to change. Brett wasn't that boy on the high dive anymore, and suddenly I knew what I had to do. I knew how to make Dad listen.

I went to my bedroom and booted up my computer. I logged on to my blog. Dad's demands to stay quiet and his promise to punish Luke swirled in my head.

"No," I said out loud. "No, Dad. I'm not staying quiet. I'm not keeping this inside."

For only a second, I hovered the cursor over the button confirming my blog was private before I clicked it and went public.

I logged on to my Beacon account and selected everyone on the list server; the entire staff and all students in the school. I typed the address of my blog into an e-mail and hit Send. Now the entire school had a direct link to the real story.

I closed my eyes and prepared myself for what I hoped was the start of the end. I'd done it. With just a click, I jumped, sang, and told the world everything in a voice so loud there was no way Dad or anyone else could act as if they didn't hear me.

I heard from Julia less than an hour after I sent the e-mail.

"What is this blog?" Julia asked when I answered the phone.

"My story. I started writing it shortly before I came to Beacon. I kept it private, but now . . ."

"Now you want to use it to show everyone what happened."

"Exactly," I told her. "Do you think it'll work?"

Julia paused before answering.

I picked at a hangnail and waited to see what she thought.

"It'll definitely get people's attention. Although I'm not sure it's the attention you want."

"But you think people will read it?"

I heard Julia typing on her keyboard. "Oh, yeah," she said. "People are going to read this."

"Good. I sent it out to the entire school. I wanted to make sure everyone sees it."

"To everyone? Do you know what you're getting yourself into?"

"I hope so."

"What about your dad?"

"What about him?" I wondered how long it would take him to read the blog. He'd find out I sent the e-mail to everyone at school and freak out, but I didn't care. I wanted him to read all of it.

"How do you think he's going to react?"

"I tried to tell him, Julia. He wouldn't listen then, so I hope he listens now."

"He'll hear you now, and so will the rest of the school. Prepare yourself."

I walked to my computer. I opened my blog and scrolled through my entries. They all told a story: my story at Beacon, and I wanted everyone to know that story. "I've never been more ready in my life."

"I hope so, because you're about to get yourself noticed."

82

Julia was right. People were reading my blog. Shortly after I hung up with her, my phone started vibrating. I ignored it until the screen notified me that I had twenty text messages and I knew I had to see what people were saying . . . good or bad.

I held my breath as I read the first message. I slowly let it out as I clicked through each text. The messages were full of hate and contempt. They kept coming: ugly, messy words from people I once thought were my friends:

"WTF? WHY WOULD YOU SAY SOMETHING LIKE THAT?"

"YOU'RE NOTHING BUT A SLUT."

"JACK NEVER LIKED YOU. HE WAS USING YOU BECAUSE OF WHO YOUR FATHER IS."

"HOW PATHETIC CAN U B?"

"DON'T COME BACK."

"FIRST U SHOW UR TITS, NOW THIS

BULLSHIT. GET REAL."

"YOU R FINISHED."

"WATCH YOUR BACK, TRAITOR."

I imagined my e-mail box would be filled with the same. I vowed not to open any more messages. I closed my phone and got a bag of ice from the freezer. I curled up on my bed and placed the ice over my bruise. It was cold and stinging at first, but it wasn't an ache caused by destruction. Instead, I imagined the cold could heal. I pretended I could erase the words from everyone that slammed over and over me that day, sharp biting bullets and prickly burrs leaving me bruised and wounded. I let their words and actions slip off me. I had spoken out to Beacon. I had told the truth. Now I let go of everything until I held onto nothing but the words I wanted to say between Dad and me. The words that needed to be said.

I woke hours later to darkness outside. Dad would be home soon. I forced myself to go downstairs and confront him. I wouldn't hide in my room any longer. I waited for him in the living room, sitting in the ugly, worn, gold chair. He didn't come back until after midnight, the start of a new day, the day after.

The beams of his headlights swept across the front lawn. It reminded me of all the times I'd waited for Jack in the mornings before school, watching. Unlike Jack's visits, though, this time I wasn't full of anticipation and giddiness. This time my body shook with fear as the lights made shadows on the wall, warped and menacing tree branches reaching out to snatch me with gnarled fingers.

I forced myself to stay in the chair even though I wanted to run and hide and delay talking to Dad. But I knew it couldn't wait any longer. I needed to face him. I heard him pull in to the driveway and enter the house.

I sat straight up.

He saw me. He looked right into my eyes and said, "You need to take your blog down."

"No, Dad—"

"Take the blog down. I don't want to see it." He turned away from me and started to walk out.

"Have you even read it?"

"Quiet," he said in a voice I had to strain to hear.

There was no blowup, no shouting. There was just one word.

I watched Dad and realized he didn't even look like my dad. He was stooped over and haggard. His shirt was untucked, his pants wrinkled.

I opened my mouth, and he shook his head. "I need you to be quiet. For tonight, be quiet."

He walked past me and into his office. His words evaporated in the air. I spoke out loud, loud enough for him to hear, but the only one who seemed to listen was me. "I've been quiet, Dad. Don't you understand? And I can't be quiet anymore."

84

I looked at my phone and saw the mailbox was full.

I cried out, wishing I could toss it out the window. Instead, I ignored the fact that it was 1:00 a.m. and dialed Julia's number.

She picked up before the second ring and didn't sound sleepy at all. "What's going on? I've been trying to call you for hours."

"I haven't checked my phone."

"Why not?"

"I made a mistake," I told her.

"What are you talking about?"

"The blog. It didn't work. My phone is full of messages about how much people hate me, and my dad can't even stand to be in the same room with me now."

"Have you checked your blog lately?"

"Not since I went public with it. I should sign on and delete it. I thought I could handle this, but—"

"I think you need to look at it first."

I fell back onto my bed, letting my pillows cushion my fall. "I know what everyone's saying. They've been calling my phone all night."

"Sign on."

I sighed and walked to my computer. "I can't take much more of this."

"Go to your blog," she said, her tone growing impatient.

I typed in my address and stared at the familiar words, the letters I started to write to myself less than a year ago. Letters I thought would chronicle a happy new start, not the story they now told. "Okay," I told her. "I'm there."

"Click on November 19."

I went to the entry. It was the one I'd written about Brett enlisting and how scared I was.

"Click on the comments."

There were twenty-three. My hands shook as I opened them.

"I really don't need to read how much everyone hates me. The messages on my phone are already telling me that."

"Read them, Kate. I promise it'll be okay."

I was prepared for words of hate, but the messages from my classmates weren't anything like the reaction I received when I walked through the hallways. These were full of hope, prayers, and well wishes:

Brett is sooo brave.

My prayers R W/ U, Brett.

Hang in there, Kate. It'll be OKAY!

Brett is doing an amazing thing. He's a hero.
Be STRONG. Have FAITH.

"Oh my gosh," I said. "Brett wrote something."

"I told him to read your blog. I hope you don't mind."

My eyes raced over his words:

"Kate, don't be afraid of me going into the Army. This is what I need to do. This is what's right to me."

"I can't believe Brett read this."

"Of course he did. He's your brother. He cares

about you," Julia said. "That isn't his only message. He wrote under some of your other entries too. People are listening. People hear you."

"I can't believe this."

"There's other dates you probably want to go to," Julia said. "Find October 29."

I scrolled back and went to the entry. It was the day Jack took my homework from me and I wrote about cheating. I read the comments. There were some expected ones that told me how wrong I was and that the team didn't cheat:

I've had classes for years with members on the team, and I know they don't cheat. Stop spreading lies.

UR the stupid 1. Stop trying 2 make other people look bad.

But there were others too. Messages different from the ones above:

I saw Danny complete a multiple choice test in less than a minute, then put his head down and sleep. When he got the test back, there was an A across the top.

I get paid $50 to write papers for players on the team.

I was sitting next to a group of players who were passing around a copy of the midterm they were taking the next day.

"What is going on?" I asked Julia, scanning the other comments. "There must be at least twenty postings from people about the team cheating."

"Go to November 13."

It was my post describing how Jack wanted to have sex with me. Again, the comments against the team shocked me.

At least Jack asked to have sex with you. I went to homecoming with Scott White, and he tried to screw me in the backseat of his car. He ripped my dress, and I had to kick him to get out.

Sex is nothing to the guys on the team. When I

started the dance team my freshmen year, it was ex-pected that we sleep with a member of the team at a party they had. It was some sick initiation thing they did. Most of us slept with them, and the girls who didn't had to put up with so much shit that they quit.

I was at a party once and walked in on 2 Beacon players in a bedroom with a girl passed out. They had her top off and one was pulling off her belt. They acted like I was the one doing something bad by interrupting them. ASSHOLES!

"This is crazy," I said as I clicked on different entries.

"I know," Julia said. "And you're not the only one who has bad stuff to say about Luke."

"What do you mean?"

"Go to your last entry."

I did, and when I saw what was written to me, I smiled for the first time in what had felt like weeks.

Kate, we hear u. Don't stop making noise.

Luke is a piece of shit!

U R not the only 1 Luke's done this to. U R the only 1 brave enough to say something.

F*** Luke . . . he deserves what he gets.

There's a lot of us at Beacon who see through the bball team. We'll stand behind you if you continue this fight.

"This is incredible," I said, staring at the words in front of me. "People believe me."

"Of course they do. So do you still want to delete your blog?"

"No way." I couldn't hide my excitement. "Not until every single person has gotten to read it and post. I'm not touching this."

And I wasn't. No matter what Dad told me to do.

I hung up and printed out the comments. I cut out the ones supporting me and hung them on my walls around my bed. When I turned off the lights to go to sleep, the white paper was visible in the faint glow from streetlights outside my window. They surrounded me, each a reminder that someone was listening and I wasn't in this alone.

www.allmytruths.com

Today's Truth:
Life has winners and losers.

Basketball is a lot like life.

It's a game where there is a defined set of rules.
If you are fouled, that person is penalized.
If you score, your team wins a point.

There are always people cheering for you,
wanting you to win,
and those who want to see you fail.
People who celebrate when you fail.

Basketball has winners and losers,
but there is always a new start with each game.
You're always able to begin again.

Posted By: Your Present Self
[Wednesday, January 15, 3:38 PM]

85

Dad was in his office the next morning when I finished showering. I'd put on my uniform, even though I was unsure of what the day would bring. I wanted to go to Beacon. People supported me, classmates were willing to stand up against the team and speak out alongside me. I wouldn't let Luke, Ali, Jack, or anyone else push me out.

Dad's door was closed, and light streamed from under it. How long had he been in there? Had he gotten up a little bit before I had, or had he been up all night? Regardless, he was in there now, and the unwritten rule always had been that if Dad was in his office we were not to disturb him.

Today, I ignored his rules. Dad's office wouldn't be his place to hide from me anymore. I wasn't going to let him close the door and shut me out.

I hesitated for only a second before I knocked. The days of second-guessing myself were over.

"Come in," he said, and there was a hint of surprise in his voice.

I opened the door, and Dad's gaze went straight to my uniform. I knew he understood that I wasn't planning to stay away from Beacon.

"You can't go to school today." He didn't say it like an order. There wasn't force behind it. It was merely a statement of truth.

"Why not?"

"Beacon wants to suspend you for the time being. They don't want you in there right now."

"How can they do that? I didn't do anything wrong."

"I don't know if they can, but right now it's not something I want to fight."

"It seems to me there are a lot of things you don't want to fight lately."

"You won't be going to school," he said, a bit louder now.

"Why am I being punished for telling the truth?" I stared at Dad, incredulous that Beacon could tell me not to return.

He held my gaze, his jaw clenched. "They need

to figure out what to do about all of this stuff you posted. How to deal with it."

"Everything I wrote is true."

"True? According to you, maybe. But the school is going to want proof. People aren't going to believe you. Anyone can post whatever they want online."

"Have you even read it? Have you read the comments people posted? Because if you did, they'd show you what I'm saying is true."

"I saw enough of it, Kate."

"No," I shouted. "You haven't. You need to read it all."

Dad leaned back in his chair and ran his left hand through his hair. His wedding ring caught in the light, and I thought about Mom.

"I'm sorry," I said, but I wasn't sure if I was. How could I forgive Dad for putting his team before me? Shouldn't he be the one apologizing?

On his desk was a piece of toast he must have made for breakfast. The butter soaked through, and the middle was a soggy mess.

I tried to focus on it as my eyes filled with tears. "I had to do this. I didn't have a choice."

"You had to ruin my team? Everything I worked for?"

I stared at the plate. The words were stuck in the back of my throat. The words I'd tried to say since Mom died. I wished I could rewind things and go back before Brett enlisted in the Army and moved out of the house and I lost Jack and my friends. I wanted to go back to those days after Mom had died and force Dad to see me, to see Brett. If I could go back to the start, before we all knew what grief and sadness were, maybe things would be different.

I longed for my old life when I'd sit at the table with Mom and Dad, listening to Brett make fun of how tall I was for a seventh grader and having Dad stick up for me, telling us he's always been fond of gi-raffes. I wanted us to be a family again. I wanted us to talk to each other.

I played with the bracelet on my wrist. "What I did wasn't about you. It was about me. I did this for me."

"I don't understand," he said, and it felt as if he hadn't heard what I was trying to say. "Why did you have to publish all that stuff for everyone to read?"

"You told me you would do something, and you didn't. This was about protecting myself and standing up against what happened."

"And so you decided it would be a good idea to punish me too?"

My tears spilled out. They hit my cheek, stinging as if I had been slapped. "That's not what I was doing, Dad. It's my life that was destroyed."

He stood, but he wouldn't run away this time. I'd make him listen. I stepped in front of him.

"Do you have any idea what *your* team has done to me?" I shouted, each word coming out harsher than the last. "How much they've hurt me? Luke tried to *rape* me. I found out he put drugs in my drink. He planned what he was going to do. There's a naked picture of me on every student's phone now. I can't even walk through the hallways of Beacon without getting elbowed or called names. And do you know who did all of this? *Your* team. The boys you think are perfect. The boys you spend so much time with that you can't pay attention to how much your own kids are hurting. They're the ones who have done everything."

He sank slowly like a flower wilting under the rain. He put his head in his hands.

"Dad?"

When he brought his head back up, his eyes were glassy, wet. He spoke quietly, "What did I do?"

"Nothing." I paused, took a deep breath then went on. "You did nothing."

Dad stared at me.

"I tried to tell you about Luke, but you wouldn't listen. You told me to be quiet. You're so blinded by Beacon that you didn't even believe your own daughter." I wasn't sure I could get the rest of the words out, but I went on. "You didn't do anything, and I've been left alone. I lost Mom. I lost you. And now, with Brett gone, I'm terrified he won't come back and I'll be left with no one."

I covered my face with my hands, shaking so hard I choked on my sobs. I let out everything I had been holding in for months, for the last two years.

I waited for Dad to yell back at me, to remind me again how I'd destroyed what he cared the most about. I heard him move around his office, small, quiet movements away from the chair.

I tried to calm down, but each time I did, my mind drifted to what had happened during these last few weeks, and fresh fears and sorrows washed over me.

Dad placed a hand on my shoulder, and then he

spoke in a voice not loud or angry but full of regret. "I've messed up, haven't I?"

I turned around. His face was no longer filled with fury, only pain. The same pain that reflected in my eyes when I looked in the mirror.

"I've let you and Brett down."

I wiped my eyes with the wet fabric of my blouse sleeves. "Why haven't you been here for us? You've shut yourself away from Brett and me, and it's as if we don't even exist. Just like with Mom. We never even talk about her. All I ever wanted was to talk, to remember her, but all you seem to care about is your basketball team."

"I'm sorry," Dad said, and he had a look on his face that I'd only seen one other time: the night Mom died. He placed a hand firmly on my shoulder. "I've messed us up. Our entire family. I didn't know what to say, what to do, how to make it better, because it wasn't. I couldn't pretend to be okay."

"None of us could."

Dad turned my chair around and gave me an awkward hug, his hands around me, his body warm but unfamiliar next to me. He spoke with his head pressed against me in the hug. His words were muffled, but I understood every one of them, "It's hard to be the strong one, but I should have been. I need to be."

"You don't need to be anything, Dad. You just need to be *here*."

He held on to me for a few minutes, neither of us talking but for the first time since Mom had died, I didn't need him to.

"I'm so sorry," he finally said, his eyes welling up. He shook his head. "What I did was wrong. I protected the wrong person."

"Sometimes it's hard to see who the enemy really is," I said, not because I was letting him off the hook but because I knew how easily you could be blinded by something if you were trying to hold on to what you loved.

"It's my job to keep the enemy away from you," he said.

I thought about those months after Mom was diagnosed. Dad had been the hero for all of us. He protected, loved, and cared for Mom even when it seemed she was giving up, even when Brett and I could see how sick she was. He watched over us and remained the strong one. Dad had fought for what he loved, and he could do it again.

"You can start to fix things," I told him. "Talk to Brett. Tell him to come home."

"I need to make this better." Dad looked me straight in the eyes. "I will make this better. I'm sorry, Kate."

"Thank you," I said and didn't even try to fight the tears that formed in my eyes, because that was exactly what I'd needed to hear. It was far from the perfect apology, but none of us are perfect. It was a start, and right now a new start was exactly what my family needed.

86

Dad sat at our kitchen table with my laptop and read the comments on my blog, and I went upstairs to change out of my uniform into jeans and a sweatshirt. I wasn't going to school, but it wasn't because Beacon was keeping me out. Dad wasn't going either; the two of us were going to the police station together.

I pulled up a chair next to him. He scrolled through one of my postings as I rubbed my hand over the indentations on the worn table that had seen my family through so much.

"Did you know," he said, pointing at the screen, "that Brett posted on here?"

"Yeah, he's read it all."

Dad's face grew sad. "He's grown up, and I've missed it."

He turned back to the screen. People had been on all night. There were twenty or thirty messages below some of the posts.

"I should have listened to you, Kate. All these people, and I couldn't—"

"Dad, you're listening to me now."

And it was the truth. Dad couldn't take back what he had done. He had made his mistakes, but he recognized it now. He was listening, and that was enough for now.

Jack's truck was sitting in my driveway when we returned from the police department. The engine was on, and little puffs of smoke came out the back pipe.

Dad put his car into park. "Do you want me to stay here with you?"

I shook my head. "No, go ahead to school. I'll be fine." Dad had asked me if it was okay for him to go to work after we filed reports against Luke and Ali. I told him it was. He had a lot to deal with, and I was the catalyst of all of it. He needed to go back to Beacon, but he was no longer choosing the team over me.

"Are you sure?" he asked, still clutching the gearshift.

"Yes, go ahead. I'll be fine," I said, even though I wasn't. I had no idea why Jack was here. After everything I'd done, he probably hated me even more now.

Dad pulled out of the driveway but stopped once he reached the street. He unrolled his window and nodded at Jack. Jack nodded back, and Dad sat there, letting the car run to make sure everything really was okay.

I took a deep breath and walked to the passenger's window. I could hear the radio on even with the windows closed.

Jack opened the door but didn't move from his seat. "Hi," he said.

I looked at him. Whatever he was here for, I wasn't going to make it easy.

He jumped out of the truck. "Can we talk?" His shoulders were hunched, and he looked almost defeated. Instead of feeling glad about this, I felt sad.

"Okay," I said and pulled my key out of my purse. He followed me to the door and stood a few feet back while I opened it. I threw my stuff on the table in the front hallway and stepped back outside.

Jack gestured toward the steps outside. "Do you mind if we sit?"

I walked out and sat far from him.

"I'm probably the last person you want to see right now, but I—"

"You aren't."

"What?"

I almost laughed. "You aren't the last person I want to see. In case you forgot, Luke is at the top of that list."

Jack closed his eyes. My words had gotten to him, but instead of feeling good about it, I felt worse.

"I was such a jerk. I deserve anything you have to say to me."

Neither of us spoke, and I let his words sink in. Jack wasn't here to yell at me. He was here for something different.

"I don't know if you've heard yet, but Luke and a few other players have been suspended from the team until the investigation is over. People are coming forward about stuff."

I'd known this would happen. Dad warned me of it when we drove to the police station. He didn't say it as a threat, words he once might have said to protect his team, but as reassurance that I'd be safe. The team would be punished, and so would Ali for sending out the picture of me.

"You sure you want to do this?" Dad had asked when we'd pulled in to the station.

"Positive," I said, even though I was trembling.

Dad got out first and came around to my side, placing a hand on my back. "We're doing this together, okay?"

I nodded, glad to know he was behind me. Instead of feeling as if he were bringing me down, I imagined we were holding each other up.

I shifted my focus back to Jack. "My dad and I went to the police today. To press charges against Luke."

Jack was the one to turn away. He played with his frayed shoelaces. "I know what I did was wrong."

"It was wrong, Jack. You abandoned me when I needed you the most. You didn't even care."

"I wasn't thinking. All I saw was you and Luke together. It's the only thing I could think about."

"And so you sided with him. You didn't even give me a chance."

Jack kicked at the concrete.

"Why are you here?" I said, although I wasn't sure if any response would sound right.

"I wanted to tell you I was sorry. I should have listened to you. It's just the team has been—"

"It's always going to be the team," I said, and it was the truth. Jack was always going to side with the team.

Jack shrugged. "It shouldn't be, but they're my boys. Some of us have been playing together since we were five years old."

I stood. "I'm not going to ask you to make choices. I don't think you want to."

Jack nodded. He didn't try to make any more apologies or explain. He stopped halfway down the walk. "The team is everything I know."

"It's all a lot of us know."

"I care about you, Kate. I always have."

"I cared for you too." I meant it, but my feelings for him were gone. I'd never come first to Jack, and it wasn't fair to either of us to expect something that couldn't happen.

He walked back to his truck, started the engine, and drove away.

I wanted to be mad at Jack for leaving me again, but I now understood why I couldn't be. He'd chosen Beacon a long time ago, and I'd seen firsthand through Dad how hard it was to pull your gaze away from the gleaming idol.

88

Dad called two hours later to tell me he was still at Beacon and might be for a while longer. "Do you want me to try to get away sooner?"

"I'm fine. I'll order a pizza."

"Sounds good. I'll try to wrap this stuff up and get home."

I spent a few more minutes convincing Dad I was okay at home.

I was sitting on the couch in our family room when the doorbell rang. I grabbed some money and rushed to the door. My stomach growled in anticipation of the hot pizza. But it wasn't the delivery man.

"Brett."

"Don't act so happy to see me. Were you expecting someone else?" he asked, one eyebrow raised.

"Kind of." I laughed. "The pizza man."

"Oh, well, that makes perfect sense. I'd be upset to find me too if I had been expecting pizza."

"Nah, I'll settle for you," I said and moved aside to let him in. "So you're ringing the doorbell now, huh?"

"It didn't feel right to just walk in, after everything . . ."

"Dad's not here, so you don't have to worry."

I headed into the kitchen, and Brett followed. The two of us sat at the table, the sound of our voices fading until all you could hear was the wind whipping against the windows. Brett's face grew serious, and it seemed as if today was the day for heart-to-hearts from everyone around me.

"It's not Dad I'm worried about." Brett reached out to the middle of the table and moved around the salt and pepper shakers. "Kate, I . . . I don't even know what to say. When I heard about what really happened that night, I wanted to go after Luke and smash his face in."

"But you didn't, right?" I gave him a serious look.

"Julia stopped me. She told me you were handling things and you'd come to me if you needed help."

"I did need help, but I didn't know how to let anyone know. Julia's the one who told me I needed to do something."

"Julia really cares about you."

"I know, and it doesn't make sense. I was such

a snob when I hung out with Ali and Jenna. She shouldn't like me."

"I think that's what's so great about her. She doesn't hold things against people."

"We all need to be more like her," I told Brett. I thought about how caught up I got in Dad's team, how Dad shut himself off from anything bad about the team, and how Brett didn't even consider giving the team a shot. We were all at fault.

"We need to try," Brett said.

"Will you come back home? I need you. Things are pretty messed up."

"Dad isn't going to forgive me for enlisting."

"It's not his choice. The decision has already been made."

"I'll be leaving in a few months."

The familiar fear hollowed my chest. "Why did you enlist?"

He sighed and ran his hands through his hair. "I had to, Kate."

"You didn't have to do anything."

"Okay, then, I wanted to. I don't fit in here."

I closed my eyes and tried to push down the guilt.

"I'm sorry for how I acted when I was with them."

"It's not your fault. You didn't cause this. I'd wanted to enlist for a couple of years. Mom and I used to talk about it before she got sick."

"You did?"

"Yeah, you don't think I'd do something like this without giving it a lot of thought, do you? Mom supported me, and we'd hoped you and Dad would too when the time came."

"But Mom's gone now. I need you here. If you stayed, it could be better. We could try to fix things."

"This isn't my place. My place is with the Army."

I wanted to tell him I knew what he meant, what it was like to want to be somewhere where you felt important. I wanted to say I understood. But I couldn't, because I didn't want the Army to be his important thing.

"I'm scared," Brett finally replied.

I held on to my next words for a minute. "I am too," I whispered.

"I'll be back. I'm not leaving you or anyone else."

"Promise?"

"I promise."

I knew without a doubt Brett was here for me.

89

"You don't have to go back to Beacon," Dad said a week later as the two of us maneuvered around each other in the kitchen and made breakfast. It had been a long week. Dad agreed to finish out the season with Beacon, and the school was doing whatever they could to keep their image clean. Luke was suspended from the team, and I'd filed a restraining order against him until the court moved forward with our case. Ali had charges against her for the distribution of my picture, and Julia said a speaker was brought in three days earlier to talk to everyone about the repercussions of taking and sending naked pictures. The school was looking into the accusations made on my blog and new ones from students who had stepped forward. I may not have put an end to the favored treatment of the basketball team, but it was an issue that couldn't be ignored anymore.

"I know. You've told me a hundred times, but this is something I want to do," I said as I buttered a bagel.

Dad had told us we could transfer, but I didn't want to run away. I *needed* to go back. Not going to school would be admitting defeat. I wasn't letting Beacon win. They'd pushed me around and controlled my life enough. Today I would face everyone.

A horn honked outside, so I took a big bite of my bagel.

Brett had moved in a few days ago. I knew he talked to Dad, but no one brought up the conversation and it wasn't my place to ask. I was just glad to have Brett home, and while the three of us weren't joking around like old times, Dad was making a real effort to be home more. We ate dinner together, and he didn't immediately retreat to his office. Sometimes he'd sit and watch TV with us for a while. It wasn't a big change, but to me it was huge.

I stopped eating my bagel long enough to yell, "Brett, Julia's here."

"Be right down."

Dad and I looked at the ceiling as Brett banged around in his room.

Finally, he jogged down, straightening his tie. "Let's get a move on."

Dad placed a hand on my shoulder. "I want you

to know I'll be at school all day. If anyone gives you trouble or you want to leave, come to my office. I can take you home."

"I'll be fine," I said, and I knew no matter how bad things got, I wouldn't go to his office. I had to stand up for things. I couldn't depend on help because of who my dad was. That wasn't the way it worked anymore.

Julia had the heat on full blast when we got into the car.

"How are you feeling?" She looked at my reflection in the rearview mirror.

I grimaced. "Sick to my stomach."

She gave me a sympathetic look and pulled out of the driveway. All the lights seemed to be green, the streets clear of traffic, and we made it to school in record time.

I held on to the handle, unable to pull it down and open the door. I watched students talking and laughing as they headed inside Beacon. Everyone had maroon ribbons in their hair, numbers painted on their faces, and wristbands sporting school pride.

"The team is playing Saint Edwards tonight," Julia said. "They're undefeated too. It's a big game."

"Saint Edwards?" I remembered the last time I saw Saint Edwards play, the night I first talked to Jack. I felt a brief wave of regret, but I pushed it away. Jack and I had changed. We weren't the same people.

This was a big game, but Dad hadn't mentioned it. He hadn't even seemed nervous the way he used to be.

"Just what we need," Brett muttered. "Another reason for these jerks to walk around the school like they own it."

"They aren't the only ones," I said, pushing open my door and stepping onto the concrete, onto Beacon. "Let's do this. Let's show the school they can't scare us away."

The two of them followed, and together we walked into Beacon with our heads held high, as if we owned the place.

www.allmytruths.com

Today's Truth:
We will all be okay.

People will hurt you,
but others will love you.

People will disappoint you,
but others will surprise you.

People will judge you,
but others will accept you.

People will betray you,
but others will support you.

People will leave you,
but others will return.

You will be okay.
We will all be okay.
We will make it through this life.
Together.

Posted By: Your Present Self
[Tuesday, January 21, 3:38 PM]

Acknowledgments

The Beatles sing, "I get by with a little help from my friends," but I think with *Canary*, I got by with *a lot* of help from my friends. I am grateful for the support of so many people during the process, a list that could probably warrant an entire book itself.

First, thank you to my wonderful agent, John Rudolph, who sold *Canary* amidst my wedding craziness. I never thought I'd be e-mailing my agent about a book deal the night before my wedding and back and forth on my honeymoon! Thank you to Medallion for your faith in this book, especially the editorial department, Helen Rosburg, Ali DeGray, Emily Steele, and Lorie Jones.

I had an awesome group of readers who helped shape this book into what it is now, including Christina Lee, Lisa Nowak, Krista Ashe, Emilia Platter-Zyberk, Lee Bross, Rachel Grassy, Jamie Blair, Jennifer Wood, Katherine Connolly, librarian extraordinaire Jodi Rzeszotarski, and my wonderful student readers, Arial Hedrich and Miranda Webb.

I wouldn't be surprised if I spent a small fortune at coffee houses while writing and revising this book. So I owe a special thanks to my favorite haunts, places where at some points I spent more time than at my own house: Starbucks in Rocky River and Barnes & Noble in Mentor, Caribou Coffee in Rocky

River, Arabica in Willoughby, and Panera Bread in Rocky River and Mentor. You kept me supplied with caffeine and free Wi-Fi and didn't kick me out when I set up camp hour after hour!

Writing can be such a solitary act, so I'm lucky to be a part of two great writing communities, The Kenyon Review Writers Workshop (Magic Twangers forever!) and the NEOMFA program at Cleveland State University. You give me inspiration, encouragement, and a place to share my passion with others who live to write as much as I do.

My love of writing wouldn't be what it is without all the incredible educators I've had throughout my life. I am especially thankful for my teachers and St. Angela Merici and Magnificat. You don't know how much I loved going to English class each day. It was Dr. Rice's multigenre project at Ohio University that sparked the idea for this book and my professors at Boston University who gave me the courage to share my writing with strangers. I am forever thankful for the enthusiasm of my colleagues, especially Cathy Priest and the Language Arts Department, who encouraged me throughout this entire process.

The online writing community is an amazing and welcoming place. The Lucky 13s have kept me sane throughout the publishing process, and so many other YA writers have reached out and helped me with support, answers, and virtual chocolate! And thank you, thank you, thank you to all who have followed my journey online. I love to connect with my readers, and your excitement for *Canary* has made this adventure even sweeter.

And where would I be without my own students? You make me think, laugh, and love what I do every single day.

I saved the best for last. My family. I owe a thousand thanks to all of you:

My mom, for first introducing me to my love of books.

My grandma, for sharing in my love of books.

My grandpa, for spoiling me with lots of books.

My sister, Amanda, for all our adventures that could fill volumes of books.

My pup, Radley, for keeping me company while revising this book.

And my glorious husband, Jason, for supporting (and putting up with!) all my reading, writing, and talking about books. You are the bomb diggity, old sport!